T0105543

A Tale of Three

A New Beginning

Kathy Gifford

Order this book online at www.trafford.com
or email orders@trafford.com

Most Trafford titles are also available at major online book retailers.

Printed in Victoria, BC, Canada.

ISBN: 978-1-4269-3308-0

Our mission is to efficiently provide the world's finest, most comprehensive book publishing service, enabling every author to experience success. To find out how to publish your book, your way, and have it available worldwide, visit us online at www.trafford.com

Trafford rev. 05/25/2010

www.trafford.com

North America & international
toll-free: 1 888 232 4444 (USA & Canada)
phone: 250 383 6864 • fax: 812 355 4082

People always say the best place to start a story is at the beginning, so I guess that's where I'll start. The earliest memory I have of my life is a face that I can't see. All I see is a blur and it's cold and dark. Anything before that I can't remember. How I got to where I was the day that I went home remained a mystery for a long time, but I know that the circumstances which brought me here are different, I am different. Something is wrong.

I remember the first day that I went home, a woman who was some kind of nurse took my hand and walked me down a very long corridor with many doors and the lights were so bright that you could feel the heat from them, but it was still dark in feeling. Just like the woman walking me. Her hair all tied back tight and her stone-like face showing no emotion.

We came to the end of the hall and she unlocked a door and relocked it on the other side. Once on the other side she gave me a cold stare that sent chills down my spine.

"Go sit down." she said pointing to a corner.

Someone came in I had never seen before. In his hand he carried a single small memory card that contained everything I needed to know about me. Other people were coming in, coming and staring at me, asking question after question about me. I just sat and stared. Looking at them. Wanting to ask why me, who are you and what do you want with me?

But no, I sat there and listened to these three decide my fate. Do I stay here, or go with them into a world I have never seen?

He who came in would look over at me from time to time, little emotion in his face toward his mate. His most concern was to get me out of here. He knew this place, he knew something.

"Fine we'll take her home." she finally said.

Getting up without a word being said to me, a motion of a hand to follow, and being let to a waiting vehicle outside. The burning of the sun high in the sky, it feels so good outside, no more cold walls. I look back and think of all the sleepless nights and days wanting to know, years and years of asking, now may be my chance, and I'm only a child.

A long trip down city streets, roads I've never seen, people all over the place going in and out of them. The long roads finally led into the urban areas then finally into the woods. Deeper and deeper we were going and I felt myself getting lost into the trees. A blue and purple sky with golden rays of sun shining through. The clouds are starting to come in for the night. My first day of freedom, but still, what are they going to ask me, or leave me be? Let me suffer alone, it will make me stronger.

We got out hours later. Flying birds and fresh air welcomed me. A well groomed white stone house and many windows and a long walkway to the front, flowering trees and shrubs scattered all around, carpeted by a light blue tinted grass.

These people are nothing more than strangers to me. She seemed so defined and straight, her long blond hair tied back, her skin very pale. He was older than her but he seemed to have a little more emotion than her. They don't seem to belong together, this I know for sure.

I looked around once I got inside. The room was huge, windows covered the wall and the sunset shinned right through. I've seen it a few times but not like this, not this much of a view. Nothing but trees and hills back here, a lot to explore.

"My name is Liera, this is Marlin." she stood behind me and stared at the sunset. "Your room overlooks the back, you can see the sunset from there. Would you like to see?"

Up the stairs and to the right, my room was at the end of the hall. In it was a closet full of cloths for me, for once I can wear something different. A soft bed and a computer next to it with a big window with a full view of the sunset. I could learn to like this.

"They called me Ariel." I told her as I stared at her.

"You don't have to keep that name."

"I know, but I want to."

"You can get cleaned up and come down when you are ready. Take your time, I'll understand if you do not want to come downstairs."

"Thank you."

She spoke not another word. She turned and shut the door, leaving me to explore my new world. My own clothing, my own bathroom, but outside that window is where I want to be. All I know is that I'll feel better if I were outside. I sat on the bed and held a pillow and watched the sunset, only then I decided to get cleaned up and venture downstairs, I stopped when I heard Marlin and Liera talk about me.

"Well, what do you think?" he asked her.

"Well, she's independent, and curious. That is natural, and you believe this will be fine, it's not too soon?"

"No, I don't worry."

"I hope you're right, for her sake as well as ours. She seems to be a fine girl, I want to see it stay that way."

"She will be fine." he assured her in an upbeat way.

"And if they come for her, what then?"

"Don't worry."

I really don't want to go down there but there I will get my answers. Or it may be in my best interest to remain quiet, wait and listen. Half way down the stairs the front door flew open and in runs a redheaded boy of twelve not stopping until he seen me.

"So they brought home a girl." he said staring at me. "My name is Roz."

"Ariel" A quick nod and a grin and he was on his way. "He doesn't like me," I said when I got to the bottom of the stairs, "but I don't care. This is going to be fun."

Liera didn't know what to make of my remark, she stood there shaking her head. She had an expression on her face like she was expecting the worse is yet to come. Maybe it was. Marlin was a little more calmer, he was laughing, not much, but enough to tell me that he thought my comment was amusing.

"It will be interesting." he said.

"May I go back to my room?" I asked.

"Of course. You don't have to ask to go to your room." He said.

Half way up the stairs Roz was coming down, once he was on the bottom floor he looked back up at me and all I did was smile back at him, yes this is going to be fun. For some reason he feels threatened by me. I sat at the computer and started to go through the basic research. I sat there for hours looking at the flat wall projection of information about the solar system and the other two planets that have life on them. I didn't realize that I missed the sunset until Marlin startled me when he came in.

"I knocked, but I see that you are busy." he said looking at the screen.

He sat at the edge of the bed, I knew he wanted to talk but I wasn't in the mood, not until I know what kind of people they are.

"I know you have questions, I'd be concerned if you didn't. If you do, I want you to know that you can ask me. No matter how crazy it sounds."

"And if there are no answer?" I asked when I looked at him.

"Then we'll find them, just don't do it alone."

"What does she do?"

"She researches chemicals for use with people."

"Biochemist" I whispered to myself.

"How would you know that."

"You'd be surprised at what I heard while I was awake."

"Awake?"

"Yes lots of times we were kept asleep." I told him.

"Who is we?" he asked with concern.

"Me and the other kids. I thought you might have known since you took me from there. I thought it was my time, my turn to leave."

"Do you know why you were there?"

"No"

"Do you know how many kids."

"There is always someone new. Some come, some leave."

"I'm not going to send you back. Don't say anything to anyone until I find out some things. Can you keep this a secret?"

"Yes"

"Good. Tell no one and I promise I will find out more. We're not going to send you back, and I'm not going to say anything to Liera."

"Why help me?"

"We were recommended for a child placement, now I want to know why. It will be okay."

He was trying to assure me I'm fine, it's starting to feel weird here. I waited until he went downstairs before I got up and went to the end of the hall where I could hear them talk.

"What was she doing when you went up?" she asked.

"Looking around on the computer. Learning."

"I have a feeling she may know more than we think."

"Time will tell. Don't worry about it."

They didn't say much more. Something is wrong, that I am right about. I believe I can trust Marlin better than Liera. I went back to my room and looked into the mirror, I wondered what he meant when he said that "time will tell."

The next day I spent the day outside exploring the backyard staring at the clouds going by. I stayed outside way into the dark, Marlin from time to time would just watch me. I was about to go back inside when I noticed a small light on the ground by a stone will at the end of the yard. When I moved to get a better look I noticed a shadow of a person the same size as me. Whoever it was noticed me and waved, so I waved back.

I wanted to go over and say hi but I wasn't sure if I should. Liera was watching me out the kitchen window, Marlin came out and stood in the doorway, whoever it was waved and he waved back.

"Do you know who it is?" I asked.

"I believe so. Go over and say hi if you want. I can see you from here."

"Really? Alright." I started to go over and Marlin stopped me and gave me a small light. I stopped and stared and then I realized it was another girl. She was kneeling on the ground with a small jar next to her.

"Hi, my name is Ariel."

"Clair. I'm looking for worms. I'm not supposed to be this far over here but there are a lot of worms here. And I saw you outside, I wanted to say hi."

"I'm glad you did. What do you do with the worms?"

"My dads taking me fishing in a few days."

"Fishing?"

"Yeah, worm, hook, throw it in water." she said looking up at me. "Don't you fish?"

"I've never been." just then I heard someone calling for her. "Who's that?" I asked backing off.

"It's my mom. I wish I didn't have to go."

"Me too. Maybe if we ask you could come over sometime tomorrow."

She asked her mother when she came over see what she was doing. After thinking about it for a few minutes she agreed as long as it was alright with Marlin and Liera.

I went over and asked if it would be alright if she came over tomorrow. "I don't see why not.

With the approval of both of them I went over and told Clair. I watched them walk back to their house, I kept thinking that there is something different about Clair, what it was I didn't know. I wondered if she was like me.

I smelled something good as I walked inside. "What's that smell?"

"Dinner" she said with a smile. "Help me set the table please."

"Ok, I like to help."

She handed me some dishes and pointed to a room off of the kitchen. I put the dishes down and looked around the room. I loved the window that covered the wall and part of the ceiling. The flowers were all around the base of the window. Different colors everywhere. The moon was full and the sky sparkled from the stars.

"You like the view?" Liera asked when she came in and put something on the table.

"Yes ma'am. I love the way the stars shine, and the flowers smell pretty."

"Well I can take credit for that, that is Marlins doing. I'm not good with plants." she said sniffing one of them. "Will you get the other things please?"

As I went in and picked up the other things I heard the front doors slam and Roz running up the stairs. I put them down when I saw Marlin doing something.

"What is that?" I asked. Now Marlin seemed like the nice guy of the bunch. His hair of silver gave way to a very old age. They don't belong together, but I don't dare ask yet.

"There is so much information that I need to go through some of it is stored on old fashion chips. There are so many." he said looking at cases stacked by the desk in the corner of the living room.

"About me?" I asked with interest.

"Maybe. Tell you what, ask me later and I'll let you know. Just give me time."

"Promise?"

He picked everything up and put it away, when I was done I when upstairs and got cleaned up and then by the time I came back down I didn't have much of an appetite, and I knew there wasn't any way of getting out of eating.

"You look funny," Roz said sitting at the table, "and I bet you're stupid too."

"Roz!" Liera said. "Apologize."

"That's okay. I know I know more than he does. He doesn't have to say he sorry for being stupid. It's not his fault. He's only twelve." I said staring at Roz. "Besides I know."

"You know what?" Roz asked.

"I was told that a girl has better manners than a boy does. Is this true?" I didn't care who answered it I just wanted to see what the response would be.

"Well, yes. Depending on how the children act." Liera answered when she sat down.

"And how they are raised." Marlin added.

That worked. Roz sat there with his mouth open. Liera and Marlin were trying not to laugh at him. I had won my first battle with Roz, and I hope we don't have anymore. No matter how much he thinks that I'm just a ten year old kid, but I have a lot more problems than he does.

"Let's eat." Liera said.

"What is it?" I asked. "It smells good."

"It's food." Roz said. He was either trying to start an argument with me, or trying to prove to me that he is as stupid as I already know he is.

"I know what it is." I said trying to be as kind as I could. "I never had this kind before."

"It's beef with a sauce that I made from many of the herbs that you see around here. It's a recipe that my mother taught me." Liera answered.

It did smell good. I was hoping to get out of eating. "I'm not that hungry. Can I please go to my room?"

"Ariel, do you feel alright? You really haven't eating anything since you got here." Marlin said with concern.

"I feel fine. Just not hungry."

"Tell you what, just have a little salad." Liera said.

"Okay"

The rest of supper went along fine, then I helped clean up. I wanted to go to bed early so that morning would come faster. I said goodnight to Liera and was about to do the same with Marlin but I saw that he was busy.

"Are you going to say goodnight?" he asked.

"You looked busy, I didn't want to disturb you."

"You won't disturb me." he smiled. "But I thank you for the consideration. Goodnight."

I went to my room and was about to shut the door when Roz stuck his head in. "That was a cheep shot." he said.

"It worked." I smiled.

"Yea well, mother said I should apologize."

"And you don't want to. I know you don't like me."

He was surprised. "How do you know?"

"I just do."

"Whatever. Night."

"Night" I said sweetly as I shut the door on him.

This was just the beginning. I have a strong feeling that our rivalry will never end, end I have come to a few conclusions within my first day. One is that I know Roz hates he, that much is obvious. Liera scares me. Marlin I trust, I don't know why. Oh well, I'm going to bed. I have other things to think about, and I don't look funny. My hair is long and black, my eyes are a light blue. I'm just an ordinary kid.

I love my room, I left the curtain open so I could get a better look at the night sky. It was so peaceful that I fell asleep staring at the stars.

I don't dream, if I did I never remember any of them, but one. That night I had the a strange dream. I had it before but not in this much detail. For some reason it is the only one that I ever remember.

There was this man, at least I believed it was a man, kneeling down on the ground beside a woman covered in blood. I couldn't see her very well but I did see her long black hair. The man picked up something, it looked like a baby. He wrapped it up and was about to leave, then he stopped and looked back, he took something from her. It sparkled brightly as he picked it up. He put it in his pocket and left. Everything else was fuzzy.

I couldn't see the surrounding area very well, but I didn't see the shadow of another person nearby watching the man. The rest I don't remember. That's why I really can't consider this a dream, more like a vision of some kind. Why it was the only one I remember I didn't know, as much as I detested this vision there was nothing that I could do to stop it. I have had it for so many years now, if I ever had a real dream I wouldn't know how to react to it.

When morning came I sat up in bed thinking about my dream. It really didn't bother me, but it does make me wonder. Where are my real parents? I'll think about it later. I have someone coming over today, this should be interesting. I got up and dressed and straightened up my room then ran downstairs missing every other step and went into the kitchen.

"What's your hurry?" Liera asked.

"Clair's coming over today. Is it okay if I wait outside?"

"Why don't you have some breakfast first?"

"I'm not that hungry." I told her, and she asked Marlin the same thing when he came in.

"No, I'll get something later. I want to get an early start." he told her.

Liera went over to him and whispered. "You're not setting a good example. I'm trying to get her to eat something."

"I'll tell you what, you go to work and I will fix us something for us." he told her. "Where is Roz?"

"He ate and left." she answered. "He will be over his friends for most of the day, but when he gets back he has to get going on his studies. Make something good."

"I will."

She gave him a hug and kiss goodbye, she was about to give me one but I backed off.

"It's okay, can I at least have a hug?" she asked.

I hated the idea, but I didn't want to hurt her feelings or get on her bad side so I said ok. She gave me a hug and it just didn't feel right, there is little emotion in her.

She smiled then got what she needed and left. I sat at the table, Marlin sat across from me.

"Are you hungry?" he asked.

"No"

"I have an idea," he said when he got up. "Lets have some juice."

"That sounds ok."

"I'll be downstairs for a while." he said as he poured something in a glass. "I'll be up now and then to check on you two. If you need anything let me know."

"What's down there?" I asked taking a sip.

"My office. I found that it is better to work at home."

"Why doesn't Liera work at home?"

"She needs to work with more computers." he said as he sat down, "plus she works with different chemicals and she has other people she needs to work with."

"This is okay, but it doesn't taste very good." I said after I finished it.

"Yes, but it is good for you."

"What does Roz have to study?"

"He wants to be an engineer. He has a certain amount of subjects he has to study and after he will go on to another level of learning. It's part of the educational system. We teach our children at home. That's why you have a computer in your room. When you are ready you will learn also." he explained.

"Why at home?"

"You can learn more, it saves on resources and the best part is that if someone is sick they can stay home, get better and not share their germs with others. Plus you can go at your own pace."

"What happens if you learn all you can?"

He smiled at my comment. "You never stop learning, but when you do finish your studies on the computer then we find an apprentenceship program in the field you want to go in. It will enable you to continue on with your dreams."

When he said the word dream I thought about telling him about the only dream that I have, but I changed my mind. I figured that it would be better to wait.

"I heard that our lives can be endless. Is that true?" I asked for a reason. I wanted to see what his reaction would be.

"Yes" he replied slowly. "That is why you must make very correct decisions in your early age. It will reflect on you forever."

I have heard a lot of different things but I have never questioned it, so I think I will. This will tell me if he is really telling me the truth when he said that he will answer my questions. So I guess the best ones are yet to come.

"What happens if too many people are born, won't the world be overpopulated?"

"Wouldn't you like to talk about this when you get older?"

"Not really. I would like to know everything that I can before I get too old." I said. Then I thought that I shouldn't have said it like that. "No offence." I caught him off guard with that statement. He sat there and stared at me as if he was intensely studying me.

"None taken." he said after a few minutes. "Like I said, you never stop learning. No matter how old you get."

"Then will you answer my question?"

"We are uunable to have more than one or two children, so with the size of the planet and the number of people, we don't have to worry about that for a long time."

"Why can't we have more than one?" I asked curiously.

"It's something that happened many centuries ago. When our ancesstors were on their original planet." he thought for a few minutes before answering. I knew some of the answers to my questions, but what I was trying to find out was if what I knew was right. "I like the idea that you ask questions. So I will try to answer them as simply as I can. Our ancestors came from a planet that they destroyed a long time ago."

"How?"

"With their wars and neglect. They were too blind to be thankful for what they had. They poisoned their planet, the toxic conditions caused different changes. the sick were the first to die then the elderly then the children. Everything that was done in the name of science was wrong."

"Wrong, how?"

"They came up with something to slow down the deaths. The only thing that it did was sterilize the females. People still died, the they messed with the dna to stop the strong from growing too fast. Everything they did had a serious side effect. With the toxin in the air and the chemicals they created it was a disaster. Then they decided to make a fresh start, by coming here. The natives were very far and few so they didn't see any reason why they shouldn't."

"As long as they didn't get near them"

"Yes, but the more they found out about the people of this world, the more curious they became. Especially when they discovered that the natives has a hidden power. After a while of watching them they dicided to try and gain the trust of the natives, then they made a deal with them. If they agreed not to repeat their mistakes here, then the natives would help them to restore a civilization that was almost destroyed. So after a few years of experiments and hard work a female child was born, and she showed signs of both worlds."

"I don't understand."

"She had the power of the natives and she also carried the burden of living forever. She too had a child, and it was the beginning of a new race."

"That planet was Terrina wasn't it?"

"Yes. How do you know that?" he asked inquisitively.

"I told you I heard lots of things there. Please don't tell Liera, I don't trust her."

"I know, I feel you anxiety when you're around her. We learned a very valuable lesson by our ancestors mistakes, in their search for survival they created a new world. The reason we have certain powers is because of what they did. That's why different people can do different things."

"Like the way that Liera can read my mind." I whispered to myself.

"Yes she can. How do you know that?"

"I feel it, it's easy. I can understand what she feels. She won't hurt me as long as I'm not a threat to her."

Marlin didn't seem surprised that I knew about Liera. He did however wonder how much power I possessed, once again he scrutinized me, searching within me for the answer. I was also curious as to how far I can take these powers and what else I can do with them.

"Would it be possible to have unlimited powers?" I asked totally out of curiosity.

Instead of searching me he sat there and wondered what I was searching for. I was searching, I wanted answers to where I really belong and if my life will contain an eternity of solitude and despair.

"Perhaps. It would depend on the person." he said, but before either one of us could say any more there was a knock at the kitchen door. "Clair's here?"

"I almost forgot about her. Can we talk some more about this later?" I asked when I got up to open the door.

"Sure"

I knew he had many questions the he wanted to ask me, but he wasn't sure if I would answer. I think my comfusion was keeping him from finding out anything reasonable.

"Hi. Am I early?" Clair asked.

"No you're not." I replied.

"I just wanted to make sure that it is okay for her to come over, you know how children can be." her mother said as she stood in the doorway.

"It's not problem. I'm sure that the girls will keep themselves occupied." Marlin said to her as he staired at us. "Besides, I think it will be good for Ariel to have a firend with a common interest."

"Can we go to my room?"

"Go ahead."

But before we went upstairs Clair's mother informed her that she wuld be back in a few hours. She gave her mother a hug and kiss and thanked her for letting her spend some time with me.

"How do you like it here?" she asked when we went in my room.

"I love it. Too bad Roz doesn't like me." I said when I shut the door.

"Oh well. Who cares what he doesn't like. We're friends now." she said in excitement.

"Yeah, and I have a feeling that we will be friends for a long time."

"It's going to be fun, we will be able to do a lot together when we get older." she said with a big smile.

We had a great morning. I found a disk with games and we played for the longest time. When we went downstairs Marlin was sitting on a chair reading something.

"Is it okay if we go outside for a while?" I asked.

"Sure, don't wander off. Clair's mother will be here soon."

While we were outside we walked the the back of the house and cimbed up on the stonewall and walked to the corner of the wall.

"My house is over there behind those trees." she said pointing behind me.

"I wondered what is way over there?" I said looking straight ahead.

"My mom says that the oldest living person lives in those woods."

"Have you ever seen who it is?"

"No, my mom told me not to bother her."

"How do you know it's a she?"

"I just do. Do you ever get the feeling that you know something without anyone telling you?" she asked curiously.

"Yeah. That's how I know Roz hates me." I said seriously. "What else can you do?"

"Well, I can read my mom's mind. If I try hard enough I can make things move. I haven't told her that yet. So promise you won't tell her."

"I won't. That's why Marlin said we have something in common."

"What else can you do?"

"I can read people's minds." I said sitting down. "I can also talk to animals, and I feel what other people are feeling."

"What do you mean by feeling?" she asked sitting next to me.

"What people feel and think are two different things. I can feel their feelings, like Roz, he hates me and I feel that hate. And you, you think im strange. I feel that difference in you. You came here today out of curiosity." I explained. "But I know we'll be good friends."

"That must be fun, talking to animals?" she said sitting next to me.

"It is. I bet it's real fun moving things around without having to touch them. Do you know things that happened somewhere else?"

"No, I wish I did." she said surprisingly.

"It's really neat, but sometimes it can be scary."

"Why?"

"How would you like to know something about a place that you've never been to or seen before?"

"It depends on what happened."

"I don't think it's a good idea to tell the adults too much."

"Yeah"

We sat on the wall talking about other things, then she told me how excited she was about her fishing trip she was taking tomorrow.

"I wish you could come."

"Maybe some other time."

Without moving I could tell that someone was coming closer and when I turned my head I noticed Clair's mother coming closer.

"Hi" I said to her.

"Hello Ariel. Did you two have fun this morning?" she asked.

"We sure did." Clair said when she got up to give her a hug. "Maybe next time you could come over to my house." she said.

"That sounds good to me. I'll see you later."

They both said goodbye and started walking back to their house. I stayed on the wall and watched the two of them, one thing I was curious about was the way they were walking. Her mother was holding her hand and they were enjoying whatever conversation they were having. I observed this until they were out of my sight. I walked back to the house smelling the flowers as I went, the air is sweet and the birds are flying. It's peaceful outside.

"So how was your morning?" Marlin asked when I walked in the door.

"Fun. I know that I asked earlier, but is it possible to have an unlimited amount of power? I mean is it possible to do everything?"

He came over and sat at the table, I could tell that he was starting to wonder even more about me. "Ariel, what can you do?"

"I can talk to animals, that you know. I feel what others feel, that's how I know Roz hates me." I didn't want to tell him that I know things about the past.

"Roz is a little upset, he was use to being the only one here."

"Roz's problem isn't the idea that I am here. He doesn't want to share what little affection he gets from his mother. As far as I'm concerned I don't want it. He is even envious about what she feels for you." which I knew wasn't much.

"And you know this for a fact?"

"Yes, I can read his mind very easy. He can't block me out and neither can Liera."

"Why would you do that?"

"I don't trust her. I just want her to treat me for who I am, not one of her experiments." I told him. "And she's home early."

"How do you know that?"

"I feel her." and within a few minutes we heard the front door closing and Liera announcing she's home.

"Well how did your day go?" she asked me coming into the kitchen.

"Good. Clair just left a few minutes ago." I replied.

"And since you're back early," Marlin said standing up. "I'm going to get some more work done."

"I'm sure we'll fine something to keep us busy for a while." Liera smiled.

"I'm going to get cleaned up, I'll be right back." I told her.

"I guess it's just the two of us for a while." she said when I went back into the kitchen. "I'm not going to bother with lunch, so I know you like plants, let's start there."

Well this shouldn't be too bad, I thought to myself. What harm can plants do? There was a room off of the dining room that let to an arboretum. I never even noticed that there was a door in the corner of that room, with all the plants it was well hidden.

"Wow" My eyes lit up, the fragrance of sweet flowers intertwined and filled the whole room. "I never knew this was here." I said looking around

"Well considering you got here yesterday, I'm not surprised. You haven't had time to look around."

It wasn't too bad, we spent hours talking about the flowers. It made her feel good that we were getting along so well. I didn't mind it at all. I enjoyed listening to her telling me how much work she did to get her plants to grow. She tole me all of the names of them and how long they live. I don't think that she missed anything about flowers. One thing that she didn't know that I knew was Marlin had been watching the two of us.

It was starting to get close to dinner time. Roz had come home and she tole him to get going on his studies so he can be done by dinner. I stayed where I was while she talked with him, looking at the beauty of the flowers.

She came back in and watched me as I looked at them. I think she was surprised that my interest with plants was authentic.

"You really like them?" she asked.

"Yes ma'am. I never seen real flowers before, they never taught us about them." I said.

"Really? I can never imagine why." she said.

"Can I grow one like that?"

"Anyone can make flowers grow, the secret is keeping them alive. I will show you how when I have a doy off. We should have done that today. Oh well, it gives us something to do another day." she said, and she seemed disappointed that she didn't think of it earlier.

"Let's get ready for dinner. Would you like to help me after we get cleaned up?"

I looked at her in a questioning way. "You want me to help you cook?"

"It's easy, and you have to learn sometime."

"Did I hear someone say cook?" Marlin said when he came into the room, and in the background I could hear Roz calling for his mother.

"I'll be back." she said when she left.

When Liera was out of the room Marlin asked me how it went, he should have known not to ask.

"Why don't you tell me. You were watching us." I told him.

"You will never cease to amaze me. It seems you have a few abilities them I'm not aware of yet."

"Well I didn't think that it was too bad. She said her next day off she will show me how to grow one. It was a good afternoon but I still have my doubts. I have to get cleaned up."

"You have never seen a real flower before?"

"No" I answered as we walked into the living room. "They never taught us about things like that."

"Us. Do you know how many of you there were?" he asked when he sat down.

"A lot. I saw and heard them all the time. We weren't allowed to talk with each other, but some of us did. I had a friend. His name was Derick, they took him away in the middle of the night and I never saw him again."

"We'll talk about this more when we're alone. Go get cleaned up."

While I was changing I couldn't help but to wonder how much power I do possess and how long it would be before I actually use it and know why. I felt good about today but I still questioned myself as far as where I belong, better yet, who I really am. These two questions always remain in my mind. Marlin knows I will talk to him when Liera's not around. I also wonder if he could find out what happened to Derick.

"So how was your morning with Clair?" Liera asked as we set the table.

"It was great. We talked about a lot of things, and I found a disk that had games of it and we played for a long time, then we went outside. She told me that the oldest woman in the world lives in the woods. Is that true?"

"Yes it is, and if you ever meet her try not to bother her too much. She likes company, but she also likes to be alone, to talk with nature." Marlin said when he and Roz came in.

"What do you mean?" I asked sitting down.

"She can understand what the plants are saying. Like the way you talk to animals. I believe she can do both."

"You can talk to animals?" Roz said when he sat across from me.

"Yes. Can't everyone?" I asked.

"You're lucky. I wish I could." Roz said in a disappointing way.

"Well maybe if you practiced more." Liera told him. "What else can you do Ariel?"

"Not much, I know when people are coming." I said with the hopes that she didn't know I didn't tell her much more, but it's not a lie, I just don't think I should tell her too much. I don't trust her.

"When you get older you may be able to do more." she smiled. I started to get a different feeling from her, for a moment she forgot what I was toward her.

When we finished eating I helped Liera clean everything up, asaid goodnight and went upstairs. I had a sigh of relief when I got to my room. I was about to shut the door when Roz stuck his head in.

"You know you are going to do that one of these nights and I might hit you without meaning to." I warned him nicely.

"I was wondering if you could show me how you talk to animals?" he asked.

"I don't know how I do it, I just do. But I can try to show you."

"You will, great, thanks. Night." he said excitedly.

I watched as he went into his room, he was happy that I said yes. His dislike for me is starting to go away slowly. Once again I was about to shut the door when Marlin came in.

"I just wanted to ask you, why didn't you tell Liera the truth about your powers?" he asked.

"I know that she feels uneasy about it, that's why I didn't tell her. I still don't trust her. I don't want her to send me back. Are you mad?"

He smiled and shook his head. "No, and you don't have to worry about going back there. Next time the subject comes up we'll figure out how to keep her at ease."

"Really, thank you."

Without thinking that I really don't like touching people, he gave me a kiss on the forehead and said goodnight. I sat on the bed thinking about Liera, I couldn't figure her out. Then I wondered if it would be a good idea to go down and give her a hug, show her a sign of affection, as much as I hated the idea. It might make her feel better about me.

All the lights were off when I got to the top of the stairs, I would have turned on one if I knew where the switch was. I heard Marlin and Liera outside talking, I grabbed ahold of the rail and very carefully made my way to the bottom, then very carefully going to the glass door out back.

"Ariel what are you doing down here in the dark? I'm surprised you didn't fall." Liera said.

"I just wanted to give you a hug." I said. Did she ever seemed surprised.

She came over and knelt in front of me. "I'm so glad that you did." then she gave me a tight hug.

I noticed something in the sky. "What was that?" I asked watching.

"A shooting star." Marlin said. "Would you like to sit with us and watch?"

"I don't want to interrupt you two." I replied.

"You're not interrupting." Liera said. "We sit out here every chance we get. Roz sits at hit window with a telescope." she said pointing to his window.

She pulled over a chair for me and we watched the stars flying across the sky for a long time, it was wonderful. We talked about anything we thought of. Liera went in and made some hot cocco for us.

"I'm proud of you. That was a nice thing you did." Marlin said taking my hand. "Your hands are cold. Are you warm enough?"

"I'm fine, I'm not cold at all. I just hope she doesn't expect that all the time. To be truthful I didn't like it.

Is that wrong?" before he could say anything Liera came back out.

"Here we go." she said handing me a cup. "I know you'll like this."

"This is good, I wouldn't mind this for breakfast. I never had it before."

"Never! What did they give you?" she asked.

"Nothing that was good. I got a lot of shots." I said showing them my arm. "Sometimes I wasn't hungry after that."

Marlin didn't like that idea at all, I could tell by the look on his face as he looked at my arm. "That explains why you don't eat much." he said rubbing my arm.

When I had finished I was ready for bed this time. Liera had taken my cup and gave me another hug. I don't know if it was because I was tired or what, but I got a different feeling from her. I felt her real feelings toward me, and I didn't like it. It was worse than the hatred that Roz felt for me. Marlin was different, he honestly cared.

The next few weeks went along fine. Clair and I had become close friends. We spent almost every other day doing something together. I showed Roz how to talk to animals, I think he expected to learn in one day. Liera showed me how to grow flowers, so far I have a pot of dirt sitting in the window, but I look at it every day to see if there is any changes. Marlin kept his promise about finding out why they were giving me shots, he didn't make much progress.

The people he was talking to didn't give out much information, it was like some big secret. I should have the right to know what they were doing to me. I still wondered about my real parents, the more I see Clair and her mother together, the more I want to know what it would feel like to touch my own.

Liera and I were outside looking at some plants when Marlin came out, he looked either frustrated or disappointed, I couldn't tell. His emotions were confusing.

"What's wrong?" she asked him.

"I have been trying to find out what they were doing to Ariel before we brought her home."

"Why would you want to know that?" she asked. "When we picked her up they showed us all the work on her."

"Maybe I should leave." I said.

"This concerns you, you can stay." he said.

When I sat down Liera sat down beside me. "How have you been feeling?" she asked touching my shoulder.

"Fine, I just don't feel like eating. I don't feel sick or anything like that." I told her.

"What happened the day before we picked you up?" Marlin asked.

"Well, someone got me up before daylight. She gave me something to drink and she took me in another room." I said.

"Can you remember what was in that room?" He asked.

"There were machines in there. She sat me in a chair and put wires all over me. After that she told me to lay down on a exam table and she started scanning me. When I asked her what she was doing she told me to shut up. She was very mean to me." I said.

"Do you remember how long you were in there for?" Liera asked, I started to think she cared.

"Almost all day. When she turned it off she took something from the computer she was at and left, someone else came in after her and just kept looking at me, he didn't say anything. After awhile someone came in and gave him something to look at." I explained.

"Must have been test results." Marlin said.

"They took blood out of my arm, then they put something over me. I can't remember much about that, but I do know that it hurt. After they took it off they gave me another shot in the same arm they took the blood out of. They only other thing I really remember after is when they took me out of my room to meet you two."

"I'm going to get us something to drink." Liera said. She didn't look good, she started to get uneasy and her stomach was starting to bother her.

"Can I asked you a question?" I asked Marlin.

"You know you can." he said rubbing my arm.

"Does she work for them?" I whispered.

"Yes, but maybe not for long."

"Can I trust her?"

"I think so." he whispered.

"Here we go." Liera said when she put some glasses on the table.

"What is it?" I asked.

"I know you'll like this, it's berry juice. I had this recipe for a long time."

"You made it. I like this." I said smelling it.

"I'm glad. I actually found two things you like."

"I want to know what they did." Marlin said taking a glass.

"I could find out." Liera said.

"Not yet." Marlin told her. "It's best if we wait awhile. I don't want them coming for her." but he knows Liera better than anyone. "I mean it, we need to wait. Timeing is everything with them. You know that." he told her when she sat down.

"This is frustrating. I want to leave that job. Why don't we move. We've been here for so long." she told him.

He put the glass down and smiled. "Let's wait until the kids are older, then we'll get out of here."

She took his hand. "I don't know how long I can hold on for." she whispered.

She hates her job, or she's afraid of them. That explains a lot of things. Now I wondered if there was a reason for me being here. If I can feel things about her what can they know. That has to be why she's uneasy all the time.

"Can I ask you something Liera?" I asked her.

"Of course. You just must be careful what you ask me." she said touching my face.

"Is Roz your real son?" I asked looking at her.

"Yes, but there are many of us that cannot have children."

"Then we are created in a lab, and then placed in homes?"

"Sadly yes. Most of the children you see today are cloned. We don't have much of a choice if we want to stay as natural as we can."

"I don't understand?"

"We can interbreed with other races, but some of us would rather stay with our own kind. Usually the first generation of clones can have children, and if that's the case then any left over dna is destroyed. It's supposed to be anyway. That's not my department." Liera said.

The rest of the day went along fine. When nighttime came I noticed a tiny green stem coming from the firt in the flower pot. I stood there looking at it for a long time.

"Do you see anything yet?" Marlin asked when he came in.

"Yes, it's starting to grow. There is a little stem right there." I said pointing to it.

"In no time you will have a flower."

"I hope so, then I can take it up to my room and put it in the window."

"I have something that may interest you. Come outside." he said reaching for my hand.

When we went out to the backyard I was surprised to see Roz out there, he's usually in his room at this time of night. Liera had made some juice and snacks and put them on a small table.

"I thought that since it was a nice night that we would sit outside for a while." she said.

"And when it gets darker we will be able to see both moons full tonight, and if you look in the right place we can see Kerrell tonight, and I have something that we can see it better with." Marlin said.

"What's that?" I asked.

"I found an old telescope downstairs." He said.

"Why would you have something like that in your office?" I asked.

"We have a storage room down there. I should go through that the next time I have a day off. I think you and Roz would find that interesting." Liera said.

"I'd like that." I said.

"So would I." Roz added.

Roz and I decided to catch some lighting bugs. I watched Roz try and fail many times, then I showed him a better way, or I should say a way that would make him made at me. I stood where it was the darkest and hald my hand out and invited a little bug to land on my hane. Roz watched in amazement, watching them as they sat there and glowed on my hand. When the flew off he decided to try and get one, but was scared when he had it in his hand.

"Roz, what's wrong?" Liera asked.

He went over and sat by his mother. "I don't know, for some reason I felt scared."

I stood in front of him trying not to laugh. "You were not the one who was scared. You felt what the bug felt. It was scared because you chased it and caught it." I told him seriously.

"Is that what you can do?" he asked.

"Yes, you will get use to it after a while. It's very easy."

He still didn't understand what happened. "That is why you can get them like that?"

"That and the fact that I told them that I would let them go." I informed him. "How would you like it if someone was chasing you?"

Roz learned something new tonight, and knowing fear like that is one that you never forget. I hope for his sake he won't.

"Come on, let's check out the telescope, it's interesting to see the stars closer." Marlin said.

"I'll let Roz go first." I said.

While Roz was busy I laid down on the ground and looked at the night sky, Liera came over and sat beside me.

"You know I was fifteen when I learned how to talk to talk to animals. I never tried it with bugs." she said.

"I can talk to almost any animal. It's a lot of fun."

"It seems that you are a few years ahead of yourself. That's not bad. Whatever you have make sure you use them wisely." She said very seriously.

I didn't like the way she said that. "What do you mean?"

"Sometimes you can hurt people without ever realizing what you have done. Sometimes it can be fixed, but there is always that one time when someone is beyond help. No matter who you know or how much power you possess." she explained.

"What is the worse thing that someone can do?"

"We have certain laws that we use our powers by. The worse thing that anyone can do is to bring back someone from the dead."

"But I thought that our lives were endless, that we can't die?"

"It is. A persons body can be damaged to the point where it will die. The power that one has always lives, and with some people their knowledge will live as well. It is what we like to believe is our lifeforce. It will always be there."

"That sounds like it would be interesting." I said to myself.

Marlin called me over to look at one of the stars, as much as I have enjoyed the conversation with Liera, I would find the stars more interesting. They were so wonderful to look at, to see something hanging in a large space of emptiness and shine so bright was incredible. He showed me how to use the telescope, and while I was looking at all the different things in the night sky I saw something else that looked better than the stars and satellites.

"What is that?" I asked.

"Let me see." he said as he looked into the scope. "That's Zandar. It's between us and Kerrell. We'll be able to see it for a few more days or so."

"It's beautiful."

Looking through this made Zandar appear closer than the moon was on a clear night. I could see everything from the clouds covering it to the colors of the planet itself.

"That it is. We are helping them to advance in their technology." he said.

"That's why you go over those computer disks?" I asked, but I also got the feeling he's checking something else.

"Yes. Maybe someday you can help as well." he said.

"I would like that. I like computers, they're a lot of fun."

"Plus they teach you many things. We use them in just about everything we do, but they're only as smart as the person programming them."

"So in a way they are overrated?" I asked.

He chuckled at my question. "Yes, we are too dependant on something made of plastic and wires."

Without using the telescope I looked at Zander until I started to feel sleepy. I said goodnight and went to my room, I opened the window to stare at the stars some more. I could still see Zandar but it wasn't the same. I wouldn't mind going there sometime, someday I will.

After a few weeks Liera had her day off. I helped her to clean up the breakfast dishes, which I didn't mind because all it consists of is rinsing them off and put them in the dishwasher, and the rest of the house. When we were done we went downstairs and into the storage room. I couldn't believe all the boxes that were in there.

"What are in all these?" I asked.

"I have no idea, that's what we are going to find out. If Roz ever gets down here he can help. We should start with the first box." she said picking it up. "Well what do you know, it's empty. We can use it to put stuff in it that will be thrown out."

"Where does that other door go to?"

"You mean that one over there?" she asked pointing to the left of her. "There is a generator in there. We use solar power. It's much better and cleaner for the planet, and more efficient and it's the only way to get energy. If you were on the roof you could see the solar panels that harness the suns rays. It's interesting when you understand how it works."

"Is it safe to come in here?" Roz asked when he stuck his head in.

"It's about time." Liera said.

We cleaned up a spot on the floor so we could sit down and go through all the boxes. We found a lot of boxes with meaningless papers in them, except for one.

"This is pretty." I said taking it out. The material was a soft jade color, very sleek and lightweight in design.

"That's my old dress, I thought I had given it away." she said. "I wore this on the day that I met Roz's father. It was so long ago."

"How long?" Roz asked.

"It must have been over sixty years ago, if not longer." she said sadly.

"How old are you?" I asked. I didn't mean anything by it, I was just curious.

She didn't mind answering my question. "Well, let me think. I must be close to two fifty." she said.

"That is old." Roz said.

"That's not nice, you're going to be old someday." I told him, but then I would have never guessed she was that old. So we also retain some youth.

"that's okay, there is nothing wrong with how old you are." she said.

"Have you found anything interesting yet?" Marlin asked when he came in.

"I think I did." Roz said when he took out some disks.

"What is it?" I asked. "These are bigger than the ones I have."

"These have pictures on them." Liera said. "Put them out by the door, we'll bring them upstairs and look at them tonight."

Marlin started to help us go through the boxes. The more we went through the more interested I became. There were things that I have never seen before, all kind of gadgets. We also found more disks and the last box I picked up was small and light.

"Look at this." I said opening it. "It has some jewelry in it."

"Let me see that. I think I know who this box belongs to." Marlin said.

"Oh yeah, care to tell me?" Liera asked.

"This belongs to my mother." he said pulling out a necklace.

"How did they get here?" I asked.

"My parents were staying with us for a little while when they were waiting for their house to be built." he said.

"You know what you should do, pay her a visit and take Ariel with you. You haven't seen your parents in years. I think your mother would love that." Liera suggested.

"It's also possible that those disks are theirs." he said.

We finished up and took the boxes upstairs that needed going through, Marlin took the photo's as well as some other disks that we found and started to go through them. I didn't pay much attention until he decided to sit on the couch and go through the photos.

"You are going to love this." he said.

Roz and I went over and sat beside him. "Who is that?" he asked.

"Me when I was your age." he told him.

"How long ago was that?" Roz asked.

"Over three hundred years. I wonder if she knows that these are missing."

"So we can take them back?" I asked.

"You really want to go?" he asked.

"Yeah, why not."

"How about you Roz?"

"I'd like to, but I don't think so."

"I understand. We'll go tomorrow. The sooner the better."

We finished going through the other boxes we had. Some of them were clothes that Roz wore when he was a baby, for some reason he hated looking at them. I guess he doesn't want to believe that he was that small.

Tomorrow should be fun. I can't wait to meet his parents, sometimes it's hard for me to realize that the people on this world can be so old. I think that this is going to be a good history lesson.

Morning came fast. I wore the best outsit I could find. I wasn't too interested in having breakfast, I just wanted to get going. I went into the kitchen and waited for Marlin, Liera was in there getting ready to leave for work.

"I can tell you're really looking forward to today." she said.

"Yes I am." I replied with excitement. "How come Roz doesn't want to go?"

"When you get there you will find out." she replied with a laugh. "I'm surprised he didn't tell you."

"I see you're ready." Marlin said coming in.

"Do you want anything before you two go?" Liera asked.

"I don't want anything." I said.

"And I'm all set. We'll get something later." he told her, then he whispered something to her and her reply was "no" as she gave him a kiss, then one to me as she left.

"I hate it when she does that." I said wiping off my forehead.

Marlin picked up the box that he was taking with us and put it in the back seat, and in no time we were on our way.

"How long will it take to get there?" I asked.

"Not long, a few hours."

"That's what you said when you took me home. It took a lot longer than you said. By the way, Roz didn't tell me about your mother."

"How do you know what I asked?"

"I have good ears." I told him with confidence.

"Oh really! I'll have to remember that."

"I have a question."

"Sounds like it serious. What is it?"

"It's not that serious. When we were cleaning up yesterday I picked up a dress that Liera said she wore when she met Roz's dad. I could feel her sadness, and for some reason, guilt."

"Liera and I have been together for nine years. His father was a nice guy, he had a very tragic death. Try not to ask her about it, it still upsets her."

"Is that why she said you can't bring the dead back to life?"

"It's not a good idea, even with the help of science. It's always best to let nature take it course."

The best way to go took us on a road that overlooked a good part of the city. It was nice to see it from a distance, it looked so small from here. Trees on one side and the city on the other, before I knew it the city was far behind us and we were once again in the woods. I like the country, it's so quiet. Marlin was right, but it took a little more than a few hours to get there.

"Now this is nice!" I said when we pulled up to a small house that is hidden by trees and all kinds of plants.

"Yes. This is why my parents stayed with us for a while. My mother didn't want any of the trees and plants moved. So they built abound them."

When I got out the only thing I did was to look around, taking in the beauty of the land. It was like the house and trees were living together. I could feel something very different about this place, I felt the happiness here.

"Are you ready?" he asked.

"Well, sure. Let's go." I said.

As we walked to the front door I noticed how the shrubs and flowers belonged where they were, where nature put them. When Marlin went to knock on the door a woman opened it before he could touch it.

"Well it's about time you came here." she said in a very happy voice. I could tell she loved him just by the smile she had on her face. "Why didn't you call? Your father is going to be so happy to see you."

"We figured we would surprise you." he told her.

"We!" she said. She didn't see me standing, hiding actually, behind Marlin.

"Yes. I have someone I want you to meet." he said as he stepped inside, unobstructing her view from me. "This is Ariel."

"Oh is she pretty. Your father said that you and Liera were going to adopt a child. I never imagined it would be a girl." she said when she took my hand in hers and brought me inside.

Now I know why Roz doesn't like to come here. I felt her powers when she took my hand, I also felt that she is a very nice loving person. So I seen no reason to be leery around her.

"Don't mind me child. When I get overexcited my powers tend to take control. It's so wonderful, I'm glad you came. You can call me Mynera. Where did your father go?" she asked.

"He went outside, and he's not my father." I reminded her. "We found something that belongs to you." When I made the comment that Marlin wasn't my father she gave me a strange look, but in her own way she understood.

"To me? I can't imagine what it could be."

Marlin handed her the box when he came back in. "You left this in the house when you moved."

"My jewelry box. It took you three years to find it? Now I remember, I left it there on purpose, with the intention that you would come to see me earlier. Come on, let's go sit out back. It's a beautiful day. Take her out and I'll bring us something to drink."

As we stood out on the back deck it was prettier than the front of the house. It had a great view of the lake and hills.

"What do you think?" Marlin asked when he sat down.

"I think you forgot something." I said in a way to remind him about the photos that he purposely left on the back seat. "I love it here. It's nice and quiet."

When his mother came out she had a tray in her hands and he offered to take it for her but she politely declined.

"I can't wait till your father gets back." she said sitting next to me.

"Where is he?" Marlin asked.

"He went fishing before dawn. He wasn't going to be gone long. As a matter of fact, he will be back real soon." she said, and she wasn't wrong. A few minutes later we heard a noise at the side of the house. "There he is now."

"What is that piece of junk doing taking up space in my driveway?" His voice hollered from the side of the house.

Marlin sat there trying to look around the corner to see his father walking toward us. "Hi dad." he said.

"Well it's about time you came here." he was just like her, with one exception, he likes to joke around.

"I was just as surprised as you are." she said. "He has someone with him."

"Oh yeah." he said coming toward us. "Well this is a surprise."

I didn't mind him too much, but I got closer to Marlin anyway. "She's cautious around people." he told him patting my back. "Until she gets to know you."

"I don't blame her there. Who might you be?" he asked me.

"Ariel" I replied.

"Ariel, what a pretty name for a little girl. Did Marlin give you that name?"

"No sir. That's what they called me."

"Rule number one around here is you don't call me sir. It makes me feel old." he said. Life out here must be real good, they seem very happy.

"You are old." she told him.

"I may have an old body, but I can still out run anyone." he said proudly as he sat beside her. "Don't call me grandpa or pops, that's for old people who sit back and watch everyone else run around. I like doing things. Isn't that right dear?" he asked her.

"Yes grandpa." she said picking on him.

"All I need is a young body, but you still love me anyway." he said to her. "Just call me Jacob." he told me. He is a funny old man, his hair is grey and thinning, his face showing his age but his spirit still holding on to his zest for life. "So what brings you out here." he asked Marlin.

"Ariel found mother's jewelry box yesterday when we were cleaning out the storage room." he said, still not mentioning the pictures.

"We also found some pictures." I was hoping to see them, just out of curiosity.

"Pictures?" they both said. "Go get them please." she added.

When I got up to get them I knew that Marlin wasn't to enthused about looking at them. As I passed him he whispered "thanks a lot."

"You're welcome." I smiled.

When I came back with them Jacob had disappeared, before I could ask Mynera she had already known my question. She can read my mind.

"He went to get cleaned up. How do you like it here?" she asked.

"I love it. The house looks smaller in the front than it does in the back." I said.

"It's the way we had it built. I love it when the shade hit's the house just right, then you really can't see it from the road."

"This feels better." Jacob said when he came back out, he also had something small in his hand.

"What it that?" I asked.

"Come here and I'll show you." he sat down and motioned me to sit next to him. He took the disks and put a few of them inside. "Now we can see what is on these."

"I think I'll take a walk." Marlin said getting up.

"Sit down son. If memory serves me right, which it always does, these are pictures of you, when you were a lot younger. Boy these are old." He said realizing that time has gone by fast.

"I remember this, they are old. I never knew that I had these." Marlin said.

"Do you know how long it has been since we have looked at them?" Mynera said.

"It has been years." Marlin said.

"This is one picture you have got to see." Jacob said holding me closer.

Marlin tried to look over that the picture. "What is it?" he asked.

"Not you, you can see it in a minute." Jacob said.

"Who is it?" I asked.

"That is Marlin when he graduated. You would never know it was him with his hair darker and longer. Now you got a lot more years on you." he laughed.

"It was a long time ago. I can't believe I looked like that." Marlin said taking the picture.

This was great, I enjoyed being here. The breeze felt cool and smelled fresh. I noticed that Marlin seemed different, calmer then he usually is. For a quick moment he let his guard down and I almost found out something about myself, when he realized it he quickly blocked me out. I wonder why.

"You know something, Ariel is right." Mynera said.

"Right about what?" I asked.

"I'm sorry, I forgot that you are not accustomed to being around me like Roz is. That is why he doesn't like being near me. You are a lot more relaxed since you got here." she said tapping him on the shoulder.

"My mind isn't all cluttered." he told her.

"Ariel is advanced for her age. I have a feeling that she is going to be powerful when she grows up. The powers that she does have she shouldn't have for a few more years. Some she knows about and some she doesn't even know she has." she told him. When he looked at me I got the feeling that I am in for a long talk on the way home. "Why don't you stay for dinner?" she asked.

"I think that we should get back." he replied.

"For what, to get to work?" Jacob said. "It will always be there. Besides the next time you come over will probably be in a few more years."

"And you can lecture Ariel on the way home." Mynera said.

"Oh we'll have a good talk on the way home." Marlin said looking at me.

The next few hours were fun. Jacob told me about the times Marlin had gotten into trouble when he practiced using his powers.

"Now I know what Liera meant when she tole me to be very careful about using my powers." I said to myself.

"How is she doing?" Mynera asked.

"She's fine, still working the same job." Marlin said.

"And how are the children getting along?" Jacob asked.

"Like all kids do. They have petty arguments that any children have. Other then that, the keep their distance from each other." Marlin said.

"He hates me." I defiantly reminded him.

"He will get over it." Mynera said. "Why don't you and I go inside and get dinner, leave these two alone."

As I stood in the kitchen I couldn't help but to notice the view. "This is nice, looking at the lake when you cook."

"It is a beautiful view." she said looking out the window, then she turned her attention to me. "Why haven't you told Marlin that you have been practicing your powers?"

"I wasn't ready yet."

"What exactly can you do?" she asked curiously while reaching for something in the cupboard.

"I can read minds, know when someone is coming, talk to animals and I know what people really feel. Sometimes it can be scary."

"Why do you say that?"

"It's just what I feel. Like Clair, she thinks that I am strange because I ask questions all the time and she thinks I act strange, because I don't act like her or Roz. I feel Roz's hatred toward me. Marlin is the only one who doesn't hide his feeling toward me, but I know something is different, I don't know what. I can also feel the powers of others." I explained in a serious straight tone. I don't think she know what to make of my attitude but I know it impressed her. "Liera works a lot so I don't see her much."

"She is probably doing more experiments." she said to herself.

"And there is one other thing."

"What is that?"

"I can see things that happened a long time ago, places I've never been or even heard of. And I keep having the same dream all the time. I never have anything different." I told her.

"What kind of dream?" I told her about my dream, she listened to every word. I also told her about where I came from and what they did there. "So you don't want to change your name in hopes of finding your friend again?"

"I knew him for a long time. They took him in the middle of the night and we didn't see him again."

"Don't say anything to anyone, not yet, when you get older you will know more. I know that you are curious about your parents, and I know that you have been questioning yourself about it. There is nothing wrong with that." she said while she mixed some things together in a pot.

"What are you making?" I asked standing next to her.

"Vegetable stew. No matter what time of day it is, it's always good."

"It smells good."

"I love it, plus it's real quick to cook. I will be done soon, why don't you go out and tell them that it will be ready soon."

I went out the kitchen door, there was a stone walkway going from the door to the deck and another to the front of the house. This was nice, I could smell the flowers as I walked by them.

"Did she talk your ear off?" Marlin asked when he seen me.

"No. She wanted me to tell you that dinner is ready." I said stepping onto the deck.

"That means I get to set the table." Jacob said when he got up.

"I can tell you two get along." Marlin said.

"Yes. I like her and I like it here." I replied when he picked me up. Which I didn't mind too much now that I know him a little better.

"I thought we'd have something light." she said putting a salad on the table. "I know that you like salads, so I made one."

"I like them a lot. But I don't remember seeing you make one." I said in a queer way.

"With me anything is possible." she smiled. "Let's get started.

The conversation at the table was funny. They talked about how Marlin used to get into trouble when he was my age.

I remember when you were ten," Mynera said. "You came up for you educational review. You started to argue with the man who came to evaluate your lessons."

"What happened?" I asked.

"I was right and he was wrong." Marlin answered. "And a few days later he came back and told me that I was right in the first place."

"You almost lost the credits for that. If I remember right you two debated for hours on that subject." Jacob said.

"What was the subject?" I asked.

"Interplanetary laws and regulations." Marlin said.

"Are they the same on other planets?" I asked.

"More or less. It's a good idea to know what the laws are if you travel." he said.

"I wouldn't mind doing that." I said to myself.

Jacob sat back and smiled. I figured that is what he use to do and I could tell he enjoyed it by what he was thinking.

"That is one of the best things that I did when I was younger. Other than marring you of course." he smiled to Mynera.

"Of course. I had better be in there somewhere." The way she said that was to remind him that there are other things that happened in their lives that were good.

"What did you do?" I asked Jacob.

"Many things. I traveled all around this solar system." he answered proudly.

"He used to run a transportation ship." Mynera said.

"If it wasn't for that job we would have never met." he said to her.

"What were you doing?" I asked.

"Checking land to see if it would be all right for the use of agriculture." she said.

"Playing with dirt." Jacob whispered to me as he leaned closer.

"I like watching plants grow. I have one at home that is starting to." I said.

"That's good. It's amazing to see the changes a plant has to go through when they grow." she said to me.

After we finished we sat outside for a while. Before we got ready to leave Mynera wanted to show me something. She took me into her bedroom and took out a small box that was wrapped in a soft cloth.

"I have something that I want to give to you, as long as you promise not to let anything happen to it until you're sure that you want to keep it. Then you can decide what to do with it. If anyone asks you about it, tell them that it was given to me when I was your age." she said as she unfolded the cloth.

"I promise. This is beautiful!" I said when she handed me a small silver box.

"Yes it is, and you may keep the box. It's what's inside that I wanted to give you." When I opened I it I couldn't believe what was inside, I was speechless. "What's wrong Ariel?"

I pulled out a steal chain with a gold ring attached to it. "This is the thing from my dream. How did you get this?"

She put her arm around me, I didn't know what her intent was but I could feel her powers more than I did earlier.

"It was your mothers. It took a lot of work to get it. It's such a long story, when you get older I will try to explain it to you. The only thing that matters is that you have it now."

"Then this is the thing from my dream." I whispered to myself.

"I'll be right back." she said in a coy way. "Stay here."

When she left the room I got the feeling that something was wrong. It may have been the way that I comprehended her sudden anxiety, I don't know. She came back in a few minutes later, then I knew something was up when I heard them talking in the hall.

"I don't think that this is a good time. I don't have all the information yet." Marlin told her.

"She already knows a little bit about it. You may as well tell her what you've found out."

"Mother"

"She is having dreams, the same one all the time. And if it continues without her being able to find out about it, it will drive her crazy. Besides there may be something in her dream that could help."

I sat on the bed holding the ring, I knew Marlin was uneasy about something. In a way I am glad that she gave it to me, if I can't see my real mother at least I have something that belonged to her. It had an inscription but I couldn't read the language.

"You're father gave that to your mother a long time ago." Marlin said.

"How do you know?"

"As you know, I have been trying to find out about your parents. When I discovered that I was getting nowhere with finding information on you I began to check your mother's background. When I didn't get very far with that I went to your father's background." he explained after he sat beside me.

"Did you know how long they were together?"

"Over thrity years. They never did get married."

"Why?"

"They were from two different worlds. And on this world we have a law that doesn't allow marriage to someone who is not from here."

"How did they manage to stay together?"

"They fooled everyone into thinking that they were working together. Your father is from here so it wasn't hard for him, but he knew he needed to protect her. But they also wanted a child, and that's where Liera fits in."

"She knew my mother?"

"Not personally. We can interbreed, but narrow minded people don't like change."

"I'm sure she loved you, even when you were not born." Mynera said while she stood in the doorway.

"Why don't we go outside and enjoy the day before we leave, and I promise that we will continue this when I find out more." Marlin said.

"Can I go down to the lake?" I asked with a more upbeat tone.

"Sure why not." he said.

"Can you hold this for me?" I asked putting the ring back in the box.

"I have the perfect place for it in my office. No one goes in there, it will be safely locked away. When you want to see it just let me know."

"What are you three up to? I come outside and everyone is still inside." Jacob said when we stepped onto the deck.

"We were thinking about taking a walk down to the lake before we leave. Care to join us?" Marlin asked.

"That sounds like a good idea." he said taking Mynera's have.

The deck had two steps to the ground with a very worn out path leading to the shoreline. Even this was lined with shrubs and plants. One plant stood out from the rest, it sat behind a bush and was a few feet taller. On it was the most beautiful flowers, I had to stop and look at them.

"You like them?" Mynera asked.

"What are they, did you plant them?"

"Yes. A long time ago a friend visited a star system and brought them back, he told me they were called roses. They thrive here." she said.

"You come down here a lot." I said when we continued on our way, looking at everything.

They had a little area under some trees that were fixed up with a gazebo like building, it had the bottom with seats and the open sides with climbing vines but the top was tree branches that draped over it. This was pretty, I know I wouldn't mind living here.

"Sometimes we come down here at night and watch the sky." she said.

"That and the fish jumping out of the water. Sometimes I think they do that on purpose, like they are laughing at me because I have a hard time to catch them." Jacob said.

"Why don't you stay a little while longer and sit with us?" she asked.

"I would but I'd like to get back before it gets dark. But I promise that we will come back soon." Marlin assured her. "I want to take a different way home, show Ariel some of the towns."

"She'll like that, considering she probably hasen't been out of the house since she got there." she said. "And the next time try to stay for a couple of days. It won't hurt you to miss work for a little while."

"Let me put it to you this way, when we get home I will try to finish up some work that I am doing and I will put some time aside. Maybe I can get Liera and Roz to come."

"That would be nice, then I can take that boy fishing with me." Jacob said.

"It won't be getting dark for hours, I hope you enjoy your ride back." she said smiling at me.

I was a few feet in front of them as we walked back toward the house. Even with her whispering I could still hear the conversation.

"It's good that she trusts you, she has little trust for people. Listen to her, as she gets older her powers will be stronger and then she will be able to find out more. My fear is that it may cause danger for Liera, be careful." she warned him.

"I will."

We said goodbye when we got to the front. As I got in I could feel her sorrow, she didn't want us to leave. I wished we could have stayed longer, but I really want to see what the other towns look like. I haven't been out of the house much so this will be fun for me.

The first town we went through was small. The people were outside taking care of their yards and kids. What few I saw were playing or helping out.

"This is a nice place, but there aren't many kids." I said.

"Remember what I told you about people having kids? That's why we take pride in our children and our land. They both need to be taking care of or there would be no future." he said turning a corner.

"How many people are there?"

"Well there is over fortyfive thousand people who are like us and out of that there is one thousand three hundred and twenty two children."

"How do you know the exact number?"

"When it comes to children it's easy to count them. That and the fact that you can get the numbers off of the computer."

"In the city or world?"

"World"

"What about where you took me from? There are a lot of children there."

"Yes, and they are all waiting to be placed in homes."

"Not all of them. Derick never got to have a home."

"Ariel, I have a lot more checking to do, if I can I will find him. I promise."

As we traveled down the street I noticed a strange vehicle as it passed us. I continued to stare at it until it was out of my sight.

"What was that?" I asked.

"It's a hovercraft. It's another way of transportation. They have some that go above the buildings. The laws for them are very strict. The people who are permitted to use them go through a very long intense training program. If you get one questions wrong you have to wait a long time to take it again. We have one in the garage."

"I didn't know that. Why do you need training?"

"Mostly to see if you can handle the responsibility, and to see what you would do in an emergency. The one we have Liera uses to go to work."

"Interesting, but I would rather keep my feet on the ground for now."

"I don't blame you. Would you like to get something to drink?"

"Yeah, I'm getting a little thirsty."

We pulled into a parking lot where a hugh building was. People were walking everywhere.

"What is this place?" I asked. I was curious but being around so many people didn't agree with me.

"I figured that since it's not going to get dark for a few more hours we'd spend some time here. Look around. See places where people go to shop."

When we entered the door there was a computerized voice that greated people coming and saying goodbye to the people leaving. It was interesting, stores on both sides and the roof in the middle was made of glass to let the sunlight in, plants and fountains were everywhere. We were there for hours looking in some of the stores, the last one we stopped in front of had things for outdoors. One of those things really caught my eye, so we went in to get a closer look.

"What is that?" I asked while I look at a strange machine. It was thin in design, shinny black with flames going down both sides. The rear was decked out in chrome. All of it sparkled under the lights.

"That is a single person glider." a salesman said. "It's used in racing."

"What is racing?" I asked Marlin.

"It's a contest to see who can go the fastest." he answered.

"How does it work?"

"It works on the same principle as a hovercraft, the only difference is the size and some minor modifications. This being as small as it is and the design, it can go very fast. It is a dangerous machine if you don't know how to handle it. Only very skilled pilots use them." the salesman said.

"It looks like it would be fun." I said.

"Maybe in about fifteen or fifty years. That also has a lot of responsibility to go with it." Marlin said.

"That's true. We don't sell one until a person has passed the courses that are offered with a sale." the salesman said.

Marlin thanked the salesman as we left the store, then we stopped to get something to drink. I saw him hand a small card to the woman behind the counter.

"What is that?" I asked.

"It's a card that people put into a machine that allows us to make a purchase." he answered.

"I still don't understand." I said when I took my drink, then thanking the lady that handed it to me.

"As we work, our work is credited. It's registered in a computer, when this card is put in a computer at the counter it tells the person who puts it in that you can make a purchase. It's like trading, you work and in return you get the credit that you need." Marlin explained.

"Does it tell you what you do for work?"

"No, that is a different system, and that one is very protected. No one has access to it."

"What happens if you don't work anymore?"

"With our lifeline that is almost impossible."

"Why?"

"No matter how old you get you always contribute something. It's not that bad."

"I still don't understand."

"Like my mother. Her plants are her bussiness, she cultivates many of them for sale."

"Oh, I get it now."

One thing noticed is that Marlin doesn't mind answering any of my questions, no matter how strange they are. While we walked I watched the other people and how they moved around searching the stores, what I thought was odd was the salesclerks.

"What's wrong with those people behind the counters?" I asked when we exited the building.

"I was wondering how long it would take you to ask about them. They're not real."

"Like computers." I said to myself.

"Sort of. These androids are all tied into a main computer system that is usually located in the basements of the buildings. The ones we have at home are all tied into a system in the city and that one is connected to a main system." he explained.

"So every single computer is connected into a main frame?"

"Right, you catch on fast. That's good."

"What happens if one of them stop working, won't the rest of them stop?" I asked when I got into the front seat.

"No. They have independent systems built in, so the others will continue to work. The main computer constantly monitors them. If one does stop, someone will come and see what is wrong if the computer can't fix the problem."

I was more tired than I thought, I realized it when I got comfortable. The ride was relaxing, I couldn't think of any more questions to ask so I watched the stars as they appeared in the sky. It was so relaxing that I fell asleep, when I woke up I was in my bed.

I had my dream again, it was the same as before with one difference. I could here her screem in pain, and for a moment I thought that I had felt it. I know I felt something, whatever it was I didn't like it and it kept me up all night.

Where I couldn't sleep I took advantage of the time and did some reading. Nothing too drastic, I found an interesting as well as informative disk on animals. I stayed up till dawn reading it. I didn't want to sleep, I didn't want to dream.

This morning was another good learning experience for Roz. He seems to have a great habit of getting into trouble, he never thinks before he speaks. Where I was up early I decided to go downstairs and watch out the window as the sun made it's way into the morning sky. If I had realized what was going to happen I would have stayed in my room, but then again Roz got what he deserved.

"How did you enjoy your trip yesterday?" He asked.

"I enjoyed it very much." I replied without looking at him.

"Really! Figures you would, you're a freak." He said sarcastically.

"Just because I'm better than you in many areas is no reason for you to be hostile toward me." I informed him calmly. I felt that it was better than starting an argument with him so early in the morning. When I turned to face him I saw Marlin and Liera standing at the top of the stairs, I could tell she was very angry. "You know, you're an idiot." I told him in a cold way.

"Oh yeah, what makes you think you're smarter than me?" he asked angrily.

"Many things. One of them is that I think before I say something," I replied without changing my tone, "and if you think any different, turn around."

By then they were both standing at the bottom of the stairs, Roz knew right then and there that he was in a lot of trouble.

"Would it help if I said I was sorry?" he asked her with an attitude.

"Go to your room. I'll be up in a minute." she said raising her voice.

Wow, she was mad. This is the first time that I ever heard her raise her voice. I don't think that it will be the last time. She was so mad I couldn't get a clear reading from her. I wondered what she has planned for him. Roz didn't want to walk past her, he slowly started and then ran up to his room.

"Liera..." Marlin started to say.

"Don't say it. I have the perfect punishment for him. I have a few days coming, I'll just call in and tell them that I need the time now." then she went upstairs.

"That is the first time I have heard her raise her voice." I said to Marlin in the same tone that I used with Roz.

"Me too, but Roz shouldn't piss her off." then he put more attention toward me. "Are you all right?"

"Yes. Why wouldn't I be?"

"Well for one, your tone. Another is you look tired. Did you sleep?"

"A little, I did some reading in between rest. I will be fine." I assured him, but I didn't change my tone, and with that he became concerned about me for nothing and remained that way.

He was still upset and he left the choice of punishment up to Liera, and she kept her promise. She took the next five days off and Roz was in his room the whole time with extensive studies. I think he got what he needed, time with his mother alone, but what he wanted was time with her alone but not doing studies.

I still didn't get much sleep but I did do a lot of reading. I found more things about computers, one was fascinating to me. It was a hologram program. There are some for entertainment uses but they were trying to experiment with an interface chip that could be placed into a living person for communication purposes. It sounded crazy but it was interesting.

Marlin was still concerned about my not sleeping much. He knew that I was up reading, he didn't know why and I didn't tell him. I didn't want to, not yet.

The sixth day Roz had a different attitude. Marlin was surprised when he came downstairs to apologize, his feelings were not totally truthful. We were looking at something on the computer but I decided that it wa a good time to go and do something else, sit on the couch with Liera and listen.

"Roz, don't bother to say something that you know is not true. I would rather you keep your thoughts inside your head. Its bad enough that we can read your mind. Besides your mother and I have been talking and we decided to have you supervised." Marlin explained.

"What, why?" Roz yelled.

"We have entered you in an evaluation program. Someone is coming over to talk with you this afternoon. One way or another your attitude will change." Liera said firmly. She was still mad, but she didn't show it anymore.

"But I thought that being in my room was my punishment?" he asked.

"I never gave you any reason to believe that was going to be the only punishment you got." she said.

"For how long?"

"That will not be determind by us. Go to your room until we call you down." Marlin said.

Roz went upstairs and Liera went into the kitchen. I remained on the couch thinking about what was going on. This will be interesting.

"Do you want to continue what we were doing?" Marlin asked.

"No, that's okay. Do you know that Roz just wants to be with his mother just to have fun? He doesn't know any better. She works too much."

"Yes I know." he said sitting beside me. "She just needs more time. Now, I have a few things I want to talk to you about. One thing is you haven't been sleeping. Is there a reason?"

"Not really. I get into what I read and lose track of time. I know you don't believe me."

"And I know you don't want to talk about it so I won't push it. I have been keeping an eye on what you're learning, and Liera and I were wondering if you think that you may be ready to be entered more formally into the educational system?"

I had to think about that for a few minutes before I answered him. I liked the idea and agreed, anyway I did feel that I was ready.

"What is this I hear, someone wants to take her exam?" Liera asked when she came back into the room.

"Yes she does. I figured that since she is eager to learn, she may as well be credited for it." he said.

"That is wonderful. Besides, now is a good time considering Roz is going to be with someone else. We will have time to get her started."

"What do you mean?" I asked.

"We have to update you computer system. I'll get a chip interface for the computer in your room. It will have a lot more information than you'll ever be able to read. Depending on your level of current education will depend on where you will start." Marlin explained.

"How will you know?"

"He's jumping ahead a little. First I will notify the educational board and they will send someone over who will ask you questions and give you a test to see how smart you are, and you will start from there." Liera said when she sat next to me.

"You are sure that you are ready? You have only been here a few weeks. If you want to wait a little longer we understand." he said.

"That's okay. I don't want to wait. This way I won't have to ask you questions all the time."

"Well answering questions is no big deal." Marlin smiled.

"Yes. You enjoy it when someone asks you a lot of questions. Don't you?" Liera asked him.

"I like it when someone has an interest in learning. It's good for anyone. She has an inquisitive mind."

"Like I said, I think I'm ready." I said with confidence.

Marlin and Liera seemed to enjoy that idea. Considering she joked around with him about my asking questions all the time, I knew that neither one of them minded it. I also knew that Marlin enjoyed it more.

Roz keeps to himself a lot, he tries to point out that he doesn't need either one of them. Considering deep down inside he does. I know this has some effect on Liera, she doesn't feel close to Roz like she wants to, and with Marlin, not having Roz close to him doesn't bother him that much.

As for me, I'm constantly asking about something, with Liera working Marlin is usually the only one I have to ask if I can't find the answer myself, and he doesn't mind it at all. I haven't been able to tell if that bothers Liera, she's good at keeping her feeling from me.

I don't like to wait too long for some things to happen, but this afternoon will be one to remember. It should be quite interesting to see what is going to happen to Roz. I was sitting in the living room reading over some disks that I have been looking at the last few days. What really helped was that Liera gave me a hand sized reader for the disks, I like the idea that it's portable. She sat on the other side of the couch quietly waiting for the time to pass, Marlin was at the computer working as always.

"You like that hand reader?" she asked me. When she touched my shoulder I felt how calm she was now that she is away from Roz.

"Yes" I replied. "This will come in very handy when I'm in bed. Thanks for getting it for me."

"You don't have to thank me. I had it in my office for the longest time doing nothing but collecting dust. I meant to give it to you when I brought it home last week but I forgot."

"They do come in handy, but there is also another device that goes onto the computer in your room so you don't have to be right in front of it to use it. I can get one for you when you start your lessons." Marlin said.

"Really! How does it work?" I asked.

"I'll show you when we see what happens after you take your exam. It's really simple, the best part about it is it's a very lightweight headset that you wear, and depending on what you're doing you don't need to look at the screen. You can interact with the computer through the headset. The best part is the range, and can be outside and do your lessons." Marlin explained.

"That would be useful." I said, then I looked toward the door. "Someone is coming.'

"You know you can spoil the element of surprise." Liera said.

When she went to open the door I wanted to stay out of pure curiosity, so I thought that if I continued to read then they wouldn't pay attention to me.

I was surprised when Liera opened the door. The woman who was standing there was like the ones at the stores, artificial in every way. I put down what I was reading and sat there trying to figure out why I knew she was coming, and I had no explanation. I was staring at her, studying her, not paying any attention to what they were talking about, until she said something to me, twice. It took that long to realize that she had spoken to me.

"Is something wrong?" the woman asked me.

"No ma'am." I replied. "I didn't expect one of your kind." I was totally fascinated with her. Her hair was blond with tints of pink in them. Her fingers long and slender like her body. She was dressed in white adorned with a single pin as if to identify her position at her job. The only thing she carries was a breifcase that held nothing more than a small computer.

"You may call me Sara if you like."

"You are very pretty."

"Appearences mean nothing. It is what you can accomplish that makes you who you are." she replied. "She has an early ability. Can Roz tell if I am not real?" she asked Liera.

"I don't believe so." she answered.

"Call him down, but do not tell him what I am. I want to see how he reacts. If he actually thinks that I'm human, let him keep thinking that. I have my reasons." she said.

I like her, and I know that this is going to be a great experience, especially for Roz.

"What?" he asked with his unchanged attitude as he came down the stairs.

"We want you to meet Sara. She is going to be your supervisor for the next few days." Liera told him.

The look on his face is one that I will never forget. He didn't know what she was and to make it worse, he hated the fact that Sara was a female.

"But she's a she." he said rebelliously.

"My being a female intimidates you?" she asked. I like her tone, she is kind and warm, and it made Roz madder.

"Well they could have sent over a guy." he replied with his attitude.

"Roz, you are being very impolite." Marlin said with a hint of disgust. "Apologize to Sara."

"Your mother has told me a lot about your actions. You are not sorry. Do not apologize to me until you are truthfully sorry."

"Good, I won't." he replied sarcastically. "I'll say goodbye if you want."

"I am not leaving. I will be right by your side day and night for as long as it takes."

"Does that mean that you're going to live with us?" I asked while I continued to read.

"Until my work with Roz is done." Sara said.

"Wow, you're going to be here a long time." I told her, and Marlin and Liera knew that I was right. Roz has a serious problem.

"I will be teaching you discipline, manners, as well as evaluating you constantly. You can not do or say anything without my knowledge of it. When I feel you no longer require my services, then I will leave."

"Can I go to my room?" he asked his mother.

"That's another thing I didn't tell you. You have to ask Sara anything that you would ask me. It's up to her." Liera told him.

"What! You mean I have to take orders from her? You're kidding." He yelled.

"As of this moment Liera and Marlin have no say in what happens to you. It part of the program, and they know it. Oh, one more thing, DO NOT raise your voice at me." Sara informed him. "All your actions will be monitored and recorded.

Roz got what he asked for and he hates it with a passion, but I'm going to enjoy every minute of it. Roz went to his room, Sara, Liera and Marlin talked a little longer about what will be happening over the next few weeks and what they might expect from Roz. She has her work cut out for herself. I kept thinking that it's a good things that she's a machine, if she were alive she may get the urge to strangle Roz, I know I have at times. But I like demeaning him when he tries to start something with me, sometimes it puts him in his place and shuts him up.

After they finished talking Sara went up to Roz's room to begin her assignment with him.

"I'll go and get Ariel set up for her review." Liera said. "Then after we can get dinner going."

With Roz out of her hair, she seemed a bit more relaxed. Although she isn't home most of the time, I couldn't figure out why he would be such a bother to her. I was going to finish what I was reading but I couldn't keep my mind on it.

"Go ahead, ask." Marlin said when he sat beside me.

"Most of my questions are for Sara."

"I know. She is a very interesting machine."

"Yes, but what I was wondering is why I knew she was coming? There is nothing to feel from a machine, bit I still knew. I don't understand it." Marlin didn't say anything, he sat back and smiled. "What?"

"It's all part of your powers. What you felt is her energy."

"Roz will never figure her out."

"I have good news for you." Liera said coming into the room. "Someone is going to come over in the morning to see you."

Liera and I took our time getting dinner, our conversation was a pleasant one. She asked me how the past few day were for me without Roz trying anything with me to provoke a fight or argument. After we got everything ready Roz reluctantly came down to join us, and Sara stood behind him the whole time. He hated every minute of it, he was afraid that if he said the wrong thing that she would hold it against him. No one was really talking so I decided to ask about tomorrow.

"What kind of test will I have to take."

"It will be a long one, that I do know. You will have to answer many different questions." Marlin said.

"What does she have to take a test for?" Roz asked, it's the first thing that I have heard him say since Sara got here. At least his tone was a little different.

"So she can start her education." Marlin answered.

"Why bother, she already thinks that she's smarter than anyone else." he said.

"Roz have you forgotten what we talked about?" Sara asked him.

"No ma'am." he replied without moving.

"Repeat what you were told."

"Think about what I say and no to demean anyone just because of what they are or what they want to do or want to learn." he said. He couldn't remember the exact way that Sara had told him, and she knew that Roz is not serious about his situation. For some reason he thinks that it's a joke.

"You have forgotten. Next time I tell you something I want you to repeat it in the same way." she said sternly. "Ariel, I would like to talk to you when you have the time."

"You can use my office. No one will bother you in there." Marlin said.

"Thank you." Sara said as she nodded.

Through the rest of dinner my mind was on Sara and how much she fascinated me. Her personality was incredible, she could change her tone accurately where it would make anyone believe that she was a real person.

After dinner I rushed to help Liera clean. I couldn't wait to hear what she wanted to talk about. The only thing I really care for was being in his office. I know how much he values his privacy when it comes to his work, that's why I try not to ask him too much about it. I hesitated when I went to the door of the basement.

"What's wrong?" Marlin asked when he noticed me. "Sara is waiting for you."

"I know. I just don't want to go into your office. We could have talked outside."

"I know. But outside Roz could hear you from his window. At least down there he can't. Don't worry about it."

"I'm not worried, I just don't feel right."

"If it will make you feel any better I will go with you to show you that it is okay."

I have never been in there, it was none of my business. Marlin didn't mind and he didn't think twice about it. Sara was standing there waiting for me.

"What is wrong Ariel?" she asked.

"I have never been in here."

"It's alright, you can't get into any trouble. Don't worry so much." He said when he patted me on the back. "If you don't mind, I will be going back upstairs."

"We will not take too long." she said. "I just have a few questions."

When Marlin left I stood there and stared at Sara, I didn't know what she expected from me.

"It's okay, I just have a few questions about Roz. I know that you have certain powers that enable you to know what other people are feeling. Is this true?"

"Yes it is. I can also hear what other people are thinking sometimes."

"Yes I know. That is why I want to talk to you. Can you tell me what Roz thinks of you?"

"He hates me."

"Do you know why?"

"Yes, when Marlin and Liera brought me here, he was expecting a brother. He hates the idea that I'm a girl, and I can do more than he can." I said as I sat down.

"You mean your powers are stronger than his?"

"Yes. He can't do a lot of things, he doesn't practice is powers like he should. In his mind he thinks they should already be there. True they are, but if he doesn't bring them forth by practicing then it will be a long time before they emerge." I explained. "I don't know why he doesn't understand that."

"You are a very articulate child, I am impressed. That does explain some of his problems."

"That is no excuse for the way he acts. It's not my fault that I can do things better than him."

"That is true. Have you tried helping him?"

"Once. He wanted me to show him how to communicate with the animals. He was too aggravated because he couldn't do it right away."

"Did he do it?"

"Yes, but after it seemed to make him more angry with me. I try to avoid him, I don't need to get him any more madder at me. It's not worth it."

"I don't blame you. You have given me some answers. I would like to talk to you again. Maybe in a week you could tell me if there is any change in his attitude toward you."

"Why me, why not Malrin or Liera?"

"Liera is usually working and Marlin is busy, plus he can't tell what Roz is feeling. Reading one's mind is different than knowing what they really feel. You possess that capability toward others."

"I didn't realize that."

All this time I had never tried to tell if I could find out what Marlin can do. I thought that he would inherit his mother's powers. I guess I was wrong. This brings up more questions to ask.

"I think we are done. Unless you have a few questions?"

"I have thousands of questions, but none of them have anything to do with Roz."

"I admire your curiosity. You show enthusiam, very good in a child your age. Shall we go?"

As we are going upstairs questions were running through my mind. I did however ask her one question that made me curious.

"Sara, do you ever get lonely?" I asked as she was about to go and see Roz.

"No"

"That's strange."

"Why do you say that?"

"Everything that I have been around gets lonely at one time or another. Even the plants."

"Being alone is one feeling that I do not have to consider, and I am thankful for that. I have seen the effects that being alone has on people. Many of them who chose to live a lonely life die alone." She explained, then she continued on her way.

Liera was nowhere to be seen and as usual Marlin was at the computer working. Now I know why Mynera was concerned about him, she thinks that he overworks, he takes no time for himself and I have to agree with her.

"How did it go?" he asked.

"Great" I replied. "This is going to be fun. I wish Sara could stay with us."

"You like her. I wish Roz felt the same way."

"He never will." I said standing beside him. "Is there something wrong with Roz?"

"When you get older I will explaine, if you don't find out first. Don't worry about it." he said. "I'm curious, why did you ask Sara that question?"

"Being alone means different things for different people. Some choose to be alone because they believe that they will never find someone who will be what they want them to be, or that they will never find someone will be equal to them. I think that is what Sara was trying to explain."

"That's a shame."

"Yes it is. Sometimes the answer is right in front of them." he said in a way to make a point. "You have a busy day tomorrow."

"Yes. I'm going to bed. I want to get up early."

"It's still early, but you need it where you haven't gotten much sleep. Is there a reason?"

"I don't want to dream. I don't like the one I have."

"So that's the reason. Dreams can't hurt.'

"That's where you're wrong. This one hurts."

"Tonight you should try to forget about your dreams and sleep. Tomorrow is going to be a long day."

"I know"

"I'm glad that you are excited about learning, I hope you stay that way."

"I think I will."

I gave him a hug and went to my room. I wondered what he meant about Roz, maybe Liera did something to him. Sara is a very interesting machine, I want to know more about her. It was the one thing that kept my mind working through the night, but I did sleep. I think that this was one way to stop my dream, going to bed and thinking about the one thing that interested me the most, and Sara was defiantly it. Morning may have come early, but I felt great.

I want to get on with my education. Not for the reason of wanting to know more, but I wanted to see how much I already knew. I had gone through almost all of the disks I have, and I have been going over the ones that have kept me very and interested with the information on them. For some reason one of the disks kept me coming back, I was fascinated with the one on space. For reasons unclear to me I believe that I will be spending a lot of time there. I hope so, I love the look at the stars.

My mind was wandering as I had gotten ready for today. I was thinking about my real mother, I don't know why she had been on my mind. Maybe it was because I had something of hers, it was so strange to see that ring. Or it may be the idea that Marlin had found out a little about her, right now that little information is all that I have to know of her. Someday I hope to meet my real father, not to talk to him, but to see what he is like. I wouldn't mind taking a trip to Kerrell to find out.

I stood at my window watching the birds flying around when someone knocked at the door.

"I'm up." I said without moving.

"Are you ready for today?" Liera asked when she came in.

"Yes ma'am, and no I don't feel like having anything to eat."

"I should have seen that one coming." she said as we walked downstairs together.

"Good morning. How are you?" Sara asked. I was a little surprised to see her away from Roz.

"I'm fine. A little nervious." I said.

"Why?" she asked.

I thought about that for a few minutes, I had no real reason to be nervous about today. I had two ideas, one was the idea of seeing someone I don't know, and the other was the exam itself.

"I really don't know." I said.

I went into the kitchen and sat at the table with that thought on my mind. Marlin was sitting there reading something, as usual.

"What's wrong?" He asked.

"Nothing. Why?"

"I was just wondering. This is the first morning that you haven't said anything to me. I thought something might be wrong."

I just smiled. "Nothing is bothering me. I just want to get that test over with."

"I can't blame you there. Those tests can be long." He said. "It may take a few hours before someone gets here. Why don't you go outside for a while."

"I don't think so. I"ll go sit in the living room and read or something."

When I walked passed him he put down what he was reading and gently grabbed my arm. "Did you get some sleep last night?"

"Yes I did." I said happily.

"Good. I'm glad to hear that." he said when he gave me a hug.

I thought that if I was reading I wouldn't be paying much attention to the passing of time. It went by so slow, I was reading a disk on Natural Abilities. I had read it before but this time I was on this same page frame. I couldn't get into reading, my mind was on the test. I wondered if it is as hard as I think.

It wasn't too long after that that there was a knock at the door. When Liera answered it I had a feeling that this was going to be a long day.

"Good morning. My name is Regina. I was sent over by the Educational Center to give a test to a child by the name Ariel." she said without taking a breath.

Oh great, I thought. I'm in trouble. This woman has a personality of a rock. Sara has a better personality, as a matter of fact, so does my computer. There was something about her that I defiantly disliked, I wasn't sure if it was her personality or her bright green eyes that looked as if she could slice right through you like a sharp knife. As much as I was looking forward to today, I don't think I could stand looking at her that much.

"Please come in. This is Ariel." Liera said.

"Very good. I only need to ask you a few questions before we begin." she said as she sat right beside me, to which I moved onto the chair.

"What kind of questions?" I asked.

"It's just a bunch of formal questions we ask all the children before we start." she replied, and for some reason she moved closer to me.

At that point Marlin had come in and sat with us, it was the perfect opportunity to get away from her. I went over and sat on his lap. It was the first time that I have ever done that and it totally surprised him, but he knew by the way that I tried to keep my distance from her that I didn't like her.

"Don't be nervous. If it makes you feel at ease call me Gina. Most of the children respond better if they feel that they are in the company of a friend." she said.

"She is very cautious around people." Marlin told her.

I had no intention of considering her a friend, a teacher maybe, but not a friend.

"That's understandable." she said changing her tone to a more friendlier one. "First question is you age?"

"I don't know." I replied.

"We adopted Ariel over a quarter ago. They had no record of the day that she was born." Marlin said. "They did however tell us that she may have been born in the early quarter of spring and that she is almost ten. They gave us a hypothetical guess."

"I see. What about place of birth?"

"That is unknown." he answered.

"What about friends, do you have any?" she asked with a snotty attitude as she tried to intimidate me or demean me.

"Yes. Her name is Clair. She lives close so we spend a lot of time together." I answered in the same attitude as hers, and she didn't know what to make of it.

"That's good. I have one more question, then we will start your test. What is it you want to do the most?" she asked.

"I want to help people." I told her.

She looked at me and smiled. "That is quite a task. It takes an enormous amount of work. Well, let's get started."

"You can use the dining room, no one will bother you there." Liera told her.

"That will be fine." she said picking up a breifcase.

Liera showed her the way and I remained where I was thinking about how much I dislike this woman, and now that I heard her talk I dislike her even more.

"I know you don't like her. Try not to pay attention to her that much." Marlin told me.

"Thanks a lot." I said in a sarcastic yet meaningless way. "I wish Sara could do this." he got a laugh out of that.

I went in and sat at the table, she sat across from me after she had taken out a touch pad the size of my hand reader. I still don't like her and she knew that.

"Ariel, do I intimidate you?"

"No ma'am."

"But you do not like me. Don't worry about it, most of the children feel the same way for some reason. It is usually the ones who have never been around anyone else except for their family."

"I have been around more people than you will ever know. Being where I was I always saw a new face on a daily basis."

"But you are cautious?"

"I trust no one." I said seriously, now I intimidated her and I felt it.

"I'll only be here for a few hours and then you will never see me again. Okay, this is only part of your test." She said handing me the pad. "You have five hundred questions to answer. There is no time limit so you may take as long as you need to answer them. The first hundred are yes or no answers. Do you understand?"

"Yes ma'am."

"Then you may begin."

Gina sat there and watched me as I did the test. She didn't bother me, I started to feel something different about her. In her thoughts I discovered that she has no children and her work is her life without a mate. How sad that must be.

These questions are so simple that they were stupid. I had them done in no time. Most of them were about judgment. I think they ask these questions to make sure that you know what you are doing. The next set of questions were of basic math. Those were simple enough, there were only fifty of them. The next set of fifty were of animals and their natural habitats. I had them don't in no time. Two hundred down, three hundred to go.

"The next one hundred will be answered in short sentences. It may take you a while to answer them. There is no right or wrong answer. It is to see what your opion is on certain things." she explained. "Do you understand?"

"Yes ma'am."

"Then you may begin."

This should be interesting. The first question was about the way we live. Some of the questions I did have to think about for a few minutes, what to do when I meet people, how to react to someone who has a different opinion on subjects, stuff like that. The last question was about the way I felt about having a long life. That one I answered the best I could because the thought had never crossed my mind.

"I'm finished." I said handing her the pad. When her hand touched mine I got a different feeling from her. She was lonely and yearned for someone, ane I just smiled. "Don't worry about being alone. You will find someone soon enough." I told her.

"How do you know?" she whispered.

"I don't know. I just know certain things." I told her when I removed my hand.

"Why don't we take a break for an hour, then we will start after." She suggested. "The next fifty questions will be written to see how you penmanship is and the last set will be done on the computer." She explained when we walked into the living room.

"Okay. Where is Liera?" I asked Marlin.

"She went to work. Are you hungry?"

"No"

"She is working very hard. She also has an interesting ability. You should concentrate on that instead." she said with a smile as she looked at me.

"What did she tell you?" Marlin asked.

"She just gave me a little insight on my life."

Marlin looked at me and didn't know what to think, as for Gina, she appreciated my insight and liked it very much. I don't know why I knew, but I felt that she should know. This brings up another questions, should I tell someone what will happen to them in the future or just leave it be and let them find out for themselves. I sat on the couch for the rest of the hour thinking about some of the questions that I had, some of them I have asked before.

"What are the next questions?" I asked.

"The next ones are multiple choice. Those you will wite small essays to answer them. Are you ready?"

"Yes I want to get them done."

Wh went back into the dining room and as I sat there I still thought about the test. It wasn't that hard, then she handed me the next test. It was hard. I had to reread half of the questions. Some of them had words that I never heard of before.

I tried to see if I could read her mind, the only information I got from her was, 'don't even bother to try'. she knew what I was trying to do. I guess that there was many others who have tried this. It took me over two hours to finish this one. I knew for a fact that I didn't do well, and it bothered me. That she knew.

"It's good that you try to use your powers when you are in a bind, but remember that will not always help you." she said.

"Why didn't you say something?" I asked curiously.

"I figured you would find out for yourself." she smiled. "Why don't we go to the computer and finish the rest of your test?"

"Well, are you done?" Marlin asked when we came into the room.

"She has one more part of the test to do. It will require the use of the computer." she said.

"Go right ahead. I'm finished with what I was doing." he said as he moved so she could set it up.

Gina had inserted a processing chip and proceeded to enter the information in it concerning who it was that was doing the test.

"This is simple, you will see different diagrams and you will have to identify them with what they pertain to. In other words you have to match them with the computer terms or electrical terms that have to do with whatever the questions ask. Do you understand?"

"Yes"

I knew I was going to fail. I had some disks that did have some of the information regarding the questions here, but I only read them once. I was headed for trouble.

This would have been a great time for me to talk to Sara, if anyone knew these answers, she would. The first few were simple computer terms, those I knew with no problem. Diagrams were the hardest, they could have matched anything. I sat and stared at them for the longest time. If I keep thinking that I am going to fail, I will fail.

I had to have a more positive attitude, I will pass this if it is the last thing I do.

I sat there for six hours. I knew that if I answered wrong and go to the next question I could not go back and correst it. It had to be right. I was relieved when I had finished. I have got such a headache from looking at the screen for so long.

"Gina seemed surprised that I was done. I guess that the other children who have taken this part of the test took longer. She took the chip and put it with the rest of the exam.

"We will let you know the results of the test in about two weeks or so." she told Marlin.

"That's it, I'm done?"

"Yes. All you have to do now is wait for the results." she said as she was getting ready to leave. "Goodbye. I hope you do well on your scores."

Once she had left I stayed at the computer with my head resting on my arm. It hurt so much that I didn't feel like moving.

"Are you okay?" Marlin asked.

"No. I'm going to bed."

"I have something that you can take for your headache." he said as he put his hand on my head. "Go up and I will bring it to you."

I had no energy to move, when I got to my room the pain in my head hurt more. As many times as I have looked at the computer screen in my room it never hurt this much. I laid across the bed and put the pillow over my head. I could hear the muffled sounds of Roz and Sara in the hallway then I heard footsteps in my room.

"Here try this." Marlin said when he took the pillow off my head.

"What is it?" I asked as he handed me a glass with liquid in it. "What does it taste like?"

"Bad, but it helps."

As I took a very little sip I could smell it, and it smelled repulsive. "I'd rather have a headache than this. This stuff smells like it could give me a stomachache."

"It may tast bad, but it will make your headache go away fast. Then you may feel like hhaving something to eat."

"I don't think so. All I want to do is sleep." I said handing him back the glass. "How long did it take Roz to do his test?"

"Most of the day. No two test are alike."

"Why?"

"So you can't get the answers from anyone else."

"Makes sense. Liera's home."

"I don't hear anything."

"Believe me, she is. How come you don't know what is going to happen before it does?"

"I never had that ability. How far in advance do you know if something is going to happen?"

"Hour or so. It's easy, I could show you. Don't even ask me about Gina, for some reason I just knew what was going to happen to her. Do you think that maybe I will be able to know something about me before it happens?"

"Maybe"

"They were paraniod about me. They were searching for something."

"Searching! How do you know?"

"For as long as I can remember, once a week they would tie me to a table and do some very painful test. They never told me what they were looking for."

"Why didn't you say something?"

"I didn't want to remember, it hurt too much. A few times they put a small wire inside me and left it there. I could feel it moving. If I moved or cried I would get yelled at or hit." That was one thing I wanted to forget, as much as I tried I couldn't.

"Why would they do that?" he asked taking my hand.

"The nurse that was there told me if I move or say anything then they would have to start over. I didn't want to go through that again. I have a question. Why do you ask me questions that your powers allow you too know?"

"I want to see if you're telling me the truth. Like you do with Liera. How do you know about my powers?"

"I can feel it. When you ask me something I can tell that you already know. I also know how upset you are at Roz, it's not his fault that he acts that was, but I don't know why. Liera's powers are different."

"Different, do you know how?" he asked curiously.

"I'm not sure, I do know that she is cautious around me. I don't know why, but I know that somehow I will find out."

I have known Liera for short and I already know as much about her powers as Marlin does. What I don't know is how we are going to get along when I get older. If it stays like this then our friendship may continue to grow.

"We'll continue this some other time." he said when he heard Liera walking up the stairs. "Do you feel better?"

"Yeah. My headache is gone."

"Let's go downstairs." he smiled.

As we were going downstairs I could smell something, Liera was taking a shower so I knew it wasn't from her. It was a surprise to see that Sara had Roz try to cook. I can't imagine what her reason for it was, probably to show him what his mother does everyday. Unfortunately I don't feel like eating, but I don't want to hurt his feelings.

He has been trying very hard to get along with Sara, although he is not showing any progress I can feel that he is doing a little better, at least he is trying, I hope he does change.

I stopped at the bottom of the stairs, Marlin took my hand when he asked me what was wrong.

"No matter how bad it taste, pretend you like it. If he thinks that you don't it would hurt his feeling even more," I told him. "And I'm not hungry."

"What are you two up to?" Liera asked coming downstrairs.

"It appears Roz has made dinner." Marlin said.

"Really!" she said, then she went into the kitchen.

"Just try a little, then we can take it from there." Marlin said as we continued on our way. "You did this yourself?" he asked Roz when we went into the dinning room.

"Yeah. Sara thought it would be a good idea if I did what mom does when she comes home from work."

Sara brought something to the table that was too heavy for Roz to carry. I had no idea what it was, it sure didn't look like food, it smelled okay, but it didn't look okay. I wondered if it tasted like it smelled. As we were sitting down I wondered if Roz figured out what Sara was yet.

"It looks good." Liera lied, but Roz didn't know that.

I know I should try it, I thought as he put some on a plate then handing it to me.

"Thanks, but I'm not that hungry." I took a small bite, to my surprise it was good. "This isn't too bad."

"You really like it?" Roz was surprised that I had said that.

"Yes"

"How did you do on your exam today?" Sara asked.

"Okay, until I got to the computer test. I could have used your help." I said to her.

"Why would you want her help with that?" Roz asked.

"She knows more about computers than you ever will." I told him.

"Is that true?" Roz asked Sara.

"Yes it is. I know everything about computers. I specialize in them." she said confidently.

"I'm glad my headache is gone, that stuff was nasty. I can still taste it, and I still don't really feel good." By now I couldn't eat another bite.

"You gave her that?" Liera asked.

"She was in pain." Marlin replied.

"I think I would rather have the pain." she said as she continued to eat.

"So would I." I whispered to myself.

I forced myself to finish eating and was about to get up when Roz informed us that there was more. I didn't think it was a good idea to try anything else.

"Why don't you save me some." I said to Roz. "I really want to go to my room." I told Marlin and Liera.

"Still don't feel well?" Marlin asked.

"Not really. I'm going to bed."

"Go ahead. I'll check on you later." He said.

I stopped when I came to the middle of the living room, for some reason I went to look out the glass door.

Something was going on out there. I stepped out to see if there is indeed something happening. I heard a strange noise coming from the woods, it sounded like a faint whistle. I also thought that it may have been the wind blowing through the trees, but then again I wondered if it was from the woman that lives there. Someday I will have to check it out.

I went to me room and sat at the window to look out at the sky. I was watching the stars shooting across. I know that they are just small pieces of rock burning in the outer atmosphere, but I like to think of them as stars falling to the ground leaving a trial of stardust.

"Are you alright?" Marlin asked when he peeked around the corner.

"Yeah"

"Get some sleep, you need it."

"Are you still trying to find out more information on me?"

"I am, but I'm not getting very far."

"But don't I have the right to know?"

"I believe you do. We will see what we can find out, it will take some time, but we will find out. Now get some rest, we'll talk later."

He gave me a kiss on the forehead and left the room. I went back to the window, this time I shut the lights off so I could see better. I was sleepy, but the sky is the most beautiful thing to watch. I kept wondering what it was like of the other planets.

I have read some interesting things about them. I would love to go and see them for myself. I have read that Zandar was a planet that kept mostly to themselves. They do travel to other planets if they want to, but right now they are more interested in the discoveries that their world had to offer. As far as Kerrell, that is one place that I am over interested in. I have a feeling that I may be going there often. I have read that it is a very harsh culture, I think that the people who are from here do not fully understand them. They consider them to be a bit barbaric. I have to see that for myself, that is a must.

The next two quarters were fine. Marlin spent his free time trying to find out more about me, with very little success. The more he didn't find out, the more he wanted to know why it was such a big secret. His next step was to go back to the place where he took me from. That is a bad idea, somehow I have to discourage him from it. As for Liera, I don't bother her too much, and Roz is showing progress and he will be rid of Sara soon.

Where it was summer I took some time to venture out to the edge of the woods. I want to meet the woman who lives there, but somehow I got the feeling that now is not the time to see her. My dreams, or vision, had faded a little. When I don't see that I see nothing, I don't dream. Instead I hear words, I quess that it is some kind of way of letting me know that what I am doing is right, I'm not sure. If there is someone telling me something I wish whoever it is would tell me more clearly as to what these words mean.

I went to the stonewall at the back of the yard and sat there thinking about the best way to go about going in there when Clair came over.

"What are you doing?" she asked.

"Sitting here. What does it look like?"

"I think your think about going into the woods. She said sitting next to me.

"You're reading minds better. How do you like it?"

"I love it, mom hates it. She hates it when I answer her before she asks me a question. What have you been up to?"

"You can read minds, you tell me." I smiled.

"Thanks a lot. Nothing about your test yet?"

"No, and I don't understand why. When are you taking yours?"

"In a few weeks. I came over to see if you can come over in a few days. You're not serious about going into the woods are you?"

"Why not? Don't tell no one."

"I won't."

"I'll ask about coming over and let you know."

"Great, I have something to show you. I have to go, mom and I are going shopping."

"I will. See you later." then she ran back toward her house.

I went back inside and caught Marlin just as he was about to leave.

"I talked to Sara and she said that she wouldn't mind keeping an eye on you until Liera gets home." he said.

"That's what I want to talk to you about. I know that you are going back to the place where you got me to talk to the people there. It's not a good idea."

"How do you know that?"

"I just do, I can't tell you how I know. Now is not a good time. If you go there they will try to talk you into bringing me back for more tests." At that point I had noticed a shadow at the top of the stairs. It wasn't Roz so I knew that it had to be Sara. "Can we go for a walk?"

"What, why?" I pointed to the shadow, he got the hint that I wanted to talk without anyone around. "That sounds fine. I have an idea, there is a pond not far from here that has swans."

"Walk or drive?" I asked curiously.

"Walk. It's not that far."

He took my hand and when we walked to where I couldn't see the house anymore I decided to say something.

"The reason I know what is going to happen today is because of something that has been happening on and off at nighttime." I said.

"What's happening?"

"Once in a great while I hear things, but last night was different."

"Different, how?"

"I was talking to someone. I thought that I was asleep, but now that I really think about it, I don't think that it was. Anyway, it was a woman's voice and she told me that if you go where you are planning to go, you will be making a big mistake."

"Mistake, how can finding out about you be a mistake?"

"They can fix it so you would have no choice but to have me go back. Her exact words were that I must grow to achieve my powers as far as I can. If anything was to happen to me now I will never be the person I was intended to be." I explained. "I still don't understand that part."

We finally got to the park and sat on a bench next to the pond. A swan had made her way toward me.

"I believe that what your friend is trying to say is that you must gain all that you can without the interference of others. Does that make sense?"

"I think so." I said petting the swan.

"There is one thing that I do want to tell you." He said seriously. "A person is venerable until they reach a certain age."

"I don't understand."

"Anything can happen to you. You could die and never come back, or you could be exposed to something that could have a very serious side effect. The reason is that your body is not old enough to comprehend what is happening to it. Do you know what I mean?"

"I think so. There is one more thing she told me and that was too watch out what we say while Sara is there. She may be helping Roz but she is also recording everything else that is being said."

"Watching us. Do you know why?"

"I'm not sure, I thought you might. That's why I wanted to talk to you without anyone else around. She has super hearing, she can hear us even when we are outside."

"Spying. That I have to believe." and he was also disgusted with that, I could tell by the sound of his voice.

I wanted to change the subject, I know now that Marlin is going to wait before he does anything. I no longer worry about going back there.

"I learned something new." I smiled as I caressed the swans neck.

"What's that?"

"Give me your hand, this I showed Clair. She can't do it either."

He gave me his hand and I put it on the swan, when I put my hand over his he could feel what the swan was feeling and understood what she was thinking.

"So this is what you feel. It's amazing how you can know what an animal knows. When did you learn this?"

"A while ago, it's easy. You should listen to them, they know more about what is going on than anyone." I could tell that he was amazed at what he was hearing, it showed as he listened. I know that he wanted to know how. "All it takes is clearing you mind and focusing on them, after a while it's easy."

"I have always been too busy with my work that I have never taken the time to allow myself to be one with my inner power. I guess Mother is right, I need time to be without my work."

"She did tell me that you were always doing something, never listening to the world itself. You should listen, it has much to offer the right person." I told him in a serious tone.

I could tell that he was seriously thinking about what I said, and for once he didn't question my attitude. If he would allow himself to feel the power of the world he would be truly amazed.

"It is easy to concentrate of her." I said.

He took her head in his hand and petted her neck, she like that. I was watching her move around, she nipped carefully on Marlin's sleeve and didn't let go, she wanted us to follow her. We went to where she had led us and in the tall grass were two eggs.

"It's her nest." I said. I knelt down and picked up one of the eggs and cradled it near my ear. "I can hear it, it is a he." I told Marlin.

He sat beside me on the grass, I gave his the egg to see if he can hear anything. "I think he is almost ready to come out." he said.

I picked up the other egg and held it the same way. "Something is wrong with this one. She is ill. We can help her."

"How?" He asked putting the egg down.

"Mynera can save her. Can we bring her? If we don't she will die."

"I don't see why not, but there is no guarantee that she will survive."

"At least we can try." I took the egg and carefully wrapped it in my shirt to keep it warm, I also took one of her feathers. Her mother didn't mind, she knew my reason.

Marlin got the idea of spending some time at his parents. I thought that would be great. When we got home I went up to my room, put the egg on my pillow after I wrapped a towel around it and got my things ready. When I had finished I went downstairs and Marlin had just finished telling Liera what we were up to.

"I think it's a wonderful idea. You need some time away from work, and I think this is the only way you will do it." she said.

"We'll be back in a while. I have taken care of my work, so I don't have to worry about it."

"Is that the egg?" Liera asked me.

"Yes it is. Something is wrong with her." Something is wrong with Liera, she doesn't seem her peppy self like she usually is when she gets home early.

When we went outside I thought about putting the egg is the back with the cloths but I decided to hold it instead. I carefully sat in the seat and kept checking her to make sure that she was okay. We didn't talk much the first hour but I was curious about Liera.

"Is Liera okay?" I asked.

"She's fine, she's just tired. Why?"

"I was just wondering."

I had a strange feeling a little bit above my stomach. It wasn't a sharp pain, but it did hurt a little. I put the egg down and put my hand on my stomach.

"Are you okay?"

"I think so. I feel okay, it was just a little pain." It did go away, but I didn't like it.

"Did you eat anything?"

"No. I wasn't hungry, and I'm still not."

"We'll be there soon, get some rest."

I looked out the window and watched the trees go by. As we parked in the driveway I didn't feel like moving. Jacob was standing at the door and he came over to us before we got out.

Marlin put his hand on the side of my face. "Do you feel any better?"

"I guess so." I said getting out.

"Well this is a surprise. You don't look so good." Jacob said when he picked me up.

"I feel okay."

"You may feel it, but you don't look it." he said patting my back.

He carried me in and put me on the couch. Marlin took the egg in and put it next to me, he started thinking that it may not have been a good idea and picked it back up.

Mynera had come into the room and was very surprised to see us. "Did you miss me already?"

"We brought over something for you, but it seems that Ariel isn't feeling well." Marlin said.

She came over and sat beside me and put her hand on my forehead. "She is warm, but that is not what is wrong with her. I will tell you after." she told him. "I am so glad that you came. What is it you wanted to show me?"

Marlin handed her the egg. "I started to think that the egg was causing her to feel ill."

"No, it's not the egg. The poor thing." she said as she cradled it in her hands.

"Will she be okay?" I asked.

"She! Of course she will. I can help her. Get some rest."

Her and Marlin went outside and sat on the deck. Jacob stayed with me and was telling all sorts of interesting stories.

"It sounds like you had a lot of fun." I said. "Is it hard to find your way around space?"

"As long as you know where you are going, and your computer is working fine, other then that it's not bad. I remember one time I did get lost. Something happened to the computer and I was the only one onboard. I spent six days trying to find my way back. I learned real quick how to find my way around a computer."

"Were you scared?"

"Not really. The only bad thing is not having someone to talk to."

"How did you meet Mynera?"

"I was transporting some supplies to Zandar and as I was standing on the dock someone came over and as if I could fly a ship back to Aquarius. I figured, why not, it was better than standing here. What I didn't know was that it had three people on board. Mynera came over me and asked me how long it would take to get back here if I took the long way around. I knew then that she wanted to talk to me. After we landed we went out to eat, we didn't even clean up. She was covered in dirt and I smelled like that cargo that I was carrying. And we have been together ever since." he explained happily.

"It sounds like that she had planned it that way." I said, I thought that it was cute.

"You know something," he said as he leaned closed, "she couldn't have planned it any better."

Just then Mynera and Marlin had come back into the room. She moved me a little so she could put my head on her lap.

"Are you feeling better?" she as as she moved my hair out of my face.

"Yes. How is the egg?"

"She will be fine, wait until morning." she smiled.

Marlin sat down in a chair across from us. "So what have you two been talking about?"

"The usual, all the trouble you got into when you were a kid." Jacob said. "Actually I was telling her about the time your mother and I met."

"Do you want to eat something?" she asked me.

"Not really. I haven't been hungry lately. I feel like I could go to sleep."

"I'll take you into the bedroom, tomorrow is another day." Marlin said.

"But it's early." I said.

He came over and picked me up. "It doesn't matter. When you don't feel good, sometimes sleep is the best thing."

When he put me on the bed I was wondering what he and Mynera were talking about.

"Clair wanted me to go over in a couple of days, she wanted me to call her." I said when he sat beside me.

"I'll call her mother and tell her that the two of you are going to have to wait." For some reason he looked worried.

"What's wrong?"

"Nothing, everything is okay."

I looked at him, I knew that he was lying, but I didn't want to say anything. He kissed me goodnight and left. I got out of bed and tried to listen at the door.

"Marlin, don't be so worried. This will pass soon and Ariel will be fine." Mynera said.

"I know. She asked me if everything was alright. I told her yes, she knew that I was lying. I don't like to withhold the truth from her." he said.

"I know. Soon enough she will know what is happening to her. Right now it may confuse her." she said.

"At least she is in no danger." Marlin said, but he did sound worried.

"As she grows she will feel a little pain, but it is nothing to be afraid of. When she becomes an adult she will no longer feel it." she said.

"Is she aggressive?" Jacob asked.

"No. She's everything but. She is always trying to help, and she is always trying to learn more." then Marlin paused for a few minutes. "I am a little worried about Sara being there. She is a computer after all."

"Be careful what you say and do around her." Jacob said.

"I know it may be hard, but try to keep an eye on Ariel at all times. Don't leave her alone with Sara. If you have to go somewhere for a few days bring her here." Mynera said. "I would love to have her for a week or more." she said changing her tone to a more upbeat happy one.

That remark was a hint to Marlin. I wondered why she said that I would be confused? I went to sit on the bed, I decided that I should put my night clothes on. I wish I knew what they knew. As far as the pain, I wondered what she meant when she said that I would grow out of it. What is happening to me? Could it be from my parents? That had to be it.

I was thinking about going out, but I just wanted to be alone. Maybe if I take a nap, the sun is still out. An hour or so would be fine. I laid across the bed and put the pillow over my head. I don't know why, but that was comforting to me.

"Ariel" I strange deep voice said.

"Who are you?" I asked curiously.

"A friend."

"Am I dreaming?"

"Maybe, maybe not."

"What do you want?'

"Don't be afraid, I won't hurt you. I want to help you."

"I'm not afraid. Help me, how, why?"

"In time I will tell you why, right now I will tell you how."

Again I asked who it was, and again it replied a friend. I couldn't see anything or anyone. It was a voice in the air. I have to be dreaming, if I wasn't someone would have come in when they heard the voice.

"How are you going to help me, why are you going to help me?"

"I have to help you, don't ask me why. You had a previous visitor. Think about it."

"Think about it? The whispering?"

"Yes, but there was too much commotion. Here the energy in the air is clearier. I have chosen you. In years to come we will meet. You will not know me. I will have someone help you to go through the changes that are going to take place within."

"I don't understand. What have I been chosen for? And what kind of changes?"

"You will find out later why. As for the changes, you are the blood of two different worlds. You will feel pain, as you already have. Your guardian knows of this pain."

"I don't understand."

"Marlin will try to protect you, so will his parents. Trust them. Be cautious around all others."

"I will. When will I see you?" I asked with the anticipation of it being soon.

"In time. After a while you will realize. I must go. You will know when the time is right to tell Marlin of our conversation."

"But what about Mynera? She is very powerful, and may know."

"I have taken care of that. She will not be able to read your mind. No one but you and I know of this. She is powerful, learn from her. Goodbye."

And that was it. I went over and looked out the window. I have got to find out somehow what is going on. I couldn't sit still. I kept pacing from one side of the room to the other. This was not helping, there must be something else that will.

I went out to the other room, everyone had gone outside. I went out the front door and sat on the steps. I wish I could have found out more. One thing that kept bothering me is not knowing who I was talking to. The idea of waiting a few years really bugged me, I hate waiting. I figured that one way to get my mind off of what may happen is to concentrate of my education and powers. After all it will not help if I worry about what is going to happen, Roz may be a bit of a challenge, he can be so nosy at times. At for Marlin, I believe that he would protect me.

I decided that a walk would be nice. When I got to the end of the house I saw a furry little animal curled up under a shrub. He was so cute, when I picked him up he opened his eyes and stared at me. He had six short legs and his body itself was slender and long. His fur was thick and fluffy and he liked it when I petted him, he was still staring at me when I put him on my shoulder he made his way around my neck. I thought his eyes were light blue, it was hard for me to tell with the sun setting. He had a cute little pink nose, and I thought that I had seen him smile. It was hard to tell with all the fur on his face. I rubbed his chin as we walked along the side of the house.

"I thought you were sleeping?" Mynera said when she saw me.

"I couldn't, so I took a little walk. Look what I found. What it it?" I asked when I stepped onto the deck and showed her the animal.

"Well he's just a baby." she smiled. "I wonder where his mother is?" she took him and held him up to get a better look. He looked at her and licked her chin. "Feels like sand." she laughed.

"He is cute. Where did you find him?" Marlin asked.

"At the corner of the house under a bush." I replied.

Mynera handed him back to me and I sat on a chair, at the same time he went back around my neck and stuck his nose under my chin.

"It seems you have made a friend." Jacob said. "There used to be more of them around here. As a matter of fact, Marlin had two of them as pets."

"And they drove mother crazy." Marlin laughed.

"What is it?" I asked.

"A mistake. They were crossbred from another animal on Zandar. No one ever thought that they would survive, but for the last sixty years they have. Someone went to Zandar and had taken their pet with them. A cat is the mother and no one is really sure what the father is. So I couldn't tell you what it actually is. They are very tame and make great pets."

"How long do they live for?" I asked.

"The average life is about eight years or so." Jacob said.

"The one that I had lived for twelve years before she died." Marlin said.

"Where did you get her?" I asked, I couldn't picture Marlin with a pet.

"Thirty years ago. The reason they were with mother is I had to go somewhere and I didn't want to leave them alone in the house for a few days." his memory of them were pleasant ones.

"Can we keep this one?" I asked excitedly.

"We'll try to find his mother in the morning, if we don't find her then I see no reason why not." he said as he rubbed the little creature. "Let me see him." as I took him off my neck he let out a big yawn. "I say, you are a baby. He doesn't have all his teeth yet."

"You know it may not be a bad idea to let her have a pet." Jacob hinted to instigate his decision.

"We'll see." Marlin replied. The way he sounded made me believe that he already made his decision.

He tried to get comfortable in Marlin's lap, when he couldn't get back to sleep he made his way back around my neck. He tickled me as he put his head under my chin.

"It looks as if he already found himself a new mother." Mynera said.

"What do you mean?" I asked.

"If we don't find his mother, he will depend on you for everything." She replied.

"I don't mind that. What will he eat?"

"Anything green. Grass, leafs, stuff like that. They are no bother to take care of." Jacob said.

"I bet if you do take him home he will stay beside you. The one that I had never missed the opportunity to sleep in my lap. In a way I miss her. You can take him home." Marlin said.

"What happened to the other one you had?" I asked.

"A friend of mine fell in love with him. He had a female and wanted to breed them, so I gave him to him."

"Do you realize what time it is?" Mynera said. "We got to talking and I forgot how late it is. I'll get us something to drink."

"I'll give you a hand." Jacob said.

"I know it may be a little early, but what are you going to call him?" Marlin asked.

"She will think of something if she hasn't already." Mynera said as she and Jacob went inside.

I sat there feeling the fur on him. "I have no idea, he is so cute."

"Yes he is. What made you walk around the house?" he asked.

"I couldn't sleep, so I went outside for a few minutes. When I got to the corner, I found him."

"It may have been a good idea to do that. I don't think that this little guy would have survived for too long without any care."

"I'm glad I found him. How do you know when they are full grown?"

Marlin moved closer and took his paw. "See the color of his nail? When it turns to a dark solid color, and he has all of his teeth, he will be an adult."

"I like his fur, it's so soft." I said as I moved my head to rub against his body.

"It will get a little thicker."

"Like a big furball." when I said that the little animal lifted his head up.

"That's for sure." He said petting his head.

"Does your friend still have some?"

"Yes he does. Sometime I'll get ahold of him and tell him what we got. He may want to breed him."

He climbed down to my lap and moved his head around like he was checking his surroundings. When he felt more comfortable he went on Marlin and climbed on his shoulder.

"Where do you think you're going? You're not my pet." Marlin said to him as he tried to pick him up.

"He likes you." I said.

"I like him too." he smiled.

As I watched he kept looking down by the lake as if he was looking for something.

"Do you think that he is trying to tell us something?" I asked as I looked in the same direction. "Like his mother may be down there?"

"It may be the last place where he had seen her."

"I guess you two have made up your minds to keep him." Mynera said as she came back out, with her she has something for us to drink plus something green for the little one to eat. "Here you go." she handed us a glass and me a small bowl.

"Salad?" I asked.

"He'll eat it." she said.

"What are you going to call him?" Jacob asked.

"I don't know yet." I said.

When he had seen what I had he got off of Marlin and came back onto my lap. I held the food for him as he sniffed it and then dove his nose into the bowl. He took out what he wanted and put it between his two front paws and sat on his back four while he ate.

"He likes those. It's good for him." Mynera said when she sait down. "Poor thing must be starving."

"I think he found himself a good home." Jacob said.

He stopped and looked at Jacob, he understood every word he heard. Jacob started to rub his head, he enjoyed having his ears rubbed. I sat there and watched how he reacted to affection, he defiantly smiled. When Jacob moved his hand away he seemed a little disappointed that he had stopped, but it passed quickly as he finished his food.

After a few hours I was starting to get sleepy and wondered where I could put him for the night.

"I think I can find a box for him. We could put it beside the bed." Mynera said.

"Yes, and by morning he will be in bed with her." Marlin said jokingly.

"I don't mind as long as he don't bite." I yawned.

"I say you are tired." Marlin said to me.

"Let me take him and we will find him something." she said.

When she took him from my lap he looked at her then at me and continued to watch me as they went inside. I put the glass down and when I stood up I felt a little pain like I had felt before. This time it went as fast as it came so I had no time to react.

"I'm going to bed." I said.

"Are you going to stay there this time?" Marlin asked curiously.

"Yes. If I get up you will be the first to know." I said as I gave him a hug, then I gave one to Jacob.

"Sleep tight princess." he said.

"I will"

When I walked into the house I stopped so I could listen to them talk.

"She is something else." Jacob said.

"Yes she is. She loves animals so much." Marlin said proudly.

"And I see that she is very confident around you, which is good."

"She trust me and only me."

"Is she ever going to be surprised when that egg hatches tomorrow." Jacob said.

I went into the bedroom and Mynera was in there putting a box with food in it next to the bed. The little creature was sitting on the bed watching her and moving his head around and sniffing the air.

"Well, what do you think?" she asked. "I gave him a towel and some more food."

I sat beside her and looked. "He should sleep good in that."

"You're not ready for sleep. Is something bothering you?"

"No. I'm okay." I assured her.

She put her hand on my head. "Are you sure?"

"Yeah, I just want to sit here."

"Okay. I'll see you in the morning." she whispered.

She gave me a kiss on the cheek and shut the door as she left. I laid there and rubbed his ears and noticed how white his fur is. He rolled over so I rubbed his belly slowly. He enjoyed that.

"You don't want to go in that box do you?" I asked him.

I laid next to him and watched him sleep, every now and then he would lift his head up and smile. He moved as close as he could and curled up by my stomach. I put my head by him and tried not to disturb him. He carefully moved his head and put his nose on mine, he was very content. I was trying to put my arm around him so I could sleep. While I petted his back I discovered that he had no tail and laughed. I heard the door move a little, I wasn't surprised to see Marlin looking in at us.

"I figured that you would be awake. Can't sleep?"

"No, and nothing is bothering me." I said.

"I know, but Mother did say that you may have something on your mind. Do you?"

"I don't want to talk about it. Not right now anyway."

"That's alright." he came over and sat on the corner of the bed. "I thought that he had a box to sleep in?" he said when he looked over at the box. It was a hint to put him in there.

"Would you like it if someone stuck you in a box to sleep?"

"I guess not. Don't stay up too late, okay."

"I won't." I promised.

He got up and started to go out the door, he paused for a moment and looked at the two of us.

"He looks comfortable. Goodnight." he said with a smile as he shut the door.

The little animal was in a good spot but I'm not. I moved a little and put the blanket over me, he came over and went under the blanket and stuck his head out and put it on the pillow. I guess he can have one corner and I can have the other.

I couldn't sleep but I was restful. I watched the sunrise from the early morning sky. When it got a little brighter I got out of bed and stood at the window. I heard a little squeaking noise. I turned around and he was looking at me with his head on the pillow.

"Is that you that made that noise?" I asked. "Maybe I should call you Squeaker, don't you?" he sat up at my remark and started cleaning himself. "Okay, I'll call you Squeaker."

I went into the bathroom at the end of the hall to get ready for taday and he followed me in and sat by the door. After I took a shower I went to reach for the towel and he had it on the floor with him, he still had a corner of it in his mouth.

"Are you holding it for me, or are you hungry?" I asked as I dripped all over the floor. When I took the towel he licked my hand. "You must be thirsty."

I put him on the counter and filled the sink with water for him. After he was done he looked back at me as I got dressed and let out a squeak.

"You want to get down?" I asked when I grabbed a brush. While I was brushing my hair he just stared at me.

"Let's go. Do you want to walk or be carried?"

He tried to stand up on my leg and fell over so I carried him in my arms but he wanted to be around my neck.

"You didn't sleep at all did you?" Marlin asked when we walked into the kitchen.

"I did a little. I decided to call him Squeaker." I said to change the subject.

"Is there a reason?"

"Yes, he squeaks."

"I think he shoud go outside."

"Do you think he will go anywhere?"

"No. I'm sure he will stick around."

I went outback on the deck and put him down on the ground. He looked around for a little bit. I wanted to see if Marlin was right about him not leaving so I went back in and left the door opened a little. When I had gone back in the kitchen Marlin was making coffee and Mynera and Jacob were sitting at the table.

"Morning" she said giving me a hug. "Where's your friend?"

"Outside. I left the door opened for him. Can we go find his mother?"

"We don't have to. Marlin and I went down by the lake last night and found her." Jacob said.

"Where is she now?" I asked.

"I buried her under the rose tree." he replied.

I sat in the chair and a few minutes later Squeaker came back in and rubbed his body on my leg. "He came back." I said happily, thinking that the two of us have something in common, we don't have parents.

"Maybe after breakfast we'll have a surprise." Mynera said.

"We don't have to take her back with us." Marlin said.

"Why not?" I asked petting Squeaker.

"Because I am going to take care of her." she said.

When I stopped moving my hand Squeaker made his little noise.

"That's why you named him that." Marlin said.

"It fits him." Jacob laughted.

Mynera made breakfast and Jacob set the table. I put Squeaker on the floor but he jumped back on my lap.

"I have something for him." Mynera said as she put a bowl on the floor.

He looked under the table to see what she was doing, it didn't take him long to realize that there was food down there.

"I'm not that hungry." I said.

"I know. That's why I made up a bowl of different fruits for you. It's not that filling." she smiled.

"They smell good." it didn't take me long to finish eating. I felt Squeaker rubbing my leg again, when I looked down he jumped up.

"You will have no problem with him." Jacob said. "What about Liera?"

Marlin put down his cup and smiled. "She won't mind.

"Working is she?" Jacob asked.

"Always"

After we finished eating I helped Mynera clean up. Squeaker stayed on around my neck the whole time and Marlin and Jacob had gone outside.

"Thankyou for helping me." she said.

"I like to help."

"You have a very good attitude about things." she said as she sat down, I sat in a chair across from her.

"Can I ask you something?"

"Sure. You can ask me anything you want." she replied, just then Marlin and Jacob came in.

"We have decided to go fishing." Jacob said.

"So we are going to leave you two alone for the afternoon." Marlin added.

"Well that is good. I know that Ariel and I will have a good time without the two of you around." She said.

"I know, anything to get rid of us right? If I know you, you two will be talking about us." Jacob said.

"And the best time to do it is when you're not around." She smiled.

"That is good." She said when they left the room. "It has been a long time since those two have done anything together."

"We're leaving, try not to get into trouble." Jacob said jokingly as they were walking out the kitchen door.

"If you come back dripping wet you can change in the garage." She said.

"Wanna bet?" Jacob said.

Mynera looked at him and smiled. "Get out of here." She said raising her voice a little. I sat there and tried not to laugh.

"Now that they're gone we should go see how the egg is doing."

"Where is it?"

"I put it where the morning sun will hit it and keep it warm."

We went out to the yard where there was a clearing, in the middle was a tree stump and the egg was nesting in the towel.

"It look neat sitting there with the sun shinning on it. It's almost a shame to see it hatch." I said.

"Yes it does look lice resting there." She replied as she looked it over. "Come over here and look at this."

I put Squeaker down and looked closer at the egg. "It has a crack in it. Can we help open the shell?"

"No. It's best for the little one to open it herself. In a few minutes she will stick her head out."

I stood there and watched the egg without moving. I could hear light tapping sounds coming from inside the egg. The first thing I saw was a little point trying to break the shell. It looked like a claw but it was her beak. In no time she had her head out, then she broke the rest of the shell.

"She's bald." I said.

Mynera laughed as she told me that her feathers will grow quickly. "We'll take her on the deck and take care of her there." she said when she picked her up.

"What will she eat?"

"I have some special food for her." she replied.

I picked up Squeaker and we went to the deck, when I sat down he tried to see what Mynera had in her hand. I was thinking of putting him down but I also thought that he would get into too much trouble.

"What is that you're giving her?"

"Pieces of fish." she said feeding with a small pair of tongs.

"What are you going to do with her?"

"I was thinking of making a little area for her down by the lake. That way she can go swimming whenever she wants to. She will be free to come and go as she pleases."

"That sounds great."

We sat outside for a long time talking about nothing inparticular. Squeaker finally stopped trying to get on her lap and went to sleep under a bush near the deck. When Jacob and Marlin returned without any fish she was not surprised.

"Well?" she asked.

"Well what?" Jacob answered.

"What happened to the fish that you were going to bring home?"

"Who said anything about catching them?" he then asked.

"We sat there watching them jumping in the water." Marlin added.

"Did you take bait with you?"

"Did I take bait with me." Jacob said mimicking her. "What kind of a fisherman do you think I am?"

"Well, let me think. You have not brought home a fish in quite a few years."

"Very funny. We leave for a few hours and when we come back you're a comedian." he said.

"What is a comedian?"

"Someone who thinks they are funny." Marlin said.

"So what did you do?" she asked either of them.

"We talked the whole time we were down there. And tossed the bait a little at a time in the lake." Marlin said.

"Well, I'll get us some lunch." she stood up and handed me the chick. "Since she is asleep you don't have to do anything but hold her. And you can come help me." she told Jacob.

Marlin sat down beside me and asked how my afternoon was.

"It sounds like you had a good day." he said.

"Yes I did. I'm glad we came."

"So am I. I called Clair's mother and told her that you can go over when we get back."

"I can show her Squeaker."

"Yes you can. What did you think about watching the egg hatch?"

"It was great, watching something being born. I told you that she could help her, I think Mynera was more excited than I was. Trying to keep Squeaker away wasn't easy."

"He was just curious. You will find out that he will investigate everything that is new to him. Like the way that you ask questions."

"What do you think Liera will say?"

"She won't mind. Just don't get the idea to bring home every stray you come across. Okay?"

"Why not?" Jacob said when he came out. "We took you home."

"I was born at home." Marlin said.

"Yeah, but no one said we had to keep you." Jacob chuckled.

"I think I'll go get ready to eat." I said.

When I got up I handed the chick to Marlin without asking him if he wanted to hold her. When I went in I could still hear what they were saying.

"I think I upset her." Jacob said.

"I'll go talk to her."

"Have you found out anything yet?"

"Nothing. The only information that I have is what Ariel has told me. I wish I knew what they were trying to do to her."

"Keep digging, you'll find something. Just be careful, you know how those type of people can be."

"It's funny you should say that." Marlin said in amazement. "Ariel told me something similar."

"She has been there for a long time. If she observed them the whole time, then she should know what they are like."

I went into the bedroom and sat on the edge of the bed, Squeaker came in after a few minutes and jumped up beside me. When I put him on my lap he stared at me, he got off when I assured him that everything was all right.

"Are you okay?" Marlin asked when he peaked around the door.

"Yeah. Why wouldn't I be?"

"Well, the way that you came back inside made me wonder." he said sitting beside me. "I know you heard us. Are you upset?"

"Not really. I just wish I knew what my parents looked like."

"Someday, somehow we will find out more." he said hugging me. "Let's go see if we can help out in the kitchen."

"I like helping her. She talks about things that are interesting."

The more I thought about being with Marlin and Liera the more I wondered the reason for it. I know that Liera has her hands full, so why did she decide to bring me into her home? That didn't make sense, unless this has to do with what she does, that I don't know.

I have three things to concentrate on. One being my powers, I want to see if I can do just about anything I desire. Two is my education, that is no problem. The third is Squeaker, I believe that when he is bigger I will be able to communicate with him like I do with other animals, maybe better.

"Can I go outside?" I asked after we had lunch.

"Go ahead, don't wander off and stay away from the lake." Marlin reminded me.

Jacob came in as I went out the door, he was about to shut it when Squeaker was coming. I didn't even realize that he was following me.

"Here you go little one." Jacob said to him. He smiled at Squeaker and watched him as he got closer to me. "He will defiantly stay by your side."

"I know. At least someone will." I said.

Jacob didn't know what to make of my comment. I think I will have to choose my words more carefully from now on. It will save on the explanations later. I will defiantly be in for a lecture on the way home.

I walked around the backyard and when I came to where Squeaker's mother is I stopped and sat on the ground. He knew that she was there, he sat on the little mound of fresh dirt that was over her. It was like he was saying his last goodbye to her.

She has a qreat spot under the rose tree, it's blossoms smelled sweet, they were bigger than both my hands put together. Poor Squeaker, I feel sorry for him. Sitting here watching him move the dirt around with his nose was heartbreaking. I wonder if he will forget her. I hope not. It would be a shame to forget the memory of someone you love.

"Come on Squeaks. I'll bring you back every chance I get. Even if you can't see her you can be near her. I promise." I told him rubbing his fur.

When I got up he moved closer to me so he could walk beside me. When I turned around Marlin and Mynera were coming closer.

"I see it didn't take long for you two to find her." she said.

"We're going to sit by the lake. Father wants to show you something." Marlin said.

"Yeah I know. Fishing." I said.

"How do you know that?" he asked.

"Just a guess." Plus I saw him walking down to the lake with a few poles.

He took my hand as we walked. Squeaker would run ahead and stop to eat some green leafs on a shrub.

"Come here you." Jacob hollered in the distance when he seen us. "I want you to try something." he had a pole already set up and in the water and he was putting a worm on another that he had for me. "I want to see how good you are." he said when I stood next to him and watched, then I looked at the one that was in the water already.

"Do you know there is nothing on the other hook?" I asked.

"Yes there is." he said.

"No there isn't." I smiled.

"Yes there is." he said again.

"You should listen to her dad." Marlin said when he and Mynera sat on the bench.

"Are you sure?" Jacob asked me when he put the pole down to get the other.

"Yes" I said confidently.

He pushed the botton to reel the line in enough to see the empty hook. "Well I'll be. That little sneak." then he reeled it all the way in and looked. "That's one smart little fish." Mynera couldn't stop laughing, she always knew that when it came to hunger, a fish will get what they need without getting caught. "You think that's funny?" he said to her. "So do I." he whispered smiling.

"Yes I do and I heard that." she said.

"I can show you a better way." I told Jacob.

"Oh really? This from a girl that has never fished before. Okay show me."

"Can I go in the water?" I asked Marlin.

"What are you up to?" he asked.

"You'll see. Can I?"

"Take off your shoes."

I held on to Jacob as I walked into the water, it was warm and so clean that I could see the bottom. I stopped when it was up to my waist and waited. A few had come to me but didn't stay long enough, they didn't trust me.

"I need some worms." I said to Jacob.

"Here you go." he said handing me a bunch.

I held them under the water and waited, then one came to me and took it from me. With my other hand I stroked her back. She in turn came up to the top of the water and swam in front of me. Once she ensured my trust she let me take her out of the water.

"I told you I can show you a better way." I said holding her up.

"I guess you have. I should take you with me." he smiled.

"She's the one that ate the worm off of the hook. Do you have any more? She wants to know, she's hungry." I said.

"Yep, a whole bucket full." he said retrieving them from the shore. "Maybe I should just feed them, like you would throwing bread to the birds." he said putting the worms in the water one at a time.

"They would like that."

This fish was as long as my arm, she had different colors on her. A dark red underneath and a light blue on the top. Her fins are white and her side fins were a foot long when expanded. She had a small fin on her back. When she was back in the water a few more like her came around, the way the sun shined on the water made their scales sparkle.

"That's something." Jacob said.

When I turned around I seen Squeaker at the edge of the water, he didn't like the idea of me being in the water. As soon as I got out he was right beside me. I picked him up and carried him over to where Marlin and Mynera were.

Mynera was smiling at Jacob as he came toward her and when he sat down she started to laugh again.

"Don't even say it." he said as he put his arm around her.

"Say what? The fact that you can't catch a fish or the fact that Ariel picked one up without any effort?" She laughed.

"She's a little showoff." he said playfully.

"You both are wet." Mynera said.

"Yes and it feels like a hundred out here, it feels good." he said.

When Squeaker felt better about me being out of the water he got down and retrieved my shoes and dragged them to me one at a time. It was funny watching him because after a few feet he would have to put it down and pick it up again.

"He despised the idea of you being in the water." Mynera said. "The second he saw you in there he ran over to the edge of the water and stared."

"I was thinking that might have been what happened to his mother." I said.

"It is possible. She was wet when we found her." Marlin said.

"There is a branch that hangs over the water." Mynera added.

Terrible way to go, I thought to myself. No wonder Squeaker was worried, it must have been awful for him to watch helplessly as she lost her struggle to swim back.

"I love you." I told him after he jumped on my lap. He was playful as I moved my fingers through his fur. He would grab onto my hand with his back four paws and bat his front paws on the strands of my hair that were hanging down, trying to put them in his mouth.

As it got later in the day I went inside to shower and change before dinner. Squeaker did the same thing that he had done this morning, this time he sat on the counter and made himself comfortable on my clothes as he watched me shower.

"Keeping my clothes warm?" I asked him when I dried off. He gave me a little smirk as he stretched. "I hate to tell you but I want those." He wouldn't move so I had to carefully pick him up and put him on the floor. When I grabbed my shirt he jumped onto my pants. "You gotta move." he looked around as if he didn't hear me, so I tickled his belly, he wanted to play. "After I finish dressing. I promise."

We sat on the couch and played, when I heard Mynera moving around in the kitchen I went to help her. Squeaker stayed on the couch and fell asleep.

"He loves you." she said as she poured coffee.

"I'm glad I found him. I love his fur."

"What do you think Roz will think of him?"

"I never thought about it. I hope he likes him. We can share."

"That's true."

"How come where you're so powerful that Marlin hasn't inherited your powers?" I asked curiously.

"Its not a question of inheriting them. True, that some are a birthright, but there are others that progress by allowing them to emerge. They are there, it's up to Marlin to allow them to grow. Do you understand?"

"Yes"

"Why don't you take these out to them while I get dinner."

"Do you want some help?" I gladly offered.

She smiled and shook her head. "You can help by taking these out. He careful, it's hot." she said as I took the handles of the cups.

"I will. It's not that far." I said moving slowly to the glass door to the deck.

"I'll take that." Jacob said as he was coming into the house, taking the cup from me. "Thank you princess." then he continued on his way.

"Why does he sat that?" I asked when Marlin took the cup from me.

"Because you're special to him." he answered. "You look a little tired."

"A little, but I want to see the stars tonight." I said when I perked up.

"They are beautiful shinning over the water. When it's really dark and they sparkle bright you can see them shine on the water."

"I can't wait."

"Where's your friend."

"Sleeping on the couch. I asked Mynera if she wanted any help, but she doesn't."

"That's because I thought that we could have some sandwiches." she said when she put a tray on the table. "And I made you some salad. I think you're going to have a vegetarian on your hands." she told Marlin.

"I don't like meat, it doesn't taste right." I said.

"Why do you say that?" she asked, she also gave me a puzzled look.

"I don't know. I just don't like it."

She wondered if she might have been wrong about the origin of my parents. Before I could find out any more of what she was thinking, she realized that I heard and concentrated on something else.

"You have a strong mind for a child so young." she said.

"Ariel is a pretty amazing girl." Marlin said proudly.

"Yes, you are lucky." she told hhim.

"What are all of you jabbering about?" Jacob asked when he sat next to her.

"I was just telling our son how lucky he is to have Ariel."

"You take good care of her son or I'll come and kick your butt a good one." Jacob warned him.

"You don't have to worry about her. There is nothing that is going to hurt her." Marlin assured both of them.

Interesting, I thought to myself. They seem to know something, but are not going to tell me. Mynera is reorganizing her thoughts about what she believed was right, she is putting together a puzzle in her mind. I won't push the issue, not right now anyway.

We had a delightful conversation as we ate. Once Squeaker woke up he made his way out to us, begging for a piece of lettuce. When I gave him some he took it and went under a tree to eat. I finished what I ws eating and turned my attention to Squeaker when I noticed him climbing a tree.

He went up with no problem then proceeded to go on a limb to get some leaves. The one he wanted was in an odd spot. I watched in amazement as he hung upside down with all six of his legs wrapped around the limb. Then I felt Marlin tapping me on the shoulder.

"I've been trying to get your attention." he said.

"Look at him." I said pointing.

"That's probably what his mother was trying to do." Mynera said when she turned around to look.

Died because she was hungry, I thought to myself. I will never let Squeaker go hungry, he doesn't have to. I helped Mlynera clean up and we made something cold to drink and brought it down to the lake and sat there talking about anything.

Mynera went back to the house and got the chick and brought her down. She kept her in their bedroom so that Squeaker's curiosity wouldn't get him in trouble. When she put her in the water she also put in some bread crumbs for her to fish for. I stood by the edge of the lake watching her and Squeaker came over and got in front of me to block me from the water.

"He's protecting you." Marlin said. "That little animal is smarter than we think."

"But how is that possible?" I asked when I walked back with Squeaker at my feet.

"An animal is a very strange creature. There is no way of measuring their intelligence." Mynera said.

After I finished my drink I sat on the ground and watched the stars appear. I love it down here, there is nothing obstructing the view of the sky. Squeaker laid around my neck and burried his nose under my hair. I heard the conversation that they were having, it was nothing of major interest. I could tell that they do love it out here, so do I.

"I'm going to bed." I told Squeaker.

"That sounds like a good idea. I'll walk with you." Mynera said.

"Goodnight" Marlin said,

"Sleep titght princess." Jacob said when I have him a hug.

Princess, what a strange word, I thought to myself as Mynera and I walked toward the house. Squeaker seen the chick in her hands and kept his eyes on her the whole time.

"You are nosy." I told him.

"Like the curiosity of a child." Mynera said as she put the chick in her room.

Squeaker got between the blanket and the sheet and put his head on the pillow the same way he did the night before. I changed and made myself comfortable beside him.

"Goodnight little one." Mynera said when she peeked in at us.

"Night" I yawned when I rolled over.

I heard her laugh in amusement as she left the room. I drifted in and out of sleep, I heard Marlin come in and felt his hand on my head, then I heard him whisper as he said goodnight again.

When I finally fell asleep I had a wonderful dream about the fish that I had held earlier. I was swimming under the water with her and many more of them joined us. It was great swimming and playing with them, then they went with me to the top of the water where I had seen Squeaker sitting at the edge of the water waiting for me. When I walked to the shore he walked away from me and headed in the direction of the tree that his mother fell from.

I seen his mother try to grab a leaf and lose her grip and fall. the strangest thing was when she hit the ground, what wasw on the ground was not an animal but a woman with long black hair. The woman was from myh previous dreams, and even here she was covered in blood. I went over to touch her and as I put my hand closer a woman grabbed my hand. The same scary hag that took me into the doctors office on the day that I went home.

"You don't want to do that." she said in an angry voice.

But in my dream, instead of taking me into his office as she had done that day I left, she took me into a room, more like a lab.

"Sit down." she said without changing her tone.

"No" I yelled as I tried to loosen her tight grip.

She tightened her grip and practically pulled me off of the floor and sat me on a table. "You will do what you are told." she said.

She pushed me down on the table and put straps around me so I couldn't move. I knew it was only a dream, but I was still scared and couldn't wake up. As I screamed and cried for help she stuck a knife in my arm. I felt the pain, you're not supposed to feel pain in a dream, but I did. As I screamed for help she then hit me across the face. When she went to hit me again someone grabbed her arm and pulled her away from me.

Within seconds she was gone, I was untied and left alone in the dark. I couldn't stop crying and I became more scared. I still felt the pain and I was still in the dark not know what was going to happen next. I felt hands on me, shaking me, then I heard someone saing "wake up." when I opened my eyes I was scared, crying and had no idea where I was.

"It's okay. It was just a dream." Mynera said.

She had turned on the light and was sitting on the bed, I was still crying and shaking. I knew where I was, but I wasn't sure if I was really here. I didn't say anything, I got out of bed and ran to Marlin when I heard him walking in the hallway toward the bedroom. He picked me up when I got to him, I still didn't stop crying.

"It's alright, it was just a dream." he said as he carried me out to the living room.

"I'll make coffee, and get something for her to drink." Mynera said.

"That sounds good." he said when he sat down. I still didn't let go. I tightened my grip when I thought that he was going to put me down. "It's okay."

"I called Cileen. She'll be over to see her." Jacob said sitting beside us.

"Do you think that is really necessary?" Marlin asked.

"She has a lot of negative energy flowing through her subconscious. I wish I could help her but I can't." Mynera said when she put her hand on me. "Cileen can."

"She sees you as her security." Jacob said.

"Marlin, when I touched her I felt something different. Ariel knew that she was dreaming and couldn't wake up. Somehow she managed to enhance a strong part of her to help her fend off whatever was frightening her. She does have a strong mind, but she has been through so much. You have no idea what they did to her. She is so small and can be hurt easily." Mynera said.

"In her dream her security must have been threatened." Jacob said. Then we heard a knock at the door. "There she is now. I'll be right back."

He came back with a woman and she sat next to me and said hello, but I ignored her. Mynera told her what happened.

"Let me hold her Marlin." Cileen said as she reached for me.

"You can try, but she's not letting go."

"I know. But if I'm going to help you, I need to hold you." She said to me. She seemed nice enough but I just didn't want to. "Please" She said staring into my eyes. She had the prettiest blue eyes and a kind smile, I reluctantly let her hold me. "Your theory on her enhancing her power is not correct. She has someone or something watching her."

"She has a guardian?" Marlin asked.

"Yes. There is a trace of another energy. She's not even fully awake, she is still terrified. That must have been some dream."

"You can help her?" Jacob asked curiously.

"Yes" she said hugging me. "I felt your friend." She said stroking my hair. "Do you know who it is?" I only stared at her, wondering why she was here. "It's okay, you don't have to tell me. I just want to help you." I felt her power, it was strange, she was searching for something. While she did that I felt somewhat better, I didn't feel scared and I was no longer crying. "Now she's awake."

I got a better look at her, her hair was white, she was old but didn't look that old. She was kind, that I felt, and sincere.

"She doesn't trust people." Marlin told her.

"With all the negative energy around her in the past, I don't blame her." Cileen said. Could she be the one? I thought to myself. No she's not, I am sure of that. I still have to wait. "Could I be what little one? she asked. When she said that I pulled away. I didn't know that she could read my mind, and I didn't want her to. "I'm sorry if I intruded in something that I was not to hear." she whispered.

"It's okay." I said as I moved away from her to sit with Marlin.

"You are defiantly her security." Cileen said to Marlin when he put his arm around me. "This has never happened before?"

"She has had the same dream that has kept her awake at night, but not like this." he told her.

"That I felt. Those are not dreams. What I seen was a vision of what had happened. She is reliving that event over and over." she said.

"But she was just a baby." Jacob said.

"It doesn't matter. Even then she was aware of her surroundings. There is something about her that I do not understand, I can't explain it. She has been talking with someone."

"That I knew. As a matter of fact that is actually why we came. I was going to go somewhere else and that is when she told me that someone had told her that it would have been a mistake." then he told her what I said to him the morning we came here.

"Someone is defiantly helping her. Unfortunately whoever it is doesn't have enough power to communicate with her for a long period of time." then she paused while she gathered her thoughts. "But I sense two different, alternate, powers. That is what is confusing me." She said touching me, but I backed away. "It's okay, I won't impose. She's a little intimidated with me. She has no trust for anyone other than you three."

"She doesn't know what to make of Liera." Mynera told her when she handed her a cup.

"She doesn't like what she does." Marlin said.

"Could she have been in contact with Ariel when she was younger? Possibly have done something to her." Cileen said.

"I don't know. I do know that Liera was in contact with her father, but after that, I don't know." Marlin said.

"What about Roz?" She asked.

"Roz is angry because Ariel can do more with her powers than he can. But he is starting to understand that he has to practice." Marlin said.

"He's mad at me because I can do things easier than he can." I whispered.

"So he is intimidated because she is more advanced in some areas." Cileen said.

"But she doesn't have to practice on some things." Mynera pointed out.

"Really! Well that is something." she said in a surprise. "I've had endless hours of practice for years to get this far."

"We all have." Jacob said. "But it's amazing how she does it without realizing it." then he told her what I did at the lake today, and how easy it was. Then he seen Squeaker come out to us. "And this little one sticks by her."

As she observed when he jumped on my lap and licked my face.

"And he always will." Cileen said. Squeaker sat up and looked at her, he went to sit next to her for a closer look. "Curious little creature." She smiled. "You are taking him home, that is good. He will help ease her mind."

"At least he keeps her occupied." Mynera said.

"What does she usually do during the day?" Cileen asked.

"She keeps very busy at home. When we're not talking she is usually reading or she spends time with her friend." Marlin explained.

"Now I understand. By keeping herself busy and abserving everything else around her and trying to understand what she is seeing it is, in a small way, keeping her from remembering or concentrating on what has already happened. Do you understand Ariel?" She asked.

"What are you, a therapist?" I asked.

"Sort of." she smiled. "I can remove the negative energy that is causing your bad dreams, what I can't do is remove the vision from your mind."

"I can live with that." I told her. "Can I go back to bed?"

"Don't you think that you're being a little rude to Cileen?" Marlin asked.

"Marlin, she is intimidated by me. Don't force her." She said.

"In time that will pass." Mynera said.

"Yes. I'm not offended at the fact that she does not want to be near me. I understand her fear of someone she know nothing of. Maybe next time we meet she will be more open toward me. After all I am a stranger and she trusts no one." Cileen said.

"True" he said rubbing my back. "I'll take you back to bed."

"I can walk." I said when he got up.

"I know"

"I'll be in to check on you later." Mynera said.

When Cileen said goodnight to me I surprised her when I said it back. She smiled at me as Marlin walked passed her. I knew she wanted to help. True I am a little intimidated, not by her, but by her power. I didn't want her reading my mind, and it scared me when she did.

"You know something," Marlin said when he put me down on the bed and covering me with the blanket.

"I know. Cileen want's to help." I yawned. "And you want me to apologize."

"Yes I do, but you need your sleep. I'll tell her for you. Do you feel better?" He asked holding my hand.

"Yes"

"Do you want to talk about it?"

After thinking about it for a few minutes I reluctantly told him about my dream, how wonderful it started and how horrifying it got.

"The strangest part is that I felt pain." I told him.

"Where?"

"My arm, where they always gave me shots."

"Father was right, in your dream your security was threatened. But I don't understand how you felt pain. I will ask Cileen about that, her or Mother may know."

"I love it here. Jacob and Mynera tell great stories. I like hearing about the places they have been."

"They have been many places that's for sure. When I was your age Father would tell me a different story every night before I went to sleep."

"I know. When he was telling me about how he and Mynera met, I could tell that he missed doing that. I do like Cileen, but I don't like her power."

"She takes some getting use to. You do understand that she was only trying to help?" he asked, I nodded. "Good. You shouldn't have any more of those dreams. I'll be back later." he gave me a kiss and when he was about to close the door Squeaker finally came in. he jumped on the bed and laid at the corner of my pillow. "It is a good thing that we are taking him home." then he shut the door.

"Comfortable?" I asked him, he gave me a smile. "Me too."

I could hear the sounds of mumbling as everyone talked in the living room, I didn't hear anything clear but I new that they were talking about me. Then I heard that same voice again.

"Better?" It said.

"She's not what I thought." I said.

"No, but she did help. Night Dre."

Before I could ask why I was called Dre he was gone. I guess it's not that important, but I would like to know. I had fallen asleep and after a while I felt Mynera when she came to check on me.

When I woke up in the morning I discovered that it was afternoon. Squeaker was moving around like carzy, I knew that he had to go outside. He didn't leave me at all last night, I was surprised. The minutes Marlin opened the bedroom door he ran by him as fast as his six little feet could go.

"He's quick."

"He has to go outside." I said.

"The door to the deck is open, I imagine he's already discovered that. How do you feel?" he asked when he sat next to me.

"Hungry"

"Good. Get cleaned up an we'll get something. Dress cool, it's going to be hot today." he said before he left the room.

I kind of figured that it was going to be hot, I could feel it. I took a cool shower and when I went to get dressed Squeaker was sitting on my clothes again.

"I bet you feel better after going outside." I said after I moved him off my clothes. "I'm hungry. Let's go eat."

That was one word he understood very well. He ran down the hallway in front of me and was sitting by the kitchen table waiting for me.

"Afternoon" Jacob said when he gave me a tight hug. "You had us a little worried last night."

"Sorry" I said when he let me go.

"Nothing to be sorry about." Mynera said when she gave me a hug. "You do seem more relaxed."

"Cileen was impressed with you. She would like to see you again, if you would like." Jacob said.

"Maybe the next time you come over." Mynera said looking at me.

"We can do that." Marlin said.

"Good, besides it's been a long time since you have seen your aunt." she said.

"You're related?" I asked sitting down.

"She's my baby sister." Mynera said.

"I didn't know that."

"With the way you were last night, it didn't matter. But she would like to see you again. Next time she would like to have a much better conversation with you. She had something on her mind when she left, but she didn't say it." Marlin said.

"That's Cileen for you. She has always been like that." Jacob said.

After lunch Mynera and I took a walk around the lake, I kept thinking of how old she looks, then I thought about how old Mynera is. She looks a lot younger than her. Even though aging on the skin doesn't show, it does on the hair.

"If she is younger than you are, how come her hair is all white?" I asked.

She looked at me and laughed. "Her hair has been that color since the day she was born. When we were in our teens I would pick on her playfully about her hair. She would tell me that it made her seem "older" and that the adults would treat her as an adult. Sometimes it got confusing for her to separate herself from youth and adult. She started working with people when she discovered that she could help them to understand what was going on within their minds if they had a hard time comprehending it." she explained. "She's done a great job with people."

We walked for the longest time, the lake seemed endless, the weeks following were great. I felt great, I slept, I ate, and I actually had a few good dreams. When it was time to leave I didn't want to go. I was playing out in the front yard with Squeaker when he decided to go out in the back and sit under the rose tree. I felt so sad for him, watching him sitting there with his paws over her grave. It was like in his own way he was saying goodbye.

"In no time he won't feel so bad." Mynera said walking up behind us.

"Yeah" I said picking him up.

He got into his usual place around my neck, this time he buried his nose under the collar of my shirt. It was like he was trying to hide or get comfort fro his sorrow. I held his paw as we walked back toward the house, that seemed to help a little.

"Ready to go?" Marlin asked.

"We're leaving now?"

"It's early so I figured that we could take our time."

When we got to the front I put Squeaker down so I could give Mynera and Jacob a hug. The little chick was much bigger her feathers were white with tints of pink along the edges. Her and Squeaker kept sniffing around each other.

"Next time you come she will be full grown." Mynera said.

"I'm glad you're taking care of her. She will have a chance to grow." I said petting her.

"Grow she will. I'm glad you brought her to me. There are some who wouldn't have taken the time to help a little animal."

"I bet there are a lot of people like that. Besides if we didn't come I would have never found Squeaker. I think that he would have died, and no animal deserves that."

"Maybe next time you come you will find another animal to take home." Jacob said jokingly.

"I don't think so." Marlin replied before I could say anything.

"I put something in a bag for Squeaker, I thought that he may get hungry on the way home." Mynera said.

"Thanks" I said when she handed me the bag.

I put the bag on the front seat, Squeaker jumped in and waited for me. He knew that he was coming too. Jacob knelt down beside me and told me to stay out of trouble and be good. That was easier said than done. I gave the chick a little kiss and she nipped my finger. It didn't hurt, I guess that was her way of saying goodbye. When I got in the seat Squeaker sat on my lap.

"Take good care of him." she told me again.

"I will."

She gave me a kiss on the cheek then shut the door. I turned around to make sure I didn't forget anything. I noticed a feather in the back seat and I handed it to her through the window.

"What's this?" she asked.

"It's a feather from her mother. I forgot I had it. I think she should have it." I told her.

"I know she will love it." Mynera smiled, then she turned her attention to Marlin. "I hate to see you go."

"We'll be back." he assured her.

"And you remember what I told you." she said when she gave him a hug.

"I will, try not to worry." he said, then he whispered, "everything will be fine," in her ear.

I wonder what that was about, maybe I shouldn't have spent so much time outside while we visited. She was very concerned, not because of my nightmare, something else was bothering her. When we started to leave I wanted to ask, but figured that it was none of my business. Marlin didn't say anything until we got a few miles down the road.

"Aside from your bad dream, you had a good time." he said.

"It was great. I loved watching the chick hatch and seeing the look of Jacob's face when I held the fish, and his stories, I'll never forget it. What do you think Liera will say about bringing another stray home?"

"What do you mean by that?"

"If you think about it, Squeaker and I have a lot in common. He doesn't have his parents, and he doesn't eat meat."

"There is a difference. We didn't find you under a bush."

"I really don't see that much of a difference. Would you have taken me home if you found me outside?"

"Of course I would have. Do you think about your mother a lot?" He asked curiously.

"Sometimes. At night is when I think about her the most, I don't know why. I wish I knew what she looked like. Do you think I will ever see her, even if she doesn't come back?"

"Anything is possible. Right now why don't you concentrate on the events of the day."

"What do you mean?" that got me a little confused.

"In other words, take one day at a time. Don't worry about what is going to happen."

"I understand that. Are you going to tell Liera what happened?"

"We'll keep that between us for now. She will never know."

"What did she put in the bag?" I asked when I saw Squeaker poking at it with his nose.

"There are some vegetable greens in there."

"Cool. I bet you want to eat?" I said petting Squeaker.

"Are you hungry?"

"No, I'm a little tired."

"Relax, enjoy the ride."

"Yeah. We'll be in for it when we get home." I laughed.

And he laughed with that too. When Squeaker heard that I had food he stuck his whole head in the bag before I got the chance to open it all the way.

"What if she won't let me keep him?"

"She will. Besides we can let him go in the backyard." he said.

As much as I loved being with Mynera and Jacob I'm glad to be home. I can't wait to show Squeaker to Clair, I hope that Liera doesn't have a problem with him.

When we got inside Liera was gone and Roz was in his room, Squeaker stayed around my neck until I got to my room. He was so nosy, once he got under my bed he found something to get into,

"Hey, that's my shoe." I said to him when I seen that he had puched it out from under the bed."

He looked at me in a strange way, he thought it was funny, I guess in a way it was. As he was investigating I was putting water down in the bathroom for him. I was about to put my clothes away when I heard a knock at the door, Squeaker knew that it wasn't Marlin and hid in the bathroom.

"Hi, dad said that you brought something back with you." Roz said when I opened the door.

"Come on in. just don't tell your mother yet. We need a plan."

"Well what is it?" he asked in excitement. "He didn't say anything." then he gave me a strange look. "What do you mean a plan?"

"Yes plan, and I know why he didn't tell you. You must promise not to say anything to your mother until we can think of something."

"It sounds important. I have good news, Sara is gone. She said that I am doing fine and that she will be back once a quarter to see how I'm doing. She left something for you, it's on your desk."

I looked over and saw a disk with a note attached. "I'll look at it later."

"Done with what, what is it?" he asked. He couldn't stand the suspense anymore.

"It's something that we both can share, and if you fall in love with it too then she can't say no. sit on the bed and close your eyes." When I made sure that he did as I told him I went into the bathroom and got Squeaker. He made a little squeaking noise when I put him on Roz's lap. "Okay, open your eyes."

"Wow!" He said in surprise. "Where did you get him, can we keep him."

"That's why we have to suck up to your mom. Marlin said yes, now it's up to us. I found him when we got there, he has no one else." I said.

"Almost like you."

Sara's work with him wasn't for nothing, she did manage to get some compassion inside him. I was touched by him kindness, even if he didn't realize it.

I could tell that Roz liked him, Squeaker kept checking him out. We were in my room for over an hour. They liked playing with each other. I told Roz how I found him and why we took him home, I also told him why I named him Squeaker. We would have stayed in my room longer but we heard Liera come home.

"Well, what do you think?" Roz asked.

"We could go down there together with Squeaker, or we could leave him in the bedroom and beg her for a pet."

"I like the first one. If that doesn't work then we can beg." he said. I can tell that he would love to have him.

Roz and I went to the top of the stairs. Squeaker was around my neck. We didn't see Liera anywhere. Marlin was at the computer when he looked up and noticed us looking for her.

"She's in the kitchen." Marlin said.

"If we wait it might be worse." I told Roz.

"How do you figure?" he asked.

"If we wait she might get mad at us for keeping a secret from her. Especially this one." I replied leaning over the banister.

"What do you mean by this one?" he whispered in my ear. He didn't want Marlin to hear him.

"Nothing. Here she comes." I whispered back.

We watched her come out of the kitchen and go sit on the couch to read.

"What are you two up to?" she asked suspiciously. She didn't even notice that Squeaker was around my neck.

"Nothing" We replied together.

"Well, let's go." I said.

When we got to the bottom of the stairs Liera didn't even turn around. Marlin stop what he was doing and decided to watch us.

"You go first." I whispered.

"Why should I? Give me one good reason."

"She's your mother."

"Good reason." he said with little enthusiasm.

I stayed by the stairs and watched Roz getting closer to her, until she turned around, then he stopped.

"You two are up to something. What is it?" she asked.

"We were wondering if we can have a pet?" he asked slowly.

"Pet? Do you realize the responsibility there is to taking care of a pet? Not to mention the mess. What do you mean WE?" she asked.

When she looked at me she realized that there was something around my neck. For a few minutes she wa speechless.

"He's a friend. His name is Squeaker." I said.

"You two go upstairs." she said calmly.

Roz and I went into my room because it was closer to the stairs. I left the door open just a little, this way we could hear what they were talking about.

"In all the places I have lived I have never had a pet in any of them. How could you let her bring a pet in here?" she asked Marlin.

"Well, she's not yelling. Is that a good thing?" I asked Roz.

"We'll find out." he said.

"I was thinking the two of them will have something in common. They may get along better." he told her.

"I don't want no animal." she said.

"Why do you think mom doesn't want him here?" Roz asked.

"I think I know. I can talk to them." I said.

I figured that she was fighting a losing battle so I decided to go and see what it was that Sara had left for me. When I read the note she said that this was some information that Marlin and I might be interested in.

"What are you doing?" Roz asked.

"I don't feel like listening to your mother. I want to see what Sara left." I said.

On the screen Sara had given me instructions to place an access word that meant a lot to me. This was easy, when I put in the word mother information started to appear on the screen. I couldn't believe it, I almost started to cry.

"What is it?" Roz asked when he came over.

"Sara said that my test scores came in the day after I did them. Liera kept them from me."

"Why would she do that?" he asked, even he was confused.

"I don't know."

As we kept reading, Sara had put information about Roz in. it seems that Liera has done something to him.

"I don't understand. Do you know what she is talking about?" he asked.

"No, but I bet it won't take much to find out. I know that Marlin would like to see this. Do you think that we should interrupt the madness?"

"It seems the only madness around here is my mother." he was starting to feel anger toward her. "Let's take it down."

I put Squeaker in the bathroom and took the disk downstairs. Marlin and Liera were still talking, but at least she wasn't aggravated. When she walked passed us to go upstairs she didn't say a word.

"It seems we have won." Marlin said.

"I wouldn't be so sure about that." I whispered.

"What are you talking about?" he asked.

"We need to talk where mom won't hear us." Roz whispered.

We went down to Marlin's office, he had no idea of what was going on as far as us wanting to talk in total private.

"Okay, what's the big secret?" he asked when he shut the door.

"Secret isn't the word for it. Sara left this for us. You should look at it now." I said handing him the disk.

"What's the pass word?" he asked after he put it in the computer.

"Mother" I replied.

He looked at me and smiled. "I should have known." His expression changed as he read the information. "Why would she keep the scores from you?"

"I was hoping you would know." I replied.

"Keep reading." Roz said.

When he had read that Liera was doing something to her own child Marlin became very angry.

"This is the most sickening thing that anyone could do to a child. I'm going to have a talk with her." he said.

"Then you know what these abbreviations mean?" Roz asked.

"Yes" He said staring at the screen.

"Do you think that it's a good idea to ask her while we are here?" Roz asked, he was actually scared.

He sat there and thought for a while, and he could only come up with one plan.

"Ariel, I want you to start teaching Roz how to use his powers. I have a feeling that you're going to need them more than ever." he said to us.

"What if what she is doing is to keep me from being able to use them?" he asked.

"Could be, but why?"

"Maybe she's afraid of him. Like she is with me." I said.

"Stick together. I'll figure something out." he told us. "Roz, don't worry."

We went up to my room to see what Squeaker was going. When we went into the bathroom we couldn't see him. We searched the bathroom and stopped when we came to the tolet.

"You don't think he could of gotten in there?" he asked.

"No, he's not in there. Let's keep looking."

We were relieved when we found him in the cabinet under the sink.

"He must have a strong nose to open that." Roz said.

"I should take him out but I don't want to run into your mother." I told him.

"I don't blame you. Right now I don't care if she disappears. How could she do something like that?"

"She doesn't have a heat. Besides we don't know exactly what she did and why. Don't get me wrong, I'm not defending her, I never will. But I've been through a lot of stuff that you will never know."

We sat on the bed playing with Squeaker. I knew that I had to take him out and get him food, but I don't want to go out of my room.

"Where are you going?" Roz asked.

"I have to get him food and take him out."

"Hey if you can talk to animals, can you talk to him?"

"Yeah, why?"

"Do you think he can be tolet trained?"

"That's a crazy idea that just might work." I said looking at Squeaker. "I am impressed Roz."

"You do that and I'll get him some food."

"He's a vegetarian, anything like that."

"Cool, someone that can eat my veggies. He has to come to dinner all the time."

He went downstairs and I took Squeaker to the bathroom. It was interesting to sit him on the tolet, but after a little persuasion and holding his tail up for him, he figured out how to put his back four paws on the tolet and not fall in. I will eventually show him how to hold his tail up or in his front paws so it doesn't get wet.

"He did it?" Roz asked when he came back in.

"Yeah. I think it's great."

"Maybe that's what you should do. Work with animals. It's better than people."

"Yeah. Anything is better than people."

"I wouldn't know about that." Marlin said when he came in, scaring both of us. "Sorry. I didn't mean to scare you."

"It's okay. You didn't talk to her yet did you?" I whispered.

"No. I have another idea. I want to find out what Sara was talking about, this will take time. I just need you two to stick together." Marlin said.

"We can do that." I said.

"I don't even want to see her." Roz said.

"Hey guess what?" I said cheerfully to Marlin.

"What?"

"Squeaker can be tolet trained. It was Roz's idea."

"Really, amazing. Don't worry Roz." Marlin said when he sat next to him. "I'm going to hold on to that disk, I can hide it better."

"What about my scores?" I asked when I sat on the floor.

"I can get those." Marlin replied.

When he left my room Roz and I sat there not knowing what to think.

"I hate her." he said while he petted Squeaker.

"So do I."

"I don't trust her."

"I have an idea." I said smiling.

"What is it?" he asked curiously.

"Have you ever been in the woods?"

"No. You're not thinking about going in there are you?"

"Give me one good reason why not and I can give you one why we should."

"What about what dad said?"

"Marlin didn't say no, he just said not to bother her. Besides it will get us out of the house."

"I get it. It's good for one day. What about the other days?"

"There is a lot to explore, things to find that I have never seen with my own eyes before. Roz I grew up in a lab, I've never seen the outside until I came here."

"I like that idea. You're not so bad after all.'

"Thanks. I'm not your enemy.'

"I know. When you and dad were gone, Sara explained a lot of stuff to me that made sense. I'm glad she was here. Even if the only time she left me alone was to go to the bathroom."

When Squeaker finished what he was eating we took him outside for a little while. As we were sitting on the stonewall in the backyard Clair came over to see if I was still coming over tomorrow. When we had told her what we were up to she was wondering if she could come along with us.

"I don't see why not. Don't tell anyone." Roz said.

"Great!" She said, then she seen Squeaker when he jumped on Roz's lap. "What is that?"

"His name is Squeaker." Roz said.

"I found him when we went to Mynera's." I said.

"Can I hold him?" she asked.

"If he let's you." I said.

He didn't know what to make of her when Roz handed him to her. He didn't lick her like he usually does but he didn't mind her stroking his fur. Then we heard her father calling for her.

"I wish I didn't have to go." she said handing Squeaker back to Roz. "I'll see you tomorrow."

I don't know who liked the idea of tomorrow better, her or us. We came back in when Liera informed us that it was time for dinner. We cleaned up and as I was leaving my room Squeaker decided to stay there and sleep on my pillow, an idea that I thought was very good. I left the bathroom door open for him and the tolet seat up.

As Roz and I were sitting at the table we tried to keep a conversation going between the two of us. He told me about what went on between him and Sara and I was telling him about what we did while we were away, leaving out the part about Cileen, just for the sake of not giving Liera the chance to say anything, until she got the chance herself.

"You two are talking a lot tonight." she said.

"Is there anything wrong with that?" Roz asked.

"We just have a lot to say." I added.

"I told you that a pet would help them to get along better." Marlin told her.

"Well, I guess it will stop the two of them from bickering all the time." she said.

"What bickering? I was with Sara, I didn't have time to pick on her." Roz said.

After we were done I helped Liera. She usually knows what I'm thinking but not this time. I wondered if it had anything to do with my visitor, that has to be it. When whoever it was said that it would take care of Mynera reading my mind, it must have taken care of everyone else. If this is true I think it's great.

It was early so I took Squeaker outside. I sat on the stonewall and watched him investigate. I turned my attention toward the woods trying to find the best way in.

"Hey, what are you doing?" Roz asked when he came over.

"Looking"

"Mom wants us."

Roz didn't sound enthused about that. We had no idea as to what she wanted. She was sitting on the couch drinking coffee and Marlin was sitting on the chair reading until Squeaker jumped on his lap.

"I meant to tell you two that I have tomorrow off. How would you kids like to go shopping?" she asked.

I was stunned. The last thing that I wanted to do was to go anywhere with her. Roz felt the same way.

"But we have plans tomorrow." I told her.

"What are you up to?" she asked.

"Clair didn't really see Squeaker, and we were going to play with him, get him used to more people. Besides I don't think that it would be a good idea to leave him by himself." I said.

"He can't get into much. Marlin will be here." she said.

"I don't think that it would be fair for Marlin to take care of him, he's not his responsibility. Until Squeaker gets use to the idea of being alone, me or Roz should stay with him." I explained seriously, I didn't even take a breath.

"Well, that is very thoughtful of you. You have a good sense of responsibility." she said.

"Why don't we wait a few weeks, then we all can go." Marlin said as he petted Squeaker.

"We could make a day of it. I like the sound of that." she said.

That was easy to get out of. Roz went to his room and didn't come back out. I went along as usual, then I took Squeaker outside one more time. I couldn't wait to get to bed, the only thing on my mind was going into the woods.

I took Squeaker out bright and early, Roz also got up early. I waited by the stonewall for him to get done with breakfast. We sat there waiting for Clair, we knew that she would be along any minute. After an hour we saw her running toward us. We waited until we were sure that no one was watching us before we went to the edge of the woods.

"Have you ever been in there?" I asked.

"I wasn't allowed." He still felt that we shouldn't go.

"After what happened, does it matter?" I asked.

"Not to me."

"What happened?" Clair asked.

"We'll explain it when we can. We're trusting you not to say anything." he told her.

Squeaker stayed with us while we went in, he would eat a leaf here and there. After a while I picked him up and put him around my neck. Not too long after that we came to a field.

"Wow" I said.

"It's a meadow. We were told to stay away from this. It's so beautiful." Clair said.

"I wonder why we didn't come here before?" Roz said.

"Because you were told not to." I reminded him.

We went into the middle of the meadow. Wild flowers were growing everywhere, and the smell was the best thing that I have ever smelled.

"All this time we were told that someone lived here and it has been nothing but a lie." Roz said.

"I don't think so." I said while I was looking at the other side of the meadow. I did feel some kind of presence.

"Why do you say that?" Clair asked.

"I think we should go over there." I said pointing.

"What if it's a waste of time?" Roz asked.

"Remember your mother has the day off. Do you really want to go home and listen to her?" I asked.

"Let's go." he said when he started to walk to the other side.

We we went in I knew that we were going in the right direction. We stopped when we came to a small stream.

"How do we cross?" Clair asked.

"Take your shoes off and put them on when we get to the other side." I said when I picked up Squeaker.

"I don't think I should. It's been over two hours." Roz said.

"If you want to go home, go." I told him as I crossed.

After Roz left Clair and I continued on. We kept walking until the woods got thicker, then she didn't want to go any further.

"I think I'll go home too." she said.

"Why?"

"I don't feel right. Besides I have something to do that I want to show you later and I have to get it ready."

"Can you make it back?"

"Sure, I have a good sense of direction." she said confidently.

I watched her until I couldn't see her anymore. I took Squeaker and continued walking, stepping over the fallen tree branches carefully. I knew that if I got hurt no one would find me for a long time. I stopped when I thought I heard someone.

I looked around, but I didn't see anyone. I started walking again, this time I was more aware of the surroundings. There was something different about this place, it gave me a strange feeling. It was like being scared and excited at the same time, I really can't explain it. After I few minutes I heard it again, still no one was there.

"Who's there?" I asked when I stopped.

No one answered. The only thing I heard was a soft whispering through the trees, almost as if the trees were talking. Then I heard a question.

"Why are you here?" I heard in a womans voice whispering.

"I came out of pure curiosity." I replied.

"Some go forward and some go back."

"I don't understand." I said looking around.

"You will."

I waited a while and when I heard nothing more but the birds singing I decided that it was time to go back. When I was walking back I also got the feeling that I was not alone. I wasn't scared, I wanted to know who it was. When I got to the stream the feeling left.

"That was strange." I told Squeaker. "You felt it too, didn't you?" I said when I picked him up to carry him the rest of the way.

I put him down when I got to the kitchen door. Before I went in I heard it again, this time she told me to fear nothing. When I got inside I got something for Squeaker and went to sit on the couch. It was so quiet.

"Where have you been?" Marlin asked when he came into the room. "Roz has been back for hours."

"I went for a walk." I replied without turning around.

"In the woods. Why?"

I wasn't surprised that he knew, he had been there before. "I don't know why. It was strange."

"Strange, how?" he asked when he sat next to me.

"When you were there did you hear anything?"

"You have got to stop reading my mind." then he sat back and relaxed. "What did you hear?"

I was about to tell him what happened when Liera had come in. He knows that I won't talk around her so there will be no explaining until she is at work tomorrow.

After dinner I helped as usual, I was about to sit down when we heard a strange noise out front. Marlin and Roz and I went out to see what it was, I was very surprised to see Clair and her father sitting on a glider.

"Well, what do you think?" she asked.

"Great. Is it yours?" I asked.

"Wow. That is just, wow. I can't believe your dad got you that." Roz said while he checked it out.

"It is when she gets bigger." her father said.

"I have coffee." Marlin offered him.

"Sounds good."

The two of them went inside and left the three of us alone, she asked me how the rest of my walk went. I didn't tell her what I heard, not yet anyway.

"So what do you think?" she asked.

"About the glider. It's different." I said.

"Dad got it for me because I passed my test with no problem."

"You think your dad would let me try it sometime." Roz asked.

"You know something. Some weekend we may be able to arrange something Roz." her father said.

"Really! I would love that." he replied with excitement.

"Maybe when Clair gets to learn better you two can go for a ride together." her father told me.

"I would like that.' I replied, we stayed outside and watched them leave. "I don't think so." I said shaking my head.

"Change your mind?" Marlin asked.

"Clair as the driver. I'm not that crazy."

"I've seen her dad race. If he teaches her she'll be fine." Roz said.

Watching Clair on that was not something I wanted to picture myself doing, Roz on the other hand may have found his calling. The excitement coming from him was overwhelming.

I went to my room and got ready for bed, I was thinking about doing some random researching on the computer, but my mind just wasn't on it. I heard Liera as she was trying to help Roz with math, when he figured it out she came in and said goodnight to me.

When morning came I waited until Liera left before going downstairs. I put Squeaker outside and sat at the table, as I waited for him Marlin came in and sat across from me.

"I found out yesterday that Sara had been disassembled."

I was shocked to hear this. "Why?"

"I don't know. She may have found out something that she wasn't supposed to know. If she did, she never left any additional information."

"She was supposed to come back every now and then to check on Roz."

"They'll send a look alike. But on to something better. I asked for a copy of your test scores, and I'm proud of you. They were exceptionally high and you will be getting the proper information to start your lessons. Those will be coming in any day." he said proudly. "What do you think of that?"

"I think it's great." I said with little enthusiam.

"Hey, what's wrong?"

"Why would they do that to Sara? She was nice, it's not fair. They wouldn't do that to a real person, would they?"

"I know, they didn't have to go that far. Now about yesterday."

"It was so strange, I never heard this voice before and I felt someone. She told me that some go forward and some go back, then I didn't hear anything until I got back here and she said to fear nothing. The feeling I got was unreal. I can't explain it." I told him.

"I heard the same thing years ago when I ventured into the woods."

"Did she ask you why you came?"

"Yes. What did you tell her?"

"That I came out of pure curiosity. I didn't tell Roz or Clair what I heard."

"Well let"s not tell them unless they hear it someday."

I agreed with that. He knew what it meant but wouldn't tell me, he wanted me to find out for myself. I can live with that, he wasn't worried and neither was I.

Three days later a man came to the door carring a small box filled with preset chips for my computer. All he had to do was connect it with a wire and fill in a little information about myself and I was ready to go. I was so excited, I couldn't wait and he knew it.

Roz stood at my door smiling while the man explained what I needed to do and how to do it. I wanted to start right away.

"There you go." the man said when he stepped back. "Most of the time you don't have to use the keyboard."

"I have an extra headset she can have." Roz said.

"Thanks, that's great." I said giving him a hug.

"It's not that big of a deal." he said, then he realized that it was all new to me. "But you'll like it."

I figured that since math was the easiest that I would start there and get it over with. In one quarter I had most of that done for that level. When I got to the end of a lesson I'd get a recorded message that informed me how well I did and what areas I'd need to practice more in. It was great.

Squeaker would stay by me the whole time. On my lap or around my neck, it didn't matter, he had to be there.

Sometimes I wondered if he was also learning, I knew that he was listening. Clair would come over every now and then to see how I could figure out something so easy, and every now and then Roz would also help her. Sometimes he would go over to her house and help her there.

"Hey I have an idea." Marlin said one morning as we were having breakfast together. "I have some time off with nothing planned. And since it's going to be the hottest time of the year, I was thinking of spending it at my parents. Anyone interested?"

"Yeah. You don't have to ask me twice." I said with excitement.

"I wouldn't mind going this time." Roz said.

But Liera was a little hesitant with her answer. "I really can't go. I have so much that I am doing right now. I really can't leave it. But I think that the kids should go and enjoy themselves."

"Well, what do you think?" he asked.

"When do we leave?" I asked.

"As soon as you two are ready." he said.

"I can be packed in five minutes." I said picking up my dishes and putting them in a dishwasher.

"So can I." Roz said. He actually like the idea of going, which surprised Marlin. Lately Roz has been doing great, I think Clair also has something to do with that. He won't admit it, but he does like her.

I ran upstairs and got everything that I figured I would need for a few weeks. Where it was going to be hot I thought that it might be a good time to learn how to swim, that is if Squeaker allows me to go near the lake. I even brought something to read along the way and I hoped that Cileen would be there, I would like to see her again. Squeaker knew that something was up with the way that I rushed around the room gathering things up.

"We're going for a ride." I told him when I put him around my neck and then picking up my things. "How do you like that?"

"All set?" Marlin asked standing at the bottom of the stairs.

"Yep. Where's Roz, is he still coming?"

"He's already outside waiting for us."

Liera was outside telling Roz to mind his mannera and not cause any trouble. When I put my stuff in the back Squeaker jumped in and sat on them, he wanted to make sure that he was going too. Two full weeks without Liera around was a great idea.

"I'll get in the back." Roz said when he noticed that I was going to. "Bye mom."

"Remember what I told you." she said to him.

"I will." He said in a huff when he got in.

"We'll see you in a couple of weeks. Are you sure you don't want to come?" Marlin asked her.

"I have too much to do." she said.

As we got further down the road I started thinking that it was a great idea that Liera didn't come, Roz thought the same thing. Then I thought about Sara and how much I liked her, I wish I could of shown Squeaker to her, I bet she would have known what else he is.

"Still thinking about her?" Marlin asked.

"Once in a while, I kind of miss her." I replied as I stared out the window.

"Miss who?" Roz asked.

"Sara" Marlin said.

"You didn't tell him did you?" I asked.

"No, I wasn't sure how he would have reacted.

"What happened to her?" Roz asked, now his curiosity was starting to get the best of him.

"Sara was an andriod. She was disassembled shortly after she left us. For reasons unknown. Don't tell your mother." he said.

"I won't. Promise. Do you think that mom may have had something to do with what happened to her?"

"That I really couldn't answer. You and Sara have spent a lot of time together. Somewhere in your conversations Sara must have found out something."

"Or, she could have heard something that Liera said that no one was supposed to know. Remember she had super hearing. That would make more sense." I said.

"That's true. I want you two to be very careful when Liera is around, you never know what you may hear when she is talking with someone." Marlin said.

"I can't believe that Sara was a machine." Roz said more or less to himself. I started to laugh. "You knew?"

"I knew the minute she walked in the door, but she made me promise not to say anything." then I remembered something. "She was going to talk to me after she was with us for a while, and she never did. I wonder why, I know it didn't slip her mind."

"She knew something. She might have figured that it wasn't necessary considering that Roz was doing good."

"It's strange." then I got another idea. "Where Sara was a machine, shouldn't her memory still be in a mainframe somewhere?" I asked.

"You think too much, but yes they should. Now don't bother to consentrate on it so much. Just concentrate on things that matter to you, both of you." he said.

"Like avoiding mom." Roz said, to which I had to agree.

"As long as I am around, and if I can help it, nothing will happen to you two as for as Liera is concerned." Marlin said.

As we approached the driveway Squeaker became familiar with the surroundings. Roz was holding him until he got over excited.

"He remembers this place." Marlin said as he watched Squeaker run out the minute he opened the door. "Or either that he has to go real bad. What's wrong Ariel?"

"What if he thinks that his mother is going to be out in the back waiting for him?" I asked when I stood beside Marlin.

"Maybe he wants to make sure that she is still there." Roz said after he got out. "Boy it has been a long time since I've been here."

"It sure has." Jacob said when he came over to us. "Where have you been?" he asked Roz.

"Studying" Roz answered.

"Well that's good. So I get you three for a few weeks."

"I needed a vacation." Marlin told him when we went in.

"I thought you didn't know the meaning of the word. Someone wants to see you." Jacob said pointing to me. "She's on the back deck with Mynera."

"Cileen is here?" I asked, he nodded. "Great!" I said walking out back.

"Hello, how have you been?" she asked when she seen me, then I noticed that Squeaker was sitting on her and enjoying feeling her stroke his fur.

"Fine. Is that why he was excited and overeager about getting out as soon as the door opened?" I asked.

"Cileen is a lot like you when it comes to animals." Mynera said.

"Why do you think I have them all over my yard." she smiled.

"Someone else wants to see you. Here she comes now." she said when she turned to look down toward the lake.

I stood at the edge of the deck and looked. "Wow is she big." I said when I saw the swan.

"And she remembers you well." Mynera said standing behind me. "She comes up every morning for a piece of bread and a friendly chat."

"Something you are defiantly good at." Cileen said.

"Oh, what's that?" Jacob said when the three of them came out back.

"Mynera and talking." she said.

"That's for sure." Jacob laughed.

"Well Roz you sure have grown. I haven't seen you since you were two." Cileen said.

"That's why I don't remember you. If you don't mind my asking, who are you?" he asked.

"I'm Cileen. Mynera's sister."

"Baby sister." Mynera added.

"I haven't heard that in centuries." she said.

"How many?" Roz asked out of curiosity.

"Almost four." Cileen gladly answered.

I started thinking, wow. That is incredible, I hope I look that good if I ever get that old. I sat on the step as the swan got closer, she was beautiful just like her mother. She put her head on me so that I could stroke her long slender neck.

"She is gorgeous." I said looking in her eyes.

"That she is." Mynera said.

Roz came over and sat beside me, he wanted to touch her but he wasn't sure if he should.

"Go ahead. She won't bite." I told him.

"Really, great."

Roz moved his hand very slowly toward her, he wanted to but yet he wasn't quite sure. He was very surprised when the swan moved closer to him. She wanted to check him out.

"Ariel has a lot of love for animals." Cileen said.

"Yes she does." Marlin replied.

"How has she been doing considering what happened?" she whispered, but not low enough.

"She's doing fine. Since she has started with her lessons, plus keeping busy with Squeaker, he's tolet trained. There hasn't been anymore nightmares." he told her.

"That's good. Are you going to teach her how to swim? Considering it is going to be hot and I know she wants to." she hinted, and that's when I turned my attention to them.

"Can I? I would love to." I said with excitement.

"Well, it up to Squeaker. After all he was worried last time." Marlin said looking at him sitting all cozy on Cileen.

"What happened?" Roz asked.

"She decided to be a showoff and catch a fish." Jacob said.

"But you don't know how to fish." Roz said facing me.

"Yes she does. Without a pole." Mynera said.

"Can you show me?" he asked.

"Tell you what, after lunch we will all go down." Marlin promised.

"Why don't the three of us go and see if we can catch anything the old fashion way." Jacob said.

"What do you think Roz?" Marlin asked.

"Sure, why not."

It surprised us when Roz stopped petting the swan to get up, she didn't want him to stop and took a small piece of his shirt with her beak.

"I'll meet you down there." Roz said.

Mynera thought that it was interesting the way that the swan took to Roz so quickly, so did I.

"What would Liera think if you brought back another pet?" Cileen asked Marlin as a joke.

"She would cook her up for dinner." I said seriously as I watched Roz and the swan going down to the lake.

Once Jacob and Marlin were with Roz, Mynera got us something cold to drink. This was something that I never had before.

"What is this? It's good." I asked.

"Lemonade" She said when she put her arm around me. "You never had anything like this before?"

"No. The only time that I had anything different is when Marlin took me home." I told her.

"That place should be torn down." Cileen said. "They don't do any good for the people that they are supposed to be helping."

"That's for sure." I said to myself.

"I'm glad that you are able to sleep at night." Cileen said. "Can you tell me about the vision that you have, the one that you told me you can deal with?"

"I don't think about it during the day, I really don't want to." I told her.

"It doesn't bother you?" she asked.

"No. It's a lot better than what they used to do to me."

"Marlin told me what they did to you, and he told us what he found out regarding Liera." Cileen said in disgust.

"He doesn't leave me or Roz home alone with Liera. He needed to get away from her. But how long can he do it for?"

"He keeping his guard up, I noticed that."

The more we talked the more I liked Cileen. I discovered through the course of our conversations that no matter how old you are, you can still practice with your inner ability to achieve whatever power you wish.

Squeaker made himself at home on her but once we started talking about swimming he came over and got comfortable around my neck.

"I think we upset him." Cileen said.

"He was worried the last time that Ariel was in the water." Mynera told her.

"He's a little protector." Cileen smiled.

"I'm going to get us more to drink." Mynera said when she noticed the lemonade was gone.

"Want some help?" I asked.

"No little one. You enjoy yourself." she said getting up.

"You love it here?" Cileen asked me when I turned my attention toward the wildflowers.

"It's beautiful here."

"I wanted to ask you something."

"I know. He's a friend. Please don't ask me. I wouldn't know how to answer. I don't know what's going on. I'm not afraid."

"Well you are good at reading minds. How do you like it?" she asked.

"It depends on who I listen to. I don't intrude on Marlin, I don't think it's fair to do that to someone I'm supposed to trust. Liera's a different story."

"Liera is scary. That's why she stays away from us." Mynera said when she came back out.

"You can block people out of your mind. Like you are doing right now. Do you know how you're doing it?" Cileen asked me.

"Not really."

"Interesting. Having the power and not knowing how." she said.

When I turned my attention back to the wildflowers I saw Marlin, Jacob and Roz coming back up. Roz was wring out his shirt.

"What happened, you throw him in the lake?" Mynera asked Jacob when they came onto the deck.

"No" Jacob laughed. "He decided to go out on the rock that's out there and catch a fish, well he did. Or should I say the fish caught him."

"Pulled him right into the water." Marlin added. He wanted to laugh but he didn't know if it would hurt Roz's feeling.

"It felt good."

I thought it was funny, but Squeaker was becoming curious and went over to see why Roz was all wet. He took his shirt and dripped the water on him.

A few hours later we all went back down to the lake. I was interested in swimming but I wanted to see if I could find that fish that came to me before. Roz was good at swimming, I was impressed at how long he could stay under water. Squeaker watched me as Mynera sat on the ground petting him, he didn't like this idea at all. Cileen came over to me and watched as I tried to find that one particular fish.

"Here she is." I said as I took her out of the water to show Cileen.

"She is pretty. You didn't hold her for very long." She said when I let her go.

"Too many people around. Besides she is the one that pulled Roz in."

"That's one strong fish." Roz said when she swam by him.

The part that I enjoyed most about being in the water was that the swan had come over to me and stayed with me. In a way she was showing off with how good she swims. I watched her closely as she would float along with the waves. She did something that made me believe that she was picking, or playing, with Squeaker. She got as wet as she could and walked over to him and shook the water all over him.

Although I didn't learn how to swim today I did enjoy feeling the water cool me off. When it was night we sat around a small fire down by the lake. Squeaker was around my neck and when the swan came over to me he hissed at her, she didn't let it bother her. It was hot and I had no choice but to put him down. His fur was sheading in the heat, it was everywhere.

"Squeaker, that's not nice." I told him.

"He's either jealous or mad." Jacob said.

"I'd saw a little of both." Mynera said when she fed the swan bread.

"Well I know he's hot when I hold him. Can we shave him?" I asked.

"We can give him a trim." Marlin said.

"I'll hold him down." Roz said.

It wasn't that late but I was tired. I rested my head on Marlin's lap and Squeaker came over and curled up in a little ball by my stomach.

"Tired?" He asked.

"Not really." I replied.

"I know I am." Roz said stretching.

"You should be. You've been on the go all day." Jacob told him.

"Come on. I'll show you where to sleep." Mynera said.

Mynera and Roz went up to the house. Jacob went up a few minutes later. I did fall asleep on and off. I heard Cileen ask Marlin if what he thought about me was right. His only comment was that he is pretty sure. I wondered what that was all about? I thought to myself. Cileen realized that I wasn't fully asleep she changed the subject and whatever it was was never brought up again.

"Ready for bed?" Marlin asked me.

"It's early." I said.

"No it's not. You've been asleep for hours."

"I have to get going. I will be back before you leave." Cileen said.

"I'll walk with you." Mynera said to her, and then the two of them disappeared up toward the house.

"You've had a busy day."

"I like Cileen. How come she can't help Roz?"

"What's wrong with Roz, she can't fix. It wasn't done by nature. Now get some sleep."

The next few days were great, I learned hwo to swim a little, Squeaker became more tolerant of the water once he was shaved and felt how cool it was. He learned to swim.

I noticed that Roz was glad to be away from him mother, I also showed him how to get one of the fish by using his powers. He was amazed at how easy it was once he got the hang of it. From there he was able to figure out how to do more.

"This is great." he said when he picked up his first fish.

There was something different about this one. His fins were transparent and his scales were blue, I have never seen anything like it and neither has Jacob.

"I don't know what to tell you. Every so often, if you look hard enough, you will see many new wonders that evolve with the passing of time. This fish is just one example that you don't know what's in your yard, untill you look." Jacob said.

When I went to bed I thought about some things he said, I looked at Squeaker and wondered if he was just something new.

"Goodnight you two." Mynera said when she walked passed the door.

"Mynera I have a question."

She came in and sat on the bed next to me. "Yes"

"Do you think that Squeaker could be part of a change?"

"Well he is very intelligent, and you got him tolet trained. He learned to swim."

"I can talk to him."

"Don't let that keep you up all night."

"I won't."

I spent most of my time here learning how to swim and practicing my powers. I just want to hear what goes on around me, I like the sound of the wind. If you listen real close you can hear it whispering. Our last few days Cileen spent with us.

"You know something, when I was your age I too heard a lot of things and I never understood." She said staring at the water.

"Did you ask?"

"No, by the time we were teenagers out parents moved closer to the city. I moved back so that I could get back to nature. I missed hearing what's outside."

I went over and sat on the ground under a tree thinking about what she had said, Squeaker came over and sat on me. I watched as Roz tried to find a fish.

"You and Roz have quite a tallent for animals." Marlin said.

"As long as we don't hurt them they will come around." I said.

"Never take anything you see for granted."

"I know."

Roz never managed to catch a fish, but he did get a lot of them to come around. The morning we left I petted the swan, her and Squeaker got along a little better.

"I've been thinking about getting her a companion from Cileen." Mynera said.

"That would be great. You can have more of them." I said.

"Oh great. Now we can have more of them running around. I have a better idea, let's keep the kids and send the animals home with him." Jacob said.

"No thanks. I'll keep the kids." Marlin said.

"Next time you come we'll do something different." he said.

"Let's go hiking, and camp in the woods." I said.

"Good idea." Jacob said.

I always hate to leave here just as Mynera hates to see us go. It's a nice place, so peaceful and loving. A lot different than being at home.

I put my things away and fed Squeaker. The flower I had planted had a nice yellow and orange blossom with a sweet scent hanging off of one of the stems. Squeaker also found it interesting. I took my eyes off of him for a second and he had it in his mouth.

"Why did you do that?"

His little stare while I stood there in disappointment was funny, he didn't care, it'll grow again. Roz saw what happened and stood in my doorway laughing.

"As long as he doesn't get into the flowers downstairs." he warned.

"He knows enough to stay away from there. Plus Liera keeps the door locked now, if you haven't noticed."

"I noticed. I want to ask you something." he said sitting on my bed.

Before he could say anything we heard his mother come in the front door and make her way up the stairs.

"How was your trip?" she asked when she looked in my room.

"Great. We had a lot of fun and Jacob told a lot of stories." Roz said.

"Well good, I'm glad you two had fun. Any helpers for dinner?" she asked.

"Sure" I said.

"I'll be down in a minute." Roz told her.

Roz kept talking throughout dinner, one long story after another. I noticed that all his stories revolved around animals. He enjoyed talking with them, this would be a great area for him.

"I'm glad you enjoyed yourself Roz." Marlin told him.

"I'd like to go more often."

"I just realized something, you have been here for over a year." Marlin said to me.

"I have never given it any thought." I told him.

I started to believe that things were picking up. Clair and I spent a lot of time together. I got to know her parents better and Roz got his weekend, a couple of them, with her father at a racetrack. It was one thing thiat just never interested me so I never bothered to waste my time going. Clair even knew that I wasn't interested in gliders when I kept refusing to go for a ride with her.

I was never one for so called birthdays. Even though four years have passed I really didn't notice them. Jacob and Mynera came over of the fifth year that I was here, they thought it would be nice to see how I have made it all this time. They were amazed at how much I have grown.

I loved it when we would go visit them. She did get a mate for the swan and ended up with a flock that took over part of the shore line. I have also seen Cileen on and off throught the years. She claims that she hasn't heard anything for a long time, I on the other hand still hear the whispereing through the trees.

The worst day for me was when Roz and I were wrestling around and it got out of hand. I don't know how it happened but without meaning to I punched him in the face knocking him to the floor.

"You bitch, you cut me." he said joking, but as luck would have it Marlin had come into the room with a stranger.

"What were you two doing?" Marlin asked looking at Roz's face.

"We were just joking around." Roz answered.

"It just got out of hand. He's not bleeding that much." I said.

"Go up and get cleaned up. You sit down." He told us.

"He asked for it." I told him.

"How often does this happen?" the stranger asked Marlin.

"He's fine. We were just messing around." I said.

"Just be careful you two don't break something." Marlin said when he got Squeaker. "Remember years ago when I told you I have a friend who has some of these."

"Oh yeah. Hey I want one someday if you're still around." I told him.

"He is beautiful." he said petting him. "You did a good job raising him. My name is Reggi. Can I bring one over see how they react? I would love to breed him."

"Can we?" I asked.

"Well, sure. It would be good for him to have a friend." Marlin said.

That night I apologized to Roz for cutting him, I got him good on the face, in one way I did feel sorry, and in another I didn't. I did make amends for it. One thing I do know how to do is to fix an error. When I put my hand near his face he backed off.

"If you want this to scar for the rest of your life then I'll leave it alone." I told him.

"You can get rid of scars?"

"I don't know, but I do know that I can take care of the cut I put on the side of your face."

Over the next three years Squearker had some friends and out of those friends he had seven little ones. The last year I let him go over there for a little while, I figured he may have some fun with what there is of his own kind.

Over the next few days I noticed a change in Squeaker. He lost his appetite and didn't bother to run around like he used to. I stopped my lessons for a while and held him day and night. Then before I was ready it was time to put him with his mother. I cried the whole night, I sat on my bed and held him thinking that he had led a full life. I didn't say anything to anyone about his death, I wanted to hold him one more time. This hurt me more than anything.

When Marlin came into my room I told him that I wanted to put Squeaker with his mother. I felt that it was only fair. When Marlin left my room I could feel his sorrow. He felt as bad as I did, but he didn't show it. It's strange how an animal can bring a person to feel love. Squeaker was always with me, he never left my side, even when I spent the night at Clair's or when I was sitting at my computer. He was around my neck sleeping or watching me work. We would walk together, eat together, share the pillow at night. Whatever I did, he was there.

"Morning" Roz said as he walked by, then he came into my room. It took him a few minutes to realize why I was crying. "Sorry. I know how much you love him."

"I knew this day was coming. I wished that it had waited a few more years. We're taking him to Mynera's to put him with his mother."

"I'd go but I have to apply for some classes. If I get accepted then I'm out of here."

"I know. You've been waiting a long time."

It was a long ride to Mynera's, I cried the whole way there. I knew that it was only a matter of time before I'd never see my beloved pet again. Marlin didn't say much of anything to me, he knew I wouldn't answer.

When we arrived at Mynera's I got out and stood at the door. My face was red from crying, tears were running, I couldn't take the pain anymore. Jacob offered to take him from me but I thought that it was up to me to put him with his mother.

I went out back to the rose tree. It had grown so much since I have first seen it.

"Look at that Squeaker, it's so beautiful. You're back home." I said when I laid him down on the ground.

Mynera brought over a small blanket that he would sleep in when we visited. "How are you doing?"

"I'll be fine." I said wiping my face.

"Nothing can change the course of death, but as long as you still love him, he will always be a part of you." Marlin said when he joined us.

"Yeah I know, I was just hoping he could make it a few more years." I said while I dug his hole.

"When you leave." Marlin said when he sat next to me.

"It'll only be for a few years. Besides it may be a good way for her to make some friends." Mynera said.

Over the last few years I found out about an internship that will enable me to go to Kerrell for a few years to do some schooling. Mynera knew of a family that I can stay with while I'm there. I can't wait, I know how Roz feels about leaving, I feel the same.

What they don't know is that I'm going to observe the people, I want to see how they interact with each other on a larger scale. Life here is good, but sometimes I feel as if I don't belong. I can't wait to explore, I can't wait to get out of the house.

We walked back up to the house and visited for a few hours, I sat on the deck and looked down toward the rose tree thinking of all the fun Squeaker and I had. One of the swans tried to cheer me up, the more I ignored her the more determined she became to get my attention. She finally pulled my hair to a point where it hurt.

"What did you do that for?" I asked her when I stood up.

"I'd say she's trying to cheer you up." Mynera said.

"I don't feel like being cheerful." I said sitting beside her. The swan wasn't going to give up, she came over and put her head on my lap.

"But she knows you're sad. Animals know an awful lot." She said when she put her arm around me. "You sure have grown. I remember putting my arm around you and it wasn't this high."

When we started to go back home Marlin asked me if I wanted to stop anywhere, but I just wanted to go home. When we got there Liera was still at work and Roz was home, waiting with good news.

"I got approved to join a technical university on Zandar. The only thing we need to do is go to a conference with you and mom." he said.

"Hi, how you doing, nice to see you too." I said when I shut the door.

"Sorry. I'm just excited." he said.

This is the first time I have ever seen Roz this happy. That night I did my lessons, or just stared aimlessly at a blank screen. I couldn't help but to cry. I sat on my bed when Roz walked in.

"I was going downstairs but I figured you might want someone to talk to." he said when he sat next to me.

"I'm fine. Besides I'm thinking of using that for an excuse to getting out of here sooner. I'm tired of being careful around your mom."

"Guess where the conference is?" he said with a grin.

"I don't feel like guessing."

"Zandar. Means you're going to have the house to yourself for a while."

"It will be a long while. Unless you come with us." Marlin said when he came in my room.

"I would rather stay here. It will be good, the quiet. I'll be fine." I assured him.

"Well, I'll ask Clair's father too keep an eye on you."

"I'll be fine. Besides maybe Cileen could come and stay with me?" I asked hinting around.

"Okay. I'll ask her."

They will be gone for almost a year, it will be a taste of freedom. It may be the last taste I have for a long time, the people that I'm going to stay with come from a big family. From what Mynera has told me there are children all over their house. This I have got to see for myself.

Marlin managed to get me annoyed with his constant list of things that he thought I needed to know considering I was going to be by myself for so long. In a way I wasn't going to be alone for too long, a few days here and there I will be, but there will always be someone around. It made the last two week before they left unbearable.

I was glad when they left I had a few days to myself before Cileen was to come and stay with me. I loved it my first night alone I sat in the dark and stared at the stars, my second night is when Cileen came to stay.

She was glad to have this time with me. I didn't mind, if Marlin was determined to have someone watch me it may well someone I like. One night was fun, Clair came over and the best part was that she let slip that she likes Roz.

The last few nights I spent by myself. I took advantage of that time alone and ventured once again into the woods. Where I was older and by myself I made good time. Before the sunset I managed to find a tiny cottage in the middle of a dense part of the meadow. Why I didn't notice it the last time we were here I couldn't figure out.

I walked up to the door, it was so rustic looking. It was a little one story building a single window in the front and a walkway going out back. I followed the walkway and came up to a woman sitting on the ground with her legs crossed.

"It's about time you came to see me child." the old woman said.

"You know me?"

"Yes. Sit you're going to be here a while." she told me without moving. "I have a tale to tell you of your future, what you make of it will depend on you."

"Are you talking about me leaving here, or staying. I don't plan on staying away forever." I said when I sat next to her.

"Coming or going doesn't matter, as long as you remember what you are. It's a great pain that you will endure over a period of time. One that no one can help you with. If you continue on the path you are going you will get to where you want to be."

"Isn't that true with anyone?"

"Is it? If in time I were to ask you to take on a quest, would you?"

"What is the quest?"

"What if I told you that in a long time from now you will take a journey into the past. A simpler time."

"To do what?"

"Deliver a message."

"If it won't be for a long time then how would I remember?"

"Oh you will. You will be surprised at what you remember no matter where you go. I need a message delivered. And in time you will do that."

"How can you be sure, why don't you do it yourself?" I asked her.

"You're going off to explore soon, with this thought in mind you will never forget where you came from."

"Okay. What's the message?"

This old woman told me a story of long ago when her kind ruled the heavens. They would travel from planet to planet, but as always there is always someone stronger than you are and when faced in a war there is always a price to pay for freedom.

"Our powers were pushed to the limits. In our struggle we were separated. One of our kind is on a planet by himself. He is surrounded by others but still he yearns to be home, he belongs here. It's not that we can't get him it's just that right now he is needed where he is. Do you understand? That's why I can't go. I'm needed here." she explained.

"Alright. Even if it seems like it will take forever?"

"Go about your life, when the time is right you will know who to deliver the message to. I know it will be you. If you want to get back before dark you had better leave now."

It seemed more of a challenge to me than a quest but I took it anyway. What harm could it do. She is the elder that everyone talks about but no one bothers her. It's like she knows who is coming and when, but I think that she expected me sooner.

I did make it home by nightfall and I enjoyed the last day of quiet that I will ever have again. The morning they came back without Roz made me realize that they next time they come in a door together I'll be gone.

A few days after they got back from their trip it had gotten unusually cold for this time of year. The world is making a slight change. I spent the day outside smelling the fresh, clean, crisp air. I would take a few trips into the woods looking around, knowing that this will be the last time I see these woods for a long time.

My last trip into the woods took me long a path that ran along side the stream. The leaves had changed to a darker color, it was peaceful. I found a rock by the stream to sit on and I closed my eyes and listened to the wind.

When I opened my eyes I stared into the water. The sun made some of the stones sparkle, one stone caught my eye. I pick up a blue transparent stone, it felt slimy. When I held it up to the light it started to dry off quickly and desolve like powder in my hand. Once it was in the water it hardened again. That's one thing that I don't believe I'll ever see anywhere else. What was left on my hand sparkled, I shook it off and watched it fall into the water.

My day of leaving had finally come. Marlin had given me my mother's ring, it fit on my middle finger. Marlin and Jacob took the trip with me, Liera stayed behind. We took a small shuttle to Kerrell, a straight shot like this took only a few hours. It didn't stop Jacob from having fun and finding a fault with as much as he possibly could. He loved the idea of having a reason to take a trip in space. I thought that maybe visiting an old friend would have been good enough.

When we landed and entered the terminal itself I was overwhelmed at the amount of people making there way here there and everywhere.

We were greeted by an elderly man who just couldn't stop shaking Jacob's hand. This is the man I'm staying with?

"You can stop anytime." Jacob said freeing his hand. "This is Ariel." he said to put his attention on to me.

"Hi" I said shaking his hand.

"Well, Jen's gonna be happy to have someone with an eager mind to work with." he told me.

"I can't wait to meet her." I told him.

The ride through the city streets was a trip within itself. People were everywhere pulling in and out of traffic. They were acting like they were in a hurry to get no where fast. The buildings were hugh and old, I can't wait to find out the history of this place.

They lived on the outskirts of the city, we arrived at the time of day when the sun was going down and the front of the house had a view of the sunset. I was impressed.

A stone wall surrounded the property of a stone house. Everything was made of stone, even the driveway. The property was hugh, there was nothing major behind the house, if I ever wanted to explore I had a big chance.

The main room of the house had a big fireplace, of stone, with many artifacts and urns sitting around it.

"Jen can tell you where everything in this room came from, what it did, what it was, on and on and on. So if you ever get bored, just ask her something. My name is Seth."

He didn't realize that his wife was standing behind him and heard his little speech about his wife.

"And you are lucky you are cute. Or you would be sleeping out here tonight. Hi I'm Jen." she said walking past him and toward me. "We are going to have a wonderful time."

She was very excited about my stay. I took an interest in anthropology a long time ago. When I found out that there was credits for going some where else I decided to sign up. The best part is that I get to stay with friends of the family. They did make me feel at home.

Jacob and Seth were friends for a long time, they spent their time together while Jen and I got to know each other better and she also showed me the way around town.

There was another lecture from Malrin about safety and manners while I'm here. But there was a more cautioned tone in his voice when he told me to be careful who and where I use my powers. Not too many people would like the idea of my presence around here. Some people don't like things that are different, I found that out a long time ago.

A wall in their den was wall to floor with books, another wall was dedicated to awards from them and their children.

"We have five children. All grown with children of their own." Jen informed me.

"I have never heard of anyone having so many children." I said while I stared at their pictures.

"Mynera told me that your kind can only have one child."

"And she told me that you two are good friends."

"I'm glad that your comfortable here. When spring comes there will be an archaelogy dig, if you would like to go, you can."

"That would be great."

Over time I noticed Seth gathering up things around the house and putting them away, while I was watching this he finally stopped and ask me what I was doing.

"I'm sorry. I just was wondering what you are doing."

"Winter is coming. Soon there will be snow every where."

"Oh I get it. Snow, how long does it last?"

"You have never seen snow before have you?" he asked when he put a shovel down by the side door.

"No, this is my first winter."

"You are in for a surprise." he laughed. "I hope you like the cold. It get's cold here."

It got cold quick, coming from a warm climate I had to adapt the best way I could. The room I had in their house had a fireplace in it. Jen didn't think that it was odd that I preferred to stay in here and read all day, it was a way for me to get use to the cold and learn at the same time.

From time to time I would look out the window and see the season come in, the leaves changed color fast and fell faster to the ground. I would go out and help them rake and clean up the yard. We would watch the sunset from their front yard. The sparkle of the city lights in the distance had a hypnotic effect on me. I couldn't help but to look.

Where it was winter I didn't go out much. I spent most of my time sitting by the fire reading or learning from Jennifer. She would tell me about the places she has been and the things that she has learned. She felt that my presence here was a good excuse for her to take a working vacation, other than that she is a curator at the nearby museum.

It was also a chance for her to have some time with her daughter. One day she got a visit from a woman with seven children. I became a little uncomfortable and made my way into my room and locked the door. That was too much of a crowd for me.

I started thinking that this is a good time for me to check out the town. This place is small and everything is walking distance. I informed Jen that I was going to head to the museum for a while.

I got a good look at the buildings as I walked down the cold street. Houses and shops, bakeries and clothing stores lined both sides of the street. Vehicles and people congested both sides of the road and walkway.

"Finally" I said to myself when I came to the steps of the museum.

I had been here a few times with Jen, but I like the idea that I can just stand here and look without hearing her stories of what I am looking at. As I looked around I got the feeling that someone was looking at me, when I would stop to get a look around I would see nothing out of the ordinary.

I liked the paintings on the walls I also enjoyed the many artifacts that went with them. It was like being in Jennifer's living room. I couldn't translate some of the tickets that accompanied them so I took to scrutinizing the objects. Once again I got the feeling that I was being watched. I looked around and didn't see anything. When I turned back to look at the object again, someone was standing on the other side.

"So I was you." I said to the man. He was tall, older, dark complexion, long hair. He was very cute.

"I was dropping something off. I have seen you here with Jennifer, is she with you."

"No, her daughter with many children came to visit so I decided to leave."

"Are you enjoying the museum?" he asked when he came closer to me.

"Yes. I have also applied for a job here. It'll help to teach me how to translate some of the words."

"I have plenty of time. Why don't we see the exhibit together? That way if there is something that you can't understand, I can translate for you."

"I don't want to take up your time." I said politely.

"No problem, come on."

Without saying another word he took my hand and we walked throught the many rooms. I wasn't interested in the paintings at all, it was the various objects and artifacts that fascinated me. One item caught my attention. The writing was almost similar to the writing on my mother's ring.

"There was a time when people believed rituals that were dominated by blood sacrifices would please their so called gods, there by granting them certain powers or knowledge of the universe."

"Did it work."

"They're all dead."

"How accurate are prophecies in this world?"

"Depending on the era, very. Why?"

"The writing on this scroll looks like the writing on my ring. I don't know what it says." I told him when I took my ring off and showed it to him.

"It is similar, but it's not the same. Once you start working here maybe you'll get your answer. Let's go get something to drink."

Once again he took my hand, we walked to a little café that's nearby. The side walk was made of stone, most of the traffic here was on foot.

"How do you like it here so far?" he asked when we sat down.

"I like it. This city just has on old feeling about it. For some reason my people think this is a hostle world."

"People will believe what they want to."

I sat there holding on to a hot coffee when the snow started to fall. I thought how great it is to be in the snow for the first time. Without realizing it I was ignoring Orrin.

"You didn't hear a word I said?" he asked when he touched my arm.

"I'm sorry. I have never seen snow before."

"Come on. I'll walk with you."

On our way back we talked about a number of subjects. I could hear the children outside as we got closer. When I got close to the driveway they found it a good time to hit me with snowballs. Something that I did not think was funny. Instead of going inside I just kept walking.

"So you do realize that I am from Aquairus?" I asked him.

"Yes, and I also know a few other things."

"Really. Like what."

"That you can minipulate the elements around you."

"To a point. How do you know?"

"I just do. I"ll see you later."

I said goodbye and thanked him for a very enlightened afternoon. I made it to the door without getting hit. Once inside I took off my coat and stood over by the fire. All the children were outside, Jennifer and her daughter Debbie were in the kitchen and her baby was sleeping comfortably on the couch. Once I was warm I sat on the other end and watched her sleep.

Her face was so beautiful, she looked so content laying there. I got a little closer for a better look, her hair was so fine and blond that she looked bald. She opened her eyes and started moving around, Jennifer and Debbie were still in the kitchen. I touched her hand and studied how small it was compaired to mine. She didn't cry, she grabbed my finger tightly and tried to put it in her mouth.

"You don't want to do that do you?" I asked her. It didn't work, she bit me anyway. When I gently pulled my hand away it sounded like she was laughing. I looked at my finger, she had put two little teeth marks in it. "Well, you have teeth. I take it you're hungry." I said when I picked her up. She didn't cry, she just stared. I never seen or held a baby before, it was different.

"Would you like to feed her?" Debbie asked when they came in the room.

"I don't think so. I should go change."

"If you want you can use my shower. No one will bother you there." Jennifer said.

"Thanks" I replied when I handed Debbie her baby.

I got a change of clothes and went into her room. After being out in the cold the hot water hitting me felt good. As I showered I started thinking about two things. I'll be getting my first job soon, and Orrin. If he is from here, he's not like the others.

Where they were staying for dinner and I wasn't hungry, I helped with the children so that their mom could relax.

"How come you're not eating?" Seth asked me.

"I'm not hungry. I'll be fine." I told him.

"She went to the museum today. As a matter of fact she was out for hours." Jennifer said.

"I know. Someone I work with saw her with Orrin today." then he started snickering. "He's not married."

"I didn't ask." I said while I poured drinks for the kids.

"I thought you would like to know."

"If I wanted to know I would have asked. Besides I'm working soon and I'll have my own place soon." if time could truly freeze now was the time it did. Jennifer stopped what she was doing and looked at Seth. "What?"

"I know what this is." Debbie said. "I saw this look when I left."

"You don't have to move out. This house is more than big enough. And besides it could be more like room mates, and you can learn your way around better and get to know your friend better." Jennifer said.

"I think I get it. You don't want me to move."

"We don't want you to stay here forever, everyone needs to be on their own. Someday you will, just ease into life slowly." Seth said.

I was telling Orrin about this conversation one day when we got together. He thought it was funny, I still didn't understand why.

"You got to consider that you a friend of a friend. Think of it this way, Jennifer has someone at the house and Seth has a reason to talk to Jacob whenever he wants. Something they can reminse about when they are too old to walk. Besides, maybe when you do move out you could move in with me." he said as a hint more than a question.

I didn't know what to think, my mind went blank. "What else are you up to?"

"You want to be my room mate." he smiled.

It was a long winter, and with all long winters around here people were getting nasty. I started my job, I didn't mind cleaning things off or moving things around. I enjoyed it. We just got done cleaning out a room for a new exhibit, I was standing in the middle listening to the echos.

"So are you the new exhibit?" Orrin asked me when he came in.

"That's cute." I said facing him.

"Want to go and grab something to drink? It's getting warmer out." he said when he put his arms around me.

"Sounds good." I said when I kissed him.

"Now why did you do that?" he asked holding on to me.

"I was just curious. And I have been thinking about your question, if you still want me to move in with you."

That was the one thing that Marlin didn't react to very well, but he also knew that he couldn't control me. The building he lived in was once a factory, it was in the process of being renovated. Aside from one neighbor, there was no one else in the building. He owned the top floor.

I could tell he was glad I had said yes, I could feel his fingers gripping me tighter. As we held each other and kissed he was the only thing that I could think of. The feeling of his hand moving on my back, feeling his lips as he kissed me on the neck, the heat of his body and the passion burning inside of me was enough to drive me crazy. As I moved my hand along his chest I felt something inside him that was different.

"What is that?"

"It's what I am, it's a part of me." he said.

As time passed we got to the point where neither one of us were dressed. It wasn't a sexual gesture, it was more of a way to feel, or experience each other. With the way he moved his hands along my body, he was barely touching me, but I could feel some kind of unexplainable energy. It tingled throughout my body. The more he held me the more I became curious as to what it was that made me feel the difference in him.

"Are you human?" I asked.

He didn't answer and I didn't bother to ask again. He held me tighter and I could feel a sharp pain, it felt like something was scratching me.

"What is that?" I asked him

"Like I said, it's a part of me, a part of us."

While I was laying on top of him and feeling his hands on me I tightened my grip on his neck and cut him. He grabbed my hair and pulled my head back.

"It seems we have something in common. We both like to inflict pain. You like to play rough." he said when he moved his hand to see how bad I had cut him.

"I don't hear you complaining."

"I won't. a thirst for blood has a lot to offer the one who desires it." Then he moved his finger along my lips.

I did desire it and him, to me it felt like an obsession. I moved back to my original position, this time he held on to my hands so that I wouldn't cut him again. My desire, or obsesstion, had become aggression, perhaps too much. I had in some way overpowered him. He managed to get me off of him and pin me down on the floor.

"It's interesting when you find your hidden strenght." he said.

The way he had me on the floor made it hard for me to breath. I was out of breath as it was and this wasn't helping me, but it was him. He let go of my hand and caressed the side of my face. When he stood up he helped me off the floor and held me tightly against him.

"Sorry, guess I lost control."

"Don't be, it's when I can't fight you off that I will be sorry. I underestimated you." he smiled.

The afternoon hours quickly became night, this time we laid together on the bed. While we were once again filling our sexual desires my desire for his blood returned, this time he was prepared. He had a very firm grip on my hands, as we kissed I wanted to embrace him but there was no way he was going to let go until he was sure that I didn't have enough energy left to fight.

I still looked for any information about my parents, after a year of living together I got a name of a planet and nothing more. Orrin suggested taking a trip and checking it out. Where there was a lot to arrange I had the pleasure of Marlin visiting before we left, the best part is he brought Clair with him.

"Do you realize how long a trip like this can take." Marlin said while we sat in the kitchen.

"I know. That's another reason why I want to go. I'm also doing it for work. So it's like a working vacation." I said pouring coffee. "And I know you don't like Orrin."

"I did a background check on him and I can't find anything."

"So he has mystery to him, that's sounds familiar."

"How do you figure that's the same thing?"

"What have you found out about my parents?" I asked and didn't get an answer. "Get my point."

"May as well go." Clair said, Marlin gave her a dirty look. "All I'm saying is why not go. Your life span is longer than his. Go have fun."

"If I didn't know any better I'd say you are a little morbid." I told Clair.

"I'm just board, so I'm gonna race."

"Whenever I get back I'll come look for you."

"Just remember eternity is a long time." she said as she got ready to leave.

On the morning we were leaving I made sure I took enough to read for a long time. I heard about passenger ship, the people can be very annoying. I didn't know what was worse, the people or the crap you have to go through customs. The ship taking us to our final destination was small, and with small areas I was lucky to be on this ship with three other people. Three very annoying people.

They just had to keep talking to me. It got to the point where I was staying in our cabin. If I had stayed around them for any length of time I would have smacked one of them. They would just go on and on about meaningless things.

Two days of hiding were left, for me it was funny. Orrin knew why I stayed in here reading and one day he came in and agreed that it wasn't that bad being in here for a few more days.

When we arrived on Calderon we found ourself a secluded place on the edge of a little village, gathered everything we needed for a expedition. The only thing to get now was guide.

We spent some time around the local pubs looking for the right people. One place that we were waiting at was loud, noisey, full of rude drunk people. The one woman kept coming over and being very annoying. Orrin told her time after time to get lost, one thing we didn't need it trouble right now, we came here for one reason and one reason only, to find our guide. I was sitting on the other side of Orrin, I reached my arm over and grabbed her by the throat.

The bartender came over and gave us a ultimatum. "Take it outside or take it over to the ring and we can make some money off of it."

The bartender loved it when people would get drunk and start fighting. He had a little set up so that the drunks can beat each other till they pass out. I like this place.

"She's not even worth it." when I let her go she fell to the floor. "She would be a waste of time."

My remark caught someone attention, a woman came over and started talking to me as if we have known each other for a long time. There was nothing vindictive about her curiosity.

"How good are you?" the woman asked me.

"Excuse me. Who are you?"

"I am Tia. You have a certain aura around you. I can see it, I can see it change."

"Now there's your bar drunk." the bartender said. "She's in here all the time drinking, telling her stories."

"Mind your own business, I tell stories about the people I see." she said to him, then turned her attention back toward us. "Your arua changes with your mood. Every one knows that. But yours, yours grows stronger. I seen it happen when you were enraged with the drunk."

"So what do you want?" Orrin asked her.

"We were told of a tale of one with a hidden power coming to our world, the psychic world. Strenghten your body will strengthen your aura. Strengthen your power will stranghten us."

"For what?" I asked.

"We're getting ready for a change. We see it all the time."

"So what your telling me is that you can feed off of my power."

"Yes. Then we will be strong enough for our journey."

"Journey?" Orrin asked.

"It is foretold in the scriptures. As well as word being passed down from generation to generation. You two came here seeking answers to your people. I can take you two to someone who can answer your questions."

"Nothing malicious about her." I told Orrin. "Besides we never did say how we were going to get a guide. She could be the one."

"Fine, let's just be careful."

We left before the sun went down, the animals we were riding had an attitude of their own. They didn't like the dark but their eyes were tuned into their surroundings.

"What is this journey you're talking about?" I asked.

"We're all leaving, the problem is that we don't have the energy to open the way. You do."

"And you're sure of this?"

"It has been pasted down for over three hundred years."

These creatures traveled all night, by morning we came to a clearing near a mountain base. There was a crude tent like set up for their little village, a few people were moving about getting ready for the day.

"There is a hut you can stay in." Tia said as she led the way.

"What do you think?" Orrin asked when we were alone.

"They are on some kind of spiritual journey. For some reason she thinks I can help."

Tia came and got us a few hours later, she then led us to another tent in the center of their camp. The old man sat inside and staired into a flame from a small firepit, in his hand he held a pipe. He looked up at us and didn't move.

"Sit child." he said as he motioned me to sit next to him. Orrin sat beside me and Tia was about to leave. "You too Tia, sit down." he inhaled deep on his pipe before he said another word. "You are right, you are not the one who will help us, this is not your journey. But I see why Tia mistakened you. You have a powerful aura. What are you doing here?"

"Looking for answers. It is believed that our fathers are from here." I told him.

I told him of my story, how I came to know about this place and the people, what I didn't know is how much time has passed, he told me a different story. Aparently over two hundred years ago a ship had come here to find something. What they didn't tell anyone is that it was people they came looking for, not a slaves, but experiments. They wanted to see if our people and their people could live together.

"If what you say is true, than we are over two hundred years old." I said. "No one really comes to this planet. It's at the end of no where."

"Yes, and the things that you can see only if you open your eyes." He said handing me his pipe. You are more than welcome to stay here the only thing we ask in return is that you mention us once in a while. So that no one forgets that we were ever here."

"I could put this is the museum archives. Anyone will have access to it." I told him. What was ever in the pipe made me relaxed.

While we were talking and getting to know more about each other I staired into the flame. The old man kept passing his pipe around but after it got to a point where I have had enough and the flame was more interesting.

I had a great buzz going, after a while I didn't hear anything that was being said. I could see so many colors in the flame dancing within each other, I could see feathers and birds all in the flames, sparks of blue and green keep me mesmerized. Then I saw fire.

I just couldn't help it, I had to. I have never seen anything so beautiful and strange. Another strange event was when I woke up I was in our little hut and Orrin was sitting beside me trying not to laugh.

"What?" I asked.

"You remember nothing of last night?"

"Only that I kept seeing something strange in that flame."

"Yes that was something. Now here's something else." he said when he moved the cloth from the doorway.

There was nothing out there, not a trace of a village or another tent. Total emptyness.

"I don't get it. Where is everything, everyone." I said standing next to him.

"Gone. I brought you back here and when I was going to leave to go back out, they were gone. At least they left us transportation." He said looking at the animals.

"So you saw what I saw and I'm not going crazy. Now we are in the middle of nowhere with a couple of animals. Which way do we go?"

"I'd say where ever these animals take us." he said getting on one.

"Let's ride together. It'll be fun."

I kept thinking about what the old man said. Could it be possible that centries have passed? Something big is going on, I have a feeling it's going to be a long time before we find out.

Our ride decided to start following a stream, it wasn't that bad. We made camp and did a little fishing. The next morning we got up early and started to make our way back upstream.

By the time it was late at night we made camp again, we were sitting down around a fire talking. I felt so peacefulin my few moments of solitude, staring at the stars, then I felt someone put a hand on my shoulder.

"I want to show you something." she said in a kind voice.

When I turned to face her I didn't recognize her or her voice. She was the same height as I was and her hair was long and pure white, she looked old and tired.

"What do you want?" I asked politely.

"I want to show you something." she said again when she took my hand. "You will be interested."

I accepted her offer. We walked for a few minutes without saying a word, the surroundings became familiar and the sun was starting to shine.

"Where are we?" I asked her.

"I wanted to show you a civilization that existed long ago." she said sadly.

And she did. She showed us the beginning of an end for these people, but she showed us a specific family. It was interesting, and sad.

In the beginning on a primitive planet, considering they have no means of space transportation as we know of and their people still live in small villages, some very isolated.

There were two sisters, the younger one looked ten or eleven, the other I'd say was in her early twenty's and this creatures she was with was half human. His eyes were totally black and his hair long, black and tied back. He had an unusual marking on his neck. It was very distinctive, the color had a bluish hue to it and it spanned from the middle of his throat to the middle of his chest.

"He looks a little like you." I said to Orrin.

The young couple would meet in complete secrecy, she would sneek out of the hut at night and meet him.

"I don't understand. Why, if they love each other, do they sneek around?" I asked.

"They are different as you can see. She is human and he is not, he and his kind live underground, after many generations their kind can't take the brightness of the sun. Their flaw is genitic, because of this they are forced to hunt at night."

"So they are forced to live underground." Orrin said.

"They are not seen too much by the people who live above ground. So much time has passed that it was forgotten that they were once just like them."

What made it worse for these girsl was that the older daughter had become pregnant and tried to hide it for as long as possible. If either one of them did something wrong, no matter how stupid, they would be punished. They lived in fear.

As tensions grew the younger girl knew that something was wrong. The father became more abusive toward them, the more the mother tried to calm things down the worse it got. It got to the point where the girl could no longer hide her baby, the parents had to know.

That added fuel to the fire, her father became more angry every time he saw her. Her best bet, and the mother also knew, was to stay away from her father, hide if she had to.

"Why are you showing us this?" I asked.

She didn't answer, instead she showed me the day that the girl had her baby. It was during the day when the sun was at it's highest peak. Her father was gone and it was up to the mother to help deliver the child.

The birth was short and painful, she had passed out from the birth. The mother cleaned up the baby and held it up for a better look, she was horrified by the uglyness of it. She broke the baby's neck, wrapped it up and ordered the young girl to take the baby deep into the woods and bury it.

She agrued with her mother telling her that what she had done was the worse thing that she had ever done. The mother became angry and slapped her across the face and told her to do what she is told. She listened to her mother's request but didn't do it, what she did do was to seek out the baby's father, which wasn't easy.

She knew more or less where the entrance was to the caverns where these people lived, it took her over two hours to find it. Once inside she carefully made her way through so that not too many would see her, she was doing fine until a guard stopped her. She ignored her fear and told the man who she was looking for and why.

He took the child into a well lit chamber and left her alone, moments later he had come back, not only with the childs father but also with a group of people who would eventually decide this girls fate.

"I warned you about getting involved with someone from the surface. A child never survives." an elder said.

"But this child was born alive. My mother killed it."

They took the child from her and listened to the rest of her story. It was near dark by the time she had finished. One of the men took her into another part of the catacombs, there were little cyrstals embedded in the rock that gave off a luminous glow, just enough to light the way.

He took her into another chamber with another woman and told her that for her safety she should remain there, they still haven't determind her fate.

It was late in the night before he returned for the girl. He took her into another chamber that was used for cremating the dead.

"They believe that by burning the dead in an open flame, their soul will be freed from the entrapment of the body." she told us.

After their ritual the girl was given a choice, stay with them in a world of uncertainty or go back to her people, another world of uncertainty. She gladly accepted their offer, she knew that here she had a chance at life.

Over the years she learned their way of life, she learned what is expected of the females. If she was strong enough to protect herself she was fine, but if she wasn't then she had to learn. He taught her everything he could think of from hunting to fighting, in this world one can't survive without the other.

Within the next year she discovered that she possessed the power of healing, she found out by accident one day as she tried to help him clean up a cut that he had gotten from sharpening a weapon for huntingl he was so fascinated by this that he took her to their elser and explained what she had done. The elder thought that it was a joke and laughed, but when he said that he could prove it, he was no longer laughing.

He took a knife and cut a slit on the palm of his hand, as the blood poured out he asked the girl to do it again. The girl was afraid of the thought of it not working again, but she did it anyway. By this time there was a crowd of people watching quietly, and they were all astonished that the girl had performed her task again.

"Would I be wrong in assuming that this girl is your mother." Orrin said.

The elder not knowing what to make of this power started to believe that the girl was given a gift of healing by the mans dead child, he didn't know if it was only for him but he asked the girl to once again perform the miracle on another who would volunteer. A woman who knew the girl very well didn't hesitate to be cut, the girl explained that she didn't know anything about what made her capable of doing it.

She smiled and told her that she wasn't afraid, a cut can heal itself in time if she couldn't do it again. She was cut and she was healed. The elder declared the girl as that, a healer. She was considered very valuable in their tribe, she enjoyed her position, she enjoyed the people.

At night she would help her friend when it came to tying his hair back. Where it was long she would offer to brush it, he didn't mind and never refused her offer. She liked his hair and sometimes she would take her time and he knew that she was doing it on purpose. They enjoyed each others company.

As time passed her feelings for him were more than friendship but she wasn't sure if he felt the same. One night she looked over as he was sleeping, wondering what he thought of her, she moved closer than usual, he felt her and put his arm around her. For the next few nights that's how she slept, in the comfort of his arms.

Her curiosity was getting the best of her, she had to know. While they laid next to each other talking about nothing of great importance, she moved onto her side to face him better and to get an answer.

He lost his train of thought as she moved her hand between his legs and very slowly arousing him while she gently kissed him. He was surprised, because he too had feelings for her, but he didn't know what she had thought of him. Only a few words of affection were exchanged before he moved on top of her.

"Okay, you're made a slight point. They love each other, Now what is the purpose?" I asked.

Not too long after she gave him a son, they both loved their child and never let him out of their sight. As he grew he became very strong and curious about his mother, he was also very friendly with other children. Which is where Orrin came in.

He was just a small child and he would follow their son around everywhere. He was a few years younger but that didn't stop them from hanging out with each other and doing what boys do.

"So you did know my parents." I said to him.

One night while their son slept not too far away from them she laid on top of her mate, passionately kissed him and smiled as she looked deep into his eyes. He had no idea as to what she was thinking, but whatever it was he knew that he would like it. She told him as proud as she could that they were going to have another child, and once again he was excited by her news.

Tragedy came too quickly to their quiet world. For reason unclear, the people of the surface set out to destroy the people in the caverns.

"I don't understand." I said.

"These are not the people from the surface. This will make your vision seem more clearer, it will give you answers. Yes, these people that I have shown you are your real parents. He ordered your mother and brother to hide deep within the caverns."

"I kind of remember something, but I was so young. It's all a blur." Orrin said.

"They came in and slaughtered these people, then they took the children under a certain age. The dream that you keep having is what Orrin saw. You are not the first children to be taken without question. I know there are more. I know they destroy planets. Knowledge is power." she said.

"Do you think that they are using primitive planets for experiments?" I asked Orrin.

"Seems like it if there are more."

When I turned to ask the woman a question she was gone. Everything we seen was gone, we were back at the stream.

"Why show us this?" I asked.

"Maybe stop it."

"How?"

"She said knowledge is power. We have a lot of computers. It's time to go home."

On the way back I was trying to put a puzzle together in my head. It always came back to the same question, what are they up to? These were our people. I didn't leave the cabin once we got onboard a ship for our return home. My mind just keep thinking all sorts of things.

"Are you alright?" Orrin asked sitting next to me.

"I was just thinking, my first ten years was actually two hundred years? I only remember ten years of it. What were they doing and why?"

"Being children we wouldn't notice the time difference."

"Or put up a fight."

"Or remember, but your starting to. Your seeing something."

"This is going to be a long road." then it made me think of what his mortality rate is. I'm a half bread, that I know, but he's not. The big question is, what did they do to him? "But how long is this road for you?"

"If I have a shorter life span, then it will be a filled one." he said holding me.

"Can you imagine what it would be like if we were still there?"

"And miss all this excitement now." he said playfully as he nibbled on my neck. "We are going to be home soon. And I can't wait."

When we got home I wrote down everything that I remembered, I compaired some things that I have seen with some things in the museum's archives. I found nothing. Jennifer noticed that I was seaching for answers to something and offered to help me. She gave me a few places to look in the computer. As always one thing leads to another.

I spent years in my spare time searching for answers when I decided to tap into Marlin's computer and see what he had for information. My mistake was when I didn't get his permission, or let him know.

"I don't think I'm supposed to be here." I told Orrin.

"What did you find?" he asked when he came over.

"Access codes. Marlin's computer was tied into the Kerellian governments computer, but that was a long time ago."

"He could still be working for him, after all we don't know what he really does. Now do you? This is interesting."

As we kept reading it reviled war plans and other maneuvers, and dates. I couldn't read the rest, someone on the other end shut the system down.

"I think I made someone mad." I said.

"I know we did. There is no doubt that this will be investigated."

"Any suggestions?"

"We wait."

"For what?"

"To see who comes to the door first. Besides we have nothing to hide."

"Only the fact that we know someone is using children in experiments."

"Let's not talk about that."

That was good advice. Our computer system was inactive and if the ones where I work we to remain online then I had to be home. So in a way I got a vacation. A few days later I got a visit and this guy was asking all kinds of questions.

He wasn't even in the door and he was talking. Between my interest in computers and my abilitys, he took an interest in me. After listening to him tell me what he knew about me I figured that he had talked to Marlin.

There is something about this guy that I can't figure out, he knows about my powers, or I should say his boss knows about my powers, because this guy, I can't read his mind.

He got our computer system back online and wanted me to show him how I got into it. When I showed him he was a little upset that it was easy for me. He took a few minutes to ponder his next move.

"Get your affairs in order, just in case. I will be back in a few days." Then he left, not another word, not even a goodbye.

"Weird"

"He knows about you, he knows something." Orrin said.

Once again our computer is shut down, makes getting your affairs in order a little hard. What made it harder is Marlin caming to see me when I'm on a time limit.

"I figured that since I got an unwanted trip here, I may as well come and see you." Marlin said when I let him in. "So your under house arrest."

"I'm sorry, I didn't think when I got into your computer that this would happen."

"What do they want?"

"I don't know. They'll be back in a few days."

"Well, I don't have to leave until morning. So how was your trip?"

I told him what we found out and what we saw, I knew that he would be able to find out more considering he was alive then. But instead of using computers to get our information we were going to do it the long hard way. By word of mouth. Someone we know must remember or heard something in their travels. He also told me that Liera's been gone for awhile, he doesn't know why, she just up and disappeared.

"Just remember, we have a long time, but I have a feeling that someone else doesn't."

Time is on our hands but in a way it's not. I though the morning the man came to our door, this time he was not alone. We were asked to come with them and it was a long quiet ride, I didn't dare ask anything, I didn't like these guys. We finally stopped hours later when we came to an isolate hanger.

"We have a job for you, and your powers can be very useful for us."

"You don't want me, you want my powers." I said.

"Yes"

"Why her?" Orrin asked.

"Because, no Aquarian with her capabilities will enter the government on their own. I believe you can help us."

"Help how?" I asked.

"That we'll tell you after a short trip."

From there we took a shuttle to a space station and from there to a ship that was docked to it. What I noticed is he didn't say anything until we were to speak to two people, once again we were in an isolated room.

"Why the secrecy?" I wondered outloud.

But it didn't take long for two people to come in, one was an andriod.

"Welcome to the Orion. I hope you will enjoy your stay, and in the meantime I want you to access the computer again." The andriod said to me.

"Why. You're more than capable." I told him.

"Not enough to keep you out. I need to find what went wrong." he turned to the man he was with and nodded. Without question he left. "My name is Aries. I'm in command here. I am also tied into the computer onboard this ship. But I also know about your powers."

"You want me to spy on your crew."

"We're not supposed to be here. My ship was attacked. I am not willing to take another risk until I am certain no lives will be lost. Lucky for my crew, my ship was empty."

"Alright commander, you got my interest. Tell you what, I'll be honest with you if you are with me."

"Not a problem."

"For how long?" Orrin asked.

"Until we feel you are no longer needed."

"We, as in you and your ship?" I asked.

"And me?" Orrin asked.

"You have engineering experience. I got a job for you, I need a lot of repairs overlooked."

He escorted us to a small room that will be ours for our short stay, it only contained a computer and a small area to wash up and a place to sleep.

"Well I get to spy on the crew." I said.

"Maybe we can get some answers."

Over the next few days I tried a lot of things to get into the computer system, I decided to try an easier approach, checking out the personal files. No one took an interest in it until I tried to get into the commanders file.

"What do you think you're doing?" Aries asked me when he came into the room.

"I have walked all over this ship, been near everyone, your problem is in the computer. What kind of ship is this. It's large for a small grew."

"Cargo mostly. We can be utilized as a rescue ship if needed."

"And what where you doing this time?"

"We were not going to find that out until we got there."

"That's sounds like the same thing I heard."

"Yes, they figure the less people that know what's going on the better." he said.

"I think I'm going to walk around some more. Look in a different direction."

I walked around and mixed with the people for day's listening to them. I'm not in any trouble, they just wanted to use me, good cover. I figured if that's the way they want it I may as well be nosy, I started walking in areas that were supposed to be closed off. I ended up in a computer room, to a point, this terminal was closed off.

"So you just managed to wanter around into here." Aries said when he came in.

"You don't need me here. You're playing a game." I told him. "I want to go home."

"I have to make sure this ship takes off. This room here is an access terminal to the computers mainframe . You could say that it is the brain of the ship. This is what you got into, at the wrong time."

"But I got into this through Marlin's computer."

"Which is tied into mine."

"Why is it, I think Malrin should be part of this?" I asked suspiciously.

"Right now my computer's off line. You kind of make up for that. I just need you to keep an eye on the crew. Especially right now, there is a shuttle coming in and I want you to meet with the people that are coming."

"Fair enough."

I didn't see nothing wrong with that, there were only a few to see. Mostly they are here with equipment for the medical center. I was surprised, and glad to see Clair.

"What are you doing here?" she asked.

"Filling an obligation. You?"

"I got into medical equipment, mostly robotic. Roz got me into it."

"You two are getting closer?" I asked teasing her.

"Stop"

As we walked and talked she told me that she was only here long enough to make sure that the replacement equipment was in place, so she was on a time limit. I figured that maybe this is a good chance to hang out with her and help or just be nosy. Aries even agreed, but he still hasn't told me what is going on.

The only thing that he mentioned to me is why he wanted me here, I already knew why, but being a android was a big downfall for him, and the main computer is still off line.

"The reason this is so important is the fire system is also off line, that's where Orrin comes in." Aries told me.

"I did know that he had experience when it came to weapons. I just felt that it was never my business to ask him about it. But I have no problem asking you. What is your mission?"

"We get information as we need it. I can show you what we have so far. My contact disappeared after he gave me this." he said while he brought up information on his next mission.

I watched the grotesque scenes play out on the screen and was horrified at what I saw. It showed a lab and in this lab it showed their experiments, their creations. Some children and some adults, being murdered. These must have been what they considered undesirabloe people, I thought to myself. Then the scene changed to when they tried to create or alter a person.

"They took living embryos out of a female and kept it alive?" I asked.

"That or froze them, and in the process altered their DNA, or chemically implanted information. Some of the scientists took it upon themselves to take a few and do whatever they pleased."

"How can someone do this to a child, or an adult? What did they do with the females?" Which I noticed was a few different species.

"If they were strong, they kept them alive. If they were weak or unfit, they died."

"We are a part of a group that is going to get these people out of there. This ship has been equipped to support the sleepers."

I do agree this should come to an end. What about where I grew up? I know you've been told. What is their role in this?"

"There are powerful scientist there, this is where we have to be careful. Some of them want to help, they are in the position to help. They just need to be left alone and do their job. There are a lot of people affected by this. I have talked to Marlin, I know of your background as far as your mother. I found out that it was your grandfather that was your mother's real father. For some reason, his name is not mentioned."

"I know he's Aquairan."

"Depending on how much more digging you and Orrin do will depend on how much danger the two of you inadvertently create."

"What you're saying is stop looking for information." Orrin said when he came into the room.

"What I'm saying, or asking, is if you want information then stay and help. You will understand what is going on."

"I understand. I've known for a long time something was wrong. Why do you really want us here, to watch the people on the ship, or to watch you. Make sure that you won't harm these people, being what you are." I said to Aries.

"I see you're having the same conversation Aries and I had earlier." Orrin said.

"All I'm saying is that if you want information you will get it in time. Just remember that they can make people disappear." Aries said.

"Then what, intergrate them back into society?" I asked.

"Yes"

It gave us something to think about, it would be interesting to be closer to the source, but sometimes I wonder how close is too close. Word of mouth is the key, I don't mind helping but how much of a tight hold will someone else have on us. What would be the extent of our obligation.

"We'll worry about that later. Right now I have better ideas." Orrin said when he tightened his hold on me.

I felt his ideas even more when he held me tighter and kissed me. "I like your ideas."

We had a pretty good start to our evening, the more he made love to me the more I felt my obsession returned. I have fought with myself for a long time to control my desire for his blood, but this time I had a hard time to control it, so did he.

I guess other people would consider our sex as violent but for us it was very normal and very satisfying. It's hard to describe the feeling that you can get from blood, for us it was more of a way to show loyalty.

I love the way he holds me in his arms, I can feel the energy flowing from the both of us. It added to our desires, sometimes it was this energy that helped me to retain my appetite, but not tonight. He thought that he had the advantage over me, I did manage to prove him wrong. While we were passionately kissing I got a little carried away and bit his tongue.

"You're going to get what you want no matter what." he said when he moved his head back.

"Well if you let go of my hands then I may not have bit you." I replied playfully.

"Not a chance. I'm going to hold on to you for as long as I can." he laughed.

He didn't let go until much later, and when he did, he gave in to my desire, as always. It is a unique feeling, sometimes it draws a sense of power and feeling, but most of all it's a form of fulfillment of a specific need. It was one thing that both of us wanted from each other.

When we caught up with Aries the next morning we told him of our decision to stay.

"I'm glad to hear it. I have assigned you to one of the computer programmers. You show promise. You did manage to break into Marlin's program many times. Which caused the computer to shut down."

"And what exactly is his program?" I asked.

"Sorry, I can't tell you that. Go to the computer terminal, there you will meet Jay. I thought that you may want to pick up your interests in computers again."

Well, I guess either way I'm committed. I do want to find out more, but I also like working at the museum. I suppose it's just onother one to fall back on.

Aries couldn't have picked a better person, this was the guy that was responsible for the way that the main computer system responds to people. Computers was his life, he loved his work more than anything. He prefers to be alone in a room with a computer rather than have the company of a human. This point he had no problem getting across to me when he discovered that I was to work with him.

"You have no idea what you did do you?" he asked me.

"No"

"Well now you get to help me create a firewall. I have been tracking your every move on the computer since you tapped into Marlin's and ever since then I have been lost."

"I don't understand?"

He showed me on a screen how he's been trying to trace where the breech had occurred. Problem was if you put it in as point a being my computer, point b being Marlin's computer, he has no idea what happened. Which got me to thinking something else.

"I need to talk to your commander. I have a thought." I said when I realized the obvious.

We meet in a small conference room about an hour later. After Jay had told him what he was showing me and what we were talking about he left the room, leaving me and Aries alone.

"Now what's your idea?" he asked.

"I'm thinking that someone could have been at Marlin's computer when I tapped into it. It's the only thing that makes sense to me. Jay can't find nothing, my computer at home has probably been taken apart piece by piece." I explained.

"If what your saying is right, then it may be Marlin that is in danger. I'll contact him and see what's going on at his end."

Over the next few days I started to get minor headaches, but with a little rest they went away. I wasn't too concerned about it but Orrin tried to persuade me to go and see the ships doctor. I told him I would if they got any worse, which it didn't, so I figured whatever was bothering me was gone.

I went about my business as usual, a week had passed and I was fine. Then I started to feel pain in my side, and this wouldn't go away. That's when I decided it was time to see her.

When I walked into her office it was like she was expecting me, which she was. Orrin had told her that I may be coming to see her. She started to ask me all kinds of medical questions, most of my answers were no until she asked if I had ever been in the hospital. She wasn't surprised at my answer.

She knew that there was no way of getting my records so she, if I agreed, wanted to do tests from scratch, start with my blood and work her way up. By the time she was done, four days later, the word pregnant kept running through her mind.

"That's impossible, I can't have children." I told her when we sat in her office.

"Your not going to be able to have this one. With the different chemicals I found in your body, this thing that is forming inside you will never be human. Whatever your decision, I need an answer tonight." Chris said.

"I don't have to think about it, I just need to talk to Orrin."

I went back to our quarters and sat there waiting for Orrin, I staired aimlessly at the wall, not moving, not wanting to think. When Orrin came in I told him everything that the doctor had done and what she had found, and what she wants to talk to us about tonight.

One thing I always loved about him so much is that he is always supportive when it came to any kind of serious decisions. As he was holding on to me and talking I lost track of time. For a few minutes I gotgot about my appointment with the doctor so she came looking for me.

"I'm glad that you have made a decision. We can do this now." she said.

Once she got me back on her table she started poking me with needles while she told me what she was going to do. By the time the drugs kicked in I didn't care what she did after that. I wasn't too thrilled about being put under but I knew that he would be there.

When I woke up Orrin was sitting beside me holding my hand, his thoughts were of sorrow but I know that I can get pregnant, then question is when.

"How do you feel?" he asked when he seen I was awake.

"Fine, strange, tired, but I'm okay."

"That's good to here." The doctor said when she came in.

"Could this ever happen again?" Orrin asked her.

"That I can't answer." then she paused for a moment and looked at us. "Did you two plan this?"

"No it was a complete surprise. Why?" I said.

"Just curious. If you ever want to try again, do it under a doctor's supervision. Preferably mine, if I'm around. Get some rest, I'll let you know what I find out from futher tests on what we removed."

I laid there for a long time with my eyes closed listening to the echos around me, after awhile it seemed as if it all became one droning sound. Orrin stayed with me, holding my hand, not saying a word. To me that was more comforting.

After a couple of days Chris examined me one more time, she had a very surprised look on her face.

"I take it you're a healer." she said as I got dressed.

"Yes"

"Can you heal others?"

"It depends on what is wrong. If there is no foreign objects inside, I can. Does this mean I'm all right?"

"You are in great shape. There is one problem, I don't think you can come with us. There are a few chemicles in your system that I can't identify. No matter how much I look, I can't find them. It's like it's something new. With that I can't take the chance in you coming with us this time, giving the nature of our cargo. We can't risk a chemical reaction. I've already told Commander Aries about it." she explained.

"Wouldn't it have been easier just to tell me that you don't want me around anymore and to get out of here?" I asked with humor.

"I'm glad that you can keep your spirits up. I will tell you this, I want you to come with us at least once, just to show you what we find."

I had a few days left while arrangements were being made for my departure. Orrin was going to stay behind and go along with them, he was involved in this more than I knew. Where our time together was short we took advantage of every free moment we had left together.

I didn't realize how tired I was until one morning when I moved over to get closer to Orrin and ended up on the floor. Waking up in this manner was shocking, especially when my naked body hit the ice cold floor. I don't believe that he expected to find me on the floor when he came over to me, he found it amusing, I didn't.

"What do you find so funny?" I asked sarcastically.

"It's not what I find that is funny. It's what I see that I am enjoying." He said when he sat over me.

"And that would be what?" I asked changing my tone to a more pleasant one.

"You pinned down on the floor naked with no where to go." he smiled as he started to take his clothes off.

"An ice cold floor, so I don't like the idea too much about being on it."

He leaned closer and put his arms around me. "Really, I didn't know. Well I can make you forget about the cold."

"I bet you can."

With the heat of his body on mine, I forgot about the cold. Then a few hours later I was standing in a hot shower thinking about how much he enjoyed me squirming on the floor as he put more pressure on me. It's interesting how you can forget about things when yhou are concentrating on something that you love the most, with someone you love more than anything.

As he was going through some things on the computer I stood behind him and ran my fingers through his hair and thought about us. The things that we have done in the past and the things that may happen to us in the future. There was always one question that I occasionally asked myself, and always had to pass off because it was one that no one knew the answer to, how long do we have.

I have to pass it off, I have to keep my thoughts on our future, the child that someday we will have, and the happiness we can have. I knew this for a fact, he started to laugh in a joyous way at the thought of being a father.

"You really want to try?" he asked.

"Yes. I thought you were busy?"

"I've been done for a while. I've been listening to your thoughts."

"So what do you really think?"

He stood in front of me and put his arms around me and caressed my face. "When I get back, I promise we are going to find a way."

I smiled and held him as tight as I could. "I love you."

"And I you, more than you will ever know. I talked to Marlin about you staying with him until I get back. I would feel better if you didn't stay by yourself."

It will only be for a few years I thought to myself as I took the long trip back to Aquarius. I felt so sad that it brought on pian, pain I didn't want to feel. Once on the ground it felt good to feel the sun. I missed the warmth on my face, the smell of fresh air. I took a deep breath and buried my feeling at the same time.

I felt something different, something soothing, I couldn't find it. I stepped away from the people and got a better look at the sun as she made her way into the morning sky. It was easy for her, all she had to do is sit in an endless viod of space and let the world do the rest. She has no questions to ask or answer, just sit there and watch us. Like the way that I stand here and watch her, with only one difference, I have many questions.

"Are you all right?" Marlin asked when he approached me from behind.

"I'm fine. I didn't realize you were there." I replied without moving.

"Let's go." he said when he took my hand. "Are you okay?"

"Yeah, I'm just a little tired. I've been out of the sun for so long, I feel drained."

Once in my old room I put my stuff away and staired out the window. I wasn't looking for anything particular, just listening. Listening for something, something inside of me that had something to say. But what should I be listening for?

"Old habit that's hard to break?" Marlin asked when he stood in the doorway.

"Here it is spring, there it is winter. As long as I'm here I may as well enjoy the spring."

"I made some coffee, care for some?"

"Yea, I'll be down in a minute."

Spring is usually a warm season, but this season felt warmer. Thinking about the winter that I could be in for and thinking about here added strange feelings, I was already missing Orrin and three years is going to be a long time. When I got to the top of the stairs Marlin was looking at something outside.

"Anything interesting?" I asked as I approached him.

"There is always something interesting to see, if you know where to look. The world is changing, and I know you felt it."

"I felt something when I landed, when I stepped into the sun I felt something. It felt good."

"You get your power from the sun, take what this world has to offer. It might surprise you."

"So what is going on around here?"

"The world is changing, and we're changing with it."

I spent the first few weeks pretty much to myself, I did promise Mynera that we will be comeing by, I just needed some time for me. I leaned against the bathroom counter waiting for the water to get hot for a shower. I didn't want to think of anything right now, I wanted my mind as blank as possible.

"I'm watching you." I heard Orrin whisper in my ear.

"Stay with me." I whispered back."

"I'll be back soon enough." He said as he held me to him and moved his hand hard between my legs, stirring my emotions. "I know what it takes to make you burn. You fuel that burn with blood, that's why you attack me, to add to the feeling. That part of you will never leave, it is what you are, what we are. Focus your feelings, your power, your thoughts, your emotions on the day. You will be surprised. Take those feelings and enhance them."

"Stay with me."

"I can't, now is not my time."

I put my arms around him, looked deep within him and felt his desires. "Be with me now, don't stop these feelings. You know better."

"When I get back I promise I will make you screem." he warned me in a passionate way as he held my body tight against his, and then kissing me. "But not right now."

When I went to move my hand on his face he was gone. I miss him so much that the pain is unbearable. I took my shower and after sat on my bed reading. Marlin came in and sat beside me and put his arm around me.

"Thanks" I said.

"For what?"

"For being here."

"I will always be here."

He held me closer and kissed me, a long needed touch of affection.

"The world is changing in so many ways and in the end we will have to choose our path. All you have to do feel." he moved his hand slowly along my body then down my leg, he was barely touching me. I could feel his energy.

"What are you looking for?"

"I can feel your energy. You're getting your strength back."

Every move he made along my body added to an uncontrolled feeling that I already had. I felt his hands as he removed my clothes, the heat of his breath as he nibbled on my neck. He took his clothes off as I laid across my bed. He stared at me in intense desire when he laid on top of me, kissing and feeling.

One hand caressing the side of my face as we kissed and the other moving slowly down my body with the right amount of pressure, then between my legs. Once in a while penetrating me and moving around inside me long enough to tease. He found one spot that drives me wild. He made his way down between my legs very slowly, kissing and licking me along the way.

Very tangibly he found a spot with his tongue and very slowly drove me to the point of screaming with pleasure. I couldn't stand the burning desires inside me anymore, I wanted him in my arms holding me tight against his hot naked body, but no. he enjoyed hearing me moan with pleasure as much as I enjoyed feeling him.

The heat of his breath as he moved his tongue inside me, succulently kissing and licking me hard one more time before he held me in his arms. Most of the night consisted mostly of him touching and kissing me. It got to the point where I couldn't stand it anymore and wanted to feel him inside me and I let him know it, in return he let me know that he had other ideas. I grew suspicious when he started laughing.

"You are going to wait."

"Wait, why?" I asked.

"It's more fun this way."

When I was getting ready for bed that following night I noticed how the sunset had an interesting color combination going, practically every color in the spectrum. I also noticed that the aura around me was more visible to the naked eye, and it only lasted a few seconds.

When I slept I had a different dream, this time it was through the eyes of a child. I saw mostly women and children, or I should say women trying to hide and protect their children. I saw a mother dying to protect her child, then I seen a child being removed from a dead woman, then the child that saw this was taken. I saw nothing after that.

I couldn't go back to sleep after that, I went downstairs and made something to drink and sat on the couch in the dark staring out the window. I kept thinking that there is a movement out there someone that one by one these people are trying everything they can to put an end to this.

I fell back to sleep for a few minutes, when I woke back up it was close to daybreak, I went up and took a shower and when I came back down I made coffee. I sat back down and thought about this short vision, I am certain that the child I saw was Orrin.

I was about to get another cup when I heard knocking at the door. I debated about waking Marlin, but I figured where it was his parents Jacob would do it anyway.

"Hi, I have missed you." Mynera said with a big smile when she gave me a big hug. "How are you?"

"I'm fine." I replied choking for air. "It's good to see you." even though she didn't loosen her hold.

"You better let her go Mother, before you strangle the poor girl. So where is he?" Jacob asked.

"Sleeping still. I have coffee."

"Sounds good to me. I didn't get the chance to have any. Someone wanted to get going too early." she said as we walked into the kitchen.

"We were going to come over soon." I told her when I handed her a cup. "Do you think he deserves one?"

"For getting me up before the sun? He can get it himself."

I started laughing. "It's nice to see that you two haven't changed."

I took my cup and another out to the living room, Jacob successfully got Marlin up, he looked like he could use a few more hours.

"You look half dead. What's the matter, princess keeping you up?" Jacob asked Marlin when he sat next to Mynera.

Marlin didn't say anything, he looked at me and smiled as I handed him a cup. "Thanks"

"Where's mine?" Jacob asked.

"In the kitchen, and don't pick so early in the morning." she told him.

"What possessed you to get up so early in the morning and ride over?" I asked.

"No one's on the roads so early." Jacob said when he started to go in the kitchen. "And Mother couldn't wait."

"He has that backwards." she said.

"I figured that." Marlin said when he put his cup down. "I'll be back." then he went upstairs.

"He loves you very much." Mynera said.

"I know. They both do. I feel like I'm stuck in the middle, my feeling for both of them are unbelievable." I couldn't say anymore, Jacob came back into the room.

"We'll talk later." she said.

"I know that tone. You're either giving advice about sex or men. So which is it?" he asked.

She looked at him and shook her head. "None of your business." she said sternly.

"You two haven't changed at all." I laughed.

"And proud of it." Jacob said when he sat next to her and held her close.

"This is better." Marlin said when he sat next to me, then giving me a kiss. "Morning"

"Sleep well?" I asked, instead of answering he just smiled and put his arm around me when he sat back.

Jacob had the temptation to say something but Mynera stopped him.

"I'm not going to pick so early in the morning. I'll wait an hour or so." He assured her.

"So how have you been?" she asked.

"Great, the last few years have been fun." I said.

"So I heard. How did you manage to get into so much trouble?" Jacob asked.

"I really didn't get into trouble. Although now because of this my boss, Jennifer, was told that I am not allowed back to work for a while till they are absolutely sure that I am not going to break in to another government computer. Everything I do on the computer is tracked. In a way Marlin had a hand in it."

"How do you figure?" Marlin asked, then he thought that if his computer system had a better firewall, then I would have never gotten it. "Oh never mind. I still haven't figured that out."

"Anyway, I think that it was just an excuse to see how far I can us my powers for certain things. I saw Clair."

"Yes she likes robotics, and her glider." Marlin said.

"And Roz." Jacob laughed. "Are you going to stick with computers?" he asked me.

"As long as they don't have a personality." I said.

"Have a problem with Aries." Marlin asked.

"No, he was great. I actually thought that I may have insulted him a few times. He set me up with the head programmer and he was telling me all sorts of things that he installed. If I didn't know any better I'd say he programmed that ship to take care of itself."

"Was it online yet?" Marlin asked.

"No. I wish it was. Chris want's me to come along just once."

"If I didn't know any better I'd say you are tired." Mynera said looking at me.

"My sleep partern is messed up. I'll be fine."

"I see Orrin is treating you well." She said.

"He's great. A few years ago we took a trip to Calderon."

"Ariel, why?" Jacob asked.

"It's where we found our people, or what's left of them."

"That attack set them back thousands of years." Marlin said.

"If not more." I added. "I'm going to make some more coffee."

"I'll help you." Mynera said.

"What is wrong?" She asked when we entered the kitchen.

"Nothing that I can't figure out in time." I told her when I made more coffee.

"You do know that you don't have to figure it out for yourself, right. There is always someone here to talk to."

"I know, I'm fine with that."

"I can tell. You enjoy your life, your mate, and my son."

"Are you saying I'm wrong?" I asked when I sat across from her.

"No" She replied quickly. "I just don't want to see you hurt if you are forced to choose between the two."

"What do you mean if I am?"

"There are so many changes, so much is going on."

"What is going on here? I don't mean with the people, with the planet."

"A lot of changes are being made for the better, and the same for you."

"How?"

"Just let it happen." She said holding my hand. "Let the energy flow through you. It was much easier when you were a child. Your mind was clear and thirsting for knowledge, now you're full of more questions and confusion."

"True, some of my questions have been answered. I no longer fear being alone, thanks to Marlin, and with Orrin, I no longer question my existence."

"But you question his. You wonder if you will ever see him again if he is not included in this change."

"How do you know?"

"Believe me I know more than you think."

I was surprised. "You are not going to tell me, I have to find out for myself."

"Keep a clear mind, focus, and you will be fine." then she leaned closer. "And as for having a child, what happened to you was that your body was defending itself. It didn't know any better." I didn't know what to say, I just gave her the strangest look. "To your body, it discovered a forgien chemical and attacked."

"But sperm is organic?"

"Yes, but not to your body. It will get use to it eventually."

"We've been together for a long time?"

"But sometimes changes take a long time."

"Marlin's feelings for me, they've been there for a long time, haven't they?"

"Yes, but he didn't want to tell you. He felt that you should experience different things in life, then you met

Orrin. Marlin knew that he can wait, and wait he will for as long as it takes."

When we took the coffee back out to the living room, Marlin and Jacob were doing something with the computer and Mynera seemed a little annoyed that he would even bother. I have noticed that Marlin was working on the computer a lot and apparently he has been for a long time.

"Do me a favor, try to keep him from working all the time." she said to me.

"Now that I can handle." I said with confidence.

I always enjoyed their company, I find it relaxing, and after they left I found standing outside to watch the sunset just as relaxing. The sun from one direction and the clouds coming in from the other.

"Looks like another rainy night." Marlin said when he came out.

"Couple of days actually."

"Fine with me, I have nothing planned."

"For a change."

He did have something planned, I felt it when I put my arms around him. We stayed outside and sat on the ground and talked as the sun disappeared. I was taking advantage of what I was feeling, the grass felt nice and cool. I felt a tingling sensation in my body depending on which way I move my hand.

"This is nice."

"Yes it is. Let's go inside." he said getting off the ground.

A loving kiss and gentle touch started our evening, he made love to me as if I were a fragile doll that would crumble in his arms. It was slow and easy and very hot.

I felt the energy between us flowing, it was everywhere. In the air, water, even in our thoughts.

He held me tight against him, feeling me as we kissed. The heat of his body created a pleasing sweat that was luscious to taste. I rested my head on his chest to hear the rapid beat of his heart and listened to the shortness of his breath, then with the greatest of ease I continued on my way, kissing and licking him playfully as I aroused him.

I massaged him between his lega with my lips, seizing hold of him, sucking hard as I could without causing any pain, just pure pleasure. Then there was this little voice inside my head telling me to take the burning desire inside of me and satisfy it the way that I want to. Forget your feelings and take your desire.

I thought about that when I sat on him, I didn't know how he would react, so I had to figure out a way that he wouldn't know until it was too late. He made it hard for me, the more I moved sexually the better it felt and he held me tight against him, now I had the disadvantage.

"You are going to have to do better than that to get what you want from me." he said in between catching his breath and kissing me with a mad passion.

I didn't answer right away, I held him close as possible to feel every last pulsation of satisfaction.

"You knew?" I whispered.

"Let's just say that I was warned about your desire for blood during sex. I know that you won't hurt me."

"Then why deny me if this is true?" I asked him while I nibbled on his neck.

"A bond of blood is powerful, that is one that you share with Orrin. You have chosen him just as he has chosen you for a mate." he moved just enough to lay on top of me. "My blood would burn inside you."

"This is cozy."

"Yes it is. Can I get you anything?"

"Just you holding me is all I need."

He held me as we laid in bed and listening to the rain and wind, I thought of how peaceful the sound is for the night, a night to hold and passionately kiss with nothing more needed to satisfy us.

Over the next few weeks there was more rain than sun. The only good news that I got was from Jennifer, when I get back home I can go back to work. As I started to settle down for the night my mind became preoccupied with thoughts of Orrin and how much I miss him, the more I thought about him the more I wished I was with him. Then my thoughts go back to having a family.

"Something's making you happy." Marlin said when he sat beside me.

"I was thinking about the things that Orrin and I have done."

"I'm glad that he makes you happy."

"That he does." I said with excitement.

"Get some sleep." he started to move but I wouldn't let him. I grabbed his hand and pulled him to me.

"I have better ideas."

"I can tell, and I like your ideas. I have a few things to tend to, and then I'll be back."

He gave me a kiss and went downstairs. I laid back and put my hands behind my head, closed my eyes and thought. I thought about Orrin and how I would love to feel him holding me, feeling that burning desire grow in him. I thought back to the last time we touched and how good it felt. Then I felt hands massaging my neck and it felt good. Without opening my eyes I put my hands on the back of his.

"That feels good. Don't stop." I said.

"I don't plan to." Orrin said. I was surprised when I heard his vioce, I opened my eyes and he was sitting over me smiling. "I have missed you."

"And I have missed you. I need you."

"I know, that's why I came."

"I didn't hear you come in."

"I'm here now, for a short while." he moved his hands along my body, staring into my eyes as we kissed. We picked up where we left off the last time we were together. "I need you."

I moved my fingers through his hair and held on. "Then take me."

I needed to feel his touch, his desires. He did need me, I felt it even more when he grabbed on to me and held me tight. It was a refreshing experience to feel all his emotions and thoughts again, and this time when I took his blood he felt no pain, just pleasure. This was something new.

He put his hand on my neck and applied pressure with the tip of his fingers causing me no discomfort, he was searching for something. He continued this hold on me as he moved his hand down my chest and stopping below my heart and applying more pressure.

"What are you looking for?"

"It's a change that you haven't felt yet, but it has begun. I can feel it. I have already felt it within me. It's inside both of us and it will continue to grow until it finishes taking its place within us." he explained.

"What is it?"

"I'm not exactly sure, but I do know that it will make us stronger. I have so much more to say, but I have no time."

"I don't understand." I said with a puzzled look.

"I'll explain the next time that I get a chance to do this again. I love you. I was hoping to have more time." he said after he kissed me.

With no warning or reason he disappeared, then I realized that this was some kind of power that enabled us to actually feel, see and touch each other. I really wasn't saddened by this, in a way I was glad. It let me know that he was all right, but it still caused tears.

"Morning" Marlin said when he sat next to me. "What's wrong."

I told him what happened, he in turn told me that I was asleep all night, the sun was about to come up.

"I don't even feel like I slept. It was so amazing at how real it felt."

"It is. Every need can be satisfied. Everything you feel is real, touch, kiss, desire. It works best when there is an established bond. Like the one we share."

I loved it when the rain stapped a week later, the first morning I woke up to see the sun shining was wonderful. I didn't take the time to get dressed, I grabbed my robe and went outside and watched the sun shine brighter.

The suns rays gave me a renewed feeling, my skin was tingleing with feelings as it warmed, I needed to feel this. The more I thought of it the more I wanted to feel other things. I knew Marlin was asleep when I came out, but I didn't know if he still was. When I came back into the bedroom he was just getting out of the shower.

"Morning. Where did you go?" He asked when he sat on the edge of the bed.

"I went outside." I said taking my robe off. "it's beautiful in the sun." I playfully leaned against him, pushing him down on the bed and kissing him. "Now I want to do something better."

"And then some." he said tightening his hold. "Great way to start the day."

"My thoughts exactly."

He loved to watch me move on him just as much as I enjoy doing it, especially when he becomes aroused. I love to instigate his sexual desires, feeling the heat creating a well desired sweat. A morning filled with passion and desire is a great way to start the day.

The next few days were different. The way that I felt I could have kept going all day and night, for no reason at all. I could be reading something and then get a sudden urge to have sex. Marlin didn't mind it, he loved it. It was one way for me to keep him from working all the time.

I also felt this thing inside me move, it did feel uncomfortable sometimes but not much. I wondered if it was because of this thing that I felt over-sexed because once in a while it was pleasing to feel it move, or grow. Whatever it is, I wish I knew, right now I haven't got a clue. The only thing I do know is that it is moving and attaching itself in certain areas.

After a few days of invigorating sex I was ready to rest, my energy was exhausted. While Marlin worked at the computer I laid on the couch staring at the ceiling thinking about Roz and the stupid arguments he tried to start with me when we were younger. Then I think about him and Clair together.

"So you think Roz and Clair would have a kid?" I asked.

"Someday. I know they want to try. I thought you were resting?"

"You mean you wish I was." I laughed.

"Never" he replied confidently.

I went over and put my arms around him as I stood behind him. "Really?" I whispered as I moved my hand between his legs. "Are you sure about that?"

"If I didn't know any better I'd say you were challenging me, or trying to see how long I can keep going." he said playfully.

"Try me." I squeezed him just enough to excite him while I nibbled on his ear. "What do you say, we find out?" I said when I moved on to his lap. "Unless you're too busy." I said when I unzipped his pants and began to massage him very slowly.

"I'm never too busy."

"Prove it." I told him when I stood up.

I didn't give him a chance to think twice about it. I started to take off my clothes as I walked upstairs. He came in, held me from behind kissing and feeling me as he moved his hand between my legs and once in a while teasing me, but I didn't want to be teased. I put my hand over his and applied more pressure and continued my hold moving along with him.

"You sure have been going at it like crazy the past few days." he said.

"Just enjoying the feeling and I like what I feel. I don't hear you complaining."

"I have no reason to."

"And if I have my way, you never will."

"I will hold you to those words."

When he made love to me this time it was different, he felt possessive and acted on that feeling. True I enjoyed it but I didn't have the strenght to react to it the way I wanted and he knew it. That's when I realized what he was trying to do, he needed to find a way to control me without stirring my desire for blood. I like his possessiveness as long as he doesn't use it to my disadvantage. I thrive on aggresstion, and now I have to figure out a way to use this.

I decided to take some time and reorganize myself and my thoughts. I needed time alone. I got up early the next morning and left a note saying that I went for a walk and not to worry and that I will be back before nightfall.

I did need time alone and it felt good. I went to the field that I found years ago and stayed there for a long time watching the wildlife running free. I felt at ease here, it's peaceful with the warm breeze gently blowing. What I came here to do I didn't, my mind was blank, I thought of nothing. I laid in the shade of a tree and stared aimlessly into the sky.

"If you wish to think of nothing, think of this." That familiar formless voice said. "What would you rather choose, the power to gain the knowledge to gain the power?"

"That's a strange question, but if I had to choose I would choose the knowledge to gain power."

"Why"

"I'd like the knowledge to know the purpose of the power."

"What if there is no purpose?"

"There is always a purpose for something."

"Is there?" she then asked curiously.

"Why wouldn't there be?"

"What about your purpose?"

"I know my purpose and have accepted it just as I have been accepted by both Orrin and Marlin."

"Yes, that is part of your purpose, but it goes deeper."

"What do you mean deeper?"

"I give those who seek the knowledge the power. Like the few, you want the knowledge."

"Then I'm not wrong?"

"No"

"What of Orrin?"

"His time will come."

"I still don't really understand what's going on. Will I ever see you?"

"Just think about it. Keep listening."

She stopped talking to me after that, and I did think about it. I thought of it as I slowly walked back to the house. I looked around while I put this puzzle together, admiring the beauty of the world.

When I got to the side of the house I saw a beautiful wildflower. I was tempted to pick it but I changed my mind. What right have I got to end the life of a innocent little flower that sweetens the air. Besides it will die before the season is over.

She said that I listen, she's right. I listen to the birds, rain, any noise I can hear, my favorite one of all is the wind. The wind is her voice, I will acknowledge and respect her as that. What she said is right, one person together with others is powerful.

I had to prepare myself for the questions that Marlin will ask me when I go in, I know he's worried, he always worries about me no matter what. And I was right, when I went inside he was pacing the floor, the only time he stopped is when he seen me.

"Where have you been for so long?" he asked.

"I had the most wonderful day. I discovered so much more." then I explained what happened and what I heard and what conclusions I had come up with, and he listened word for word. "But you heard this before."

"Just about. Many years ago before I became buried in my work, then I started to ignore what I was hearing and then I stopped hearing all together."

"It's not too late to take the time to listen, no matter how involved you are with anything, including work. You have always listened to me, so what's the difference?" I asked when I put my arms around him.

"Sometimes when I get involved with something I have a hard time to stop until I am sure that everything has been taken care of."

"Including me?"

"That's different.

"How so?" I asked skeptically.

"There is a big difference between work and pleasure."

"Sometimes I use to think that your work was your pleasure. I don't think you could go a few days without doing something."

"Is that a challenge?"

"Maybe" I said when I lead him to the couch then sitting on his lap.

"I can prove it."

"How?"

"Easy, for the remainder of your time here I promise I will take that time for myself and us, and I know the best place to start." he said with enthusiasm.

"Where?"

"Have you ever been to the ocean. I've been thinking about getting away for a while.

We left before the sun came up the next day, it was a four hour ride with the way Marlin went. We hit not one town or city, only trees and wildlife and fields.

During the whole trip we saw only five people. Two were hiking together and a small family of three was seen hiking off the road into the woods a few hours later.

"That is a nice scene. Seeing a family enjoying time together." I said.

"It's things like that that kids remember for a long time. I should have taken you and Roz more." he said regrettably.

"Don't start thinking that Roz and I didn't enjoy our childhood. We have plenty of good memories." I assured him.

"And plenty of good arguments." he said with a slight laugh, which started me laughing when I thought of them.

"And they were stupid. I think Roz was trying to show some kind of dominance with his ignorance, but he always came out learning something new. Going to Zandar was the best thing for him."

"He has come a long way."

"And he has a lot further to go."

I looked out the window at the new surroundings. Fantastic was a better word for when I saw the ocean for the first time. The salty air smelled rather good as I took a deep breath to experience it for the first time. Then he took my hand and we walked down to the shoreline for a better look.

"No wonder your parents like it here so much. It's very peaceful."

"We would spend weeks at a time here." he said thinking back at his memories of the many times that they have spent here. "Mother always found something new in the ocean to observe."

The sun shinned the whole time and listening to the sounds of the waves was almost like the ocean had a voice of its own, maybe in a strange way it does, especially if you consider that the ocean contains a world of it's own. We would sit on the sand for hours listening to the sounds of the waves and seabirds, it was very relaxing.

To smell the salty air every morning was nice and at night we would go out and take long walks along the shore and watch the beautiful majestic sunsets at the same time. During one of the sunsets my aura had glowed, this time I got a good feeling from it.

"Wow" Marlin said when he seen it. "How often has this happened?"

"This is the second time, and it feels good."

We spent a good part of the last night there sitting outside talking. I surprised him when I told him that we will have a chilod that I know he will be proud of. I don't know how I knew it, it just came out in the middle of a conversation that had nothing to do with children.

"How do you know that?" he asked.

"I'm not sure, I do know that we will have a son. I don't even know why I know or what made me say that."

"Do you know when?" he asked with the anticipation that I would know.

"No, but I do know how bad you want me back."

"That I do, but I can wait."

"Please don't tell me that I'm going to feel competition from the two of you?"

He laughed at my comment. "I know how much you love him. Not a day goes by without you being in deep thought about him. Sometimes I'd ask you something and get no answer."

"Guess I didn't hear you while I've been preoccupied in my thoughts. I miss him."

"I know. It won't be long then you two will be back together."

"I worry, I can't help it."

"Don't I know it." he said kissing me.

"That doesn't bother you?"

"What?"

"That I think of Orrin when we are having sex."

"No. Your thoughts are very interesting."

"In other words, it turns you on. Among a lot of other things."

"You should know." he said as he gently pushed me on the sand. "I can't think of a better way to spend our last night here."

We spent the last night sleeping outside on the cool sand, after of course, spending hours of enjoying each others desires. The next morning we took a different way home, it was a little longer but we stopped at his parents for a visit.

"It's nice to see that you enjoyed your vacation." she said handing us something cold to drink as we sat on the deck. "First one in how many years?" she asked Marlin.

"I know Mother, you don't have to remind me." he told her as if he was a child being told that he had done something wrong. "It felt good to get away."

"He's trying to prove to me that he isn't going to do anything while I'm still here." I added for him.

"Good, then you can stay here for a while." Jacob said.

"That would be great." Mynera said quickly. "It is so beautiful this time of year with all the trees and plants at full bloom. A lot of new births come with summer."

"Speaking of which. Do you know the trouble you have caused me?" Jacob said sternly as he pointed to me.

"What did I do?"

"That swan. We have an army of them. They won't let me fish anymore." he replied.

"You don't catch any anyway." She reminded him. "Besides, you said they have a safe home here."

"Have to blame it on someone." I said.

"Why don't we take a walk. Leave these two alone." Mynera said.

We took a walk down to the lake and the only thing that I could see was swans of many different colors, but they still had the same blue tint in their feather's. my only thought was that these creatures are another part of a change.

"This is increadable." I said when one of them came toward me.

"They still make their trek back and forth from here to Cileen's, between me and her we have over thirty of them.

"Never a dull moment." I said to myself.

We sat there and talked, she was mostly interested in what I have been doing over the years since I left here. I told her just about everything, I knew that Marlin had filled her in on the rest.

"Do you think that we would ever know it all?" I asked as I petted on of the swans that came over to us.

"Someday, but right now it's fun to wonder and then to see if what we have wondered is correct, or are our imaginations running wild." she replied as she looked up in the sky.

"Do you ever miss it?"

"I believe that one has to explore their own world and understand it before they go off into space and try to understand that."

"And there is so much more to explore in our world." a very familiar and lovely voice said from behind.

"Hello stranger." Mynera said when she turned to Cileen.

"I heard you were here, and I just had to come. I stopped by your place but the two of you were gone. How are you?" Cileen asked me.

"We went to the ocean." Marlin told her when he and Jacob came toward us.

I noticed something different about her, her appearance had changed slightly since the last time that I had seen her. I studied her with a puzzled look and she knew that I had noticed.

"You are the first one. I have been here so many times, I'm surprised that Mynera hasn't said anything. This change is creating many different changes with different people." she said.

"So your getting younger?"

"Only in appearance. I have been given the chance to once again relive my life. My body will rejuvenate to a point where I will appear as I have once looked when I was a teen." she said with a slight smile, in her mind it was time for her to relive her childhood with all her knowledge and powers.

"That is wonderful." Jacob said.

"You would really be my baby sister now." Mynera said.

Cileen gave her the strangest look, she knew something about her sister and wasn't about to tell. From studying Cileen and remembering the conversations that we have had I thought that this world may be giving back something to its citizens. As I child Cileen never had the chance to experience her youth. She had been tossed into a world that was dominated by adults. Then I thought about what Mynera may have missed.

Mynera and Jacob could never conceive Marlin unless they undertook the genetics experiments themselves. Thin I thought of them having a child without anyone helping.

"You are right, but there was more to that reason than you believe. Someday you will know." Cileen said to me.

"Does she know?" I asked her as I looked at Mynera, who then became a little unsettled that we, for once, knew something that she didn't.

"Has it happened?" I asked anxiously.

"Not yet, but it will. Soon." she said when she touched her sisters shoulder.

"Will you two tell me what you two are talking about?" Mynera asked.

"No way, for once we know something you don't." I said.

"I like that thought." Cileen said as she stared into the lake. "It will be a wonderful event."

"Will I be here for it?" I asked.

"I will make sure you are, even if I have to come for you myself." Cileen assured me.

"Won't you girls at least give us a hint?" Jacob asked.

"It's only fair." Marlin said when he put his arm around me.

I looked at Cileen, I wanted to laugh at Marlin and Jacob's anticipation. I knew if Jacob knew Mynera would find out, but I didn't know about Marlin.

"When you get home, then you can tell him." Cileen whispered, then I realized that she didn't say anything at all. For once she let me read her mind.

The five of us sat there and talked way into the night hours. Jacob tried his best to catch Cileen off guard and reveal her deep secret, but she was always one step ahead of Jacob and was quick to divert him from it.

I enjoyed our visit so did Jacob, he had fun picking on Marlin about what he heard coming from the bedroom that we were staying in.

"What can I say?" I heard Marlin telling Jacob one morning when he thought that I was still asleep. I was standing right behind him as he sat at the kitchen table.

"Well I do." I said when I put my arms around his neck. "Morning"

One night it was humid to the point where I couldn't sleep at all. I took a walk down to the lake to watch all the sawns resting next to the trees. Two golden swans were in the lake getting a midnight snack. The moon was full as I looked up to the stars, wishing once again that I was with Orrin and shedding a tear at how much I miss him.

"Come swim with us." I heard a faint whisper say.

"What?" I asked looking around.

"Yes, it will be fun." I heard another voice say.

I turned my attention to two swans that were near the shore looking at me.

"So it was you." I said to them. "Why not." I said as I got undressed.

The water was much warmer than I expected when it hit my naked body. It sure felt good. I swam with them for a while then I floated on my back to look up at the stars. I noticed the stars were shining very bright tonight, more than ever for some reason.

"It's a wonder bo behold for the eyes to see." I heard a voice say, when I looked around I saw Mynera standing at the shore line. "Couldn't sleep?"

"Not really. Have you ever seen the stars so bright." I asked her when I put my robe on.

"No, but it is something to see. I'll get us something to drink." she said when we walked to the house.

I went into the bedroom and woke Marlin. "Why are you wet?" he asked.

"I went for a swim. Now we want to show you something." I told him when I left the room.

Mynera and I went outside and waited for them. We sat at the shoreline and watched, some of the swans made their way over to us and stayed around. It was interesting, it was like some the stars were getting brighter and brighter.

"So it has begun." Mynera said as she looked at the sky.

"You know what it is?" Marlin asked.

"Yes. This will be the last night that we will have one sun in the stars, but this is no ordinary sun." she said.

She right about this not being ordinary, considering what it takes for the birth of a sun. It's almost like someone put another light in a dark room, a much brighter light.

This new sun was a very unusual one, true it will be able to add extra light to all the planets but it will also be able to give warmth to the planets closer to it. I wonder about it's orbital path, what is its overall effect. I know we will have all the answers when science gets done with it.

We went home a few days after that, my mind was still wondering about this new sun. I turned my thoughts back to Orrin and how much more time I have to wait. I knew it was only a matter of time, and that will be a long time to me.

Not a day or night went by without my thoughts going toward Orrin, I wanted to see him so much and because I kept that thought in my mind, it made me miss his even more. The more I missed him the more I became distant with my surroundings. A few days after the rain returned and it made me feel worse. I tried my best to keep a good attitude but sometimes it was hard, even though Marlin was trying his best to help me stay cheerful, I still needed to know for myself that Orrin was alright.

I had started to feel a little better as the time went by. Marlin was a big help, and I mean that sarcastically, he would get me to laugh by tickling me, one thing that I like to a point. I kept thinking that if I was busy then time would go by faster.

I started out my day as usual, I took a shower and got dressed then I got something cold to drink. I stood in the doorway looking at the sun peeking through the clouds.

The warmer it got outside the more I stayed out, I like the spring air but now with summer officially here, I'll take the warmth of the sun. With the new season came new things, many things that I have never seen before, one creature caught my attention.

I was sitting outside and I noticed something moving around in the grass, so I decided to take a closer look. I got down on the ground and laid on my stomach.

"You are beautiful." I said in amazement as I picked up a little bug. It was similar to a butterfly yet its wings were transparent and when the sun hit it just right it would cause a rainbow effect. "So she does provide many lives, but you can't fly very well. I'll take you back into the woods." I said to it when I gently put it in my hand.

"What have you got?" Marlin asked when he came outside.

"Check it out. Isn't he gorgeous?"

"The wind must of blown him here."

"I was going to take him back. Come with me."

"I just thought of something, you never told me what the big secret is." he said when we started walking.

I smiled and thought about that. "Maybe I should make you wait, but then again I don't know how long before it happens."

"Before what happens?"

"They are going to get the chance to have another child, without the help of doctors."

He stopped dead in his tracts and stared at me in disbelief with the possibility. "You're serious."

"Yes I am."

"But she's so old."

"And so are you, but someday you will have a child."

He remained quiet and thought about his parents as we continued on our way. It was easy to find where the butterfly, if that is what it is, belonged. Not too far from the edge of the woods we found a bush that had thousands of them.

I moved as slow as I could toward them, I was only a few feet away when the one I had in my hand flew off. Then most of them flew off to the tree tops, they started returning after we started walking.

"That is incredible." Marlin said when he took my hand.

"They are pretty. That one could of flown back if it wanted to.

"You think so?"

"I know so."

"Soon enough they'll be in the yard anyway."

"You think so?" I laughed.

"I know so. I'm glad to see that you're in a better mood."

"It does me no good to worry, but it's hard not to. There is nothing that I can do about it except wait until I see him again. Then I will not worry."

"You look tired, you should rest. It will help you feel better."

"Yeah, I know."

Rest I did need so I didn't argue with him, only on one condition, while I rest he doesn't work. With that promise I went and laid down. I had only one question on my mind, how much longer will I have to wait?

When I woke up I felt great. My mood was a lot better and I had more energy than I knew what to do with. I was surprised that I slept the day away, when I got up it was dark. Marlin was delighted to see the change in me when he came to see how I was doing.

"I told you that some rest would help."

"I feel great, better than ever." I said when I leaned over and kissed him.

"I can see that."

The way he held me and as much as he loves me made me wonder as to what he will go through when I do leave. I knew that it was only a matter of time, a very short time.

I promised myself that I would do what it takes to assure myself that he will be alright.

"What are you going to do when I leave?"

"Don't worry about me. I'll be fine." he said confidently.

"You're positive?"

"Yes I am." he smiled. He tightened his hold on me and kissed me passionately then he let go. "Now get dressed and come downstairs. We got company."

I got dressed as fast as I could and went downstairs to see Jacob sitting on the couch.

"Well this is a surprise." I said.

"It's about time. We've been here for hours." Jacob said when he hugged me.

"Why didn't you wake me?" I asked Marlin.

"Because you needed your rest." he said.

"I can rest later. You know how much I like to visit."

"I was going to but Mother stopped me."

"Where is she?"

"Outside, we took a walk and seen your friends." Jacob said. "You should have seen her. The minute she got close to the a few of them gathered on her. They look marvelous when the sun reflects on all of them. Colors everywhere."

"It sounds like you enjoyed them more than she did." I said when I looked out the window to see what she was doing, then I notcied her talking with Orrin. "Why didn't you wake me?" I asked again.

"He got here shortly after they did, and Mother wanted to talk to him. She figured that you could wait a little while longer." Marlin said.

"About what?" I asked curiously.

"Don't know, she didn't say." I was about to go outside when Marlin stopped me. "Im sure she's almost done."

"Yes I'm sure she is."

I stood in the living room and watched out the window. Whatever the conversation was, it appeared to be pleasant, I saw him smile about something. With my desperate need to see and hold him plus my curiosity of their conversation, I went outside to find out what was going on.

Orrin was very interested in hearing what Mynera had to say, so with his back turned to me he didn't notice I was there. I wasn't too interested in her words, my interest was with Orrin. She noticed me and finished quickly to leave the two of us alone.

Neither one of us said a word. Instead we grabbed ahold of each other, he held me so tight in his arms and I felt secure once again. With my worries gone that empty space filled with an overflowing joy.

"Don't ever leave me again." I whispered.

"Never, we will never be apart again." in his voice was a sound of relief and promise. A promise that I know he will hold true to me. "I've been thinking, we should stay on this world until the birth of our child." I was surprised at this, I always thought that he would want our child born on his world. "This way I know that she will survive the birth."

"She. How do you know that our child will be a she? That's what Mynera told you."

"We'll talk about that later." a tender kiss sparked off an emotional need and the more passionate the kissing became the hotter we got. "Right now I have better ideas."

He took a tight hold of my hand and we walked aimlessly for an hour or so as we talked about what I've been doing and feeling since I've been here.

"What do you think about the new sun?" I asked him.

"It was a wonderful sight to see close up. You would of loved it."

"I figured that the night we seen it happen."

"You were watching, that was very late at night."

"It was too hot to sleep so I went for a swim, that's when I saw it."

He paused while he read my thoughts as I looked back on that day. "I think seeing you naked swimming with the swans would have been a better sight."

"And I would have never gotten into the water, but that would have been fun. Doing it in the water." I said getting playful.

As we sat in each others arms underneath a full moon and starlit sky we let our powers get reacquainted and discovered a few new unexplainable things. He was as curious as I was about one of them, I have the ability to take the energy of my aura and shape with my hands into whatever I wanted.

"Does every power have to have a purpose?" I asked.

"I don't know but this one will keep our child entertained." he laughed.

I smiled and slightly laughed at that. With my hand placed gently on the side of his face and a passionate stare I moved my face as close as I could without touching his. In a way I was searching within his thoughts, looking for the tranquility that I am feeling from him.

"What is it about this planet that makes you so peaceful here?" I asked.

I didn't get an answer, I really didn't expect one. What I got in return was a long gentle kiss with a tight embracement and a tear of joy.

I know where I belong and I know that I will never loose sight of what I hold dear to me. My love for Orrin and Marlin plus the knowledge of the two children that I will someday have.

"Promise me that no matter what happens that you will never leave me." I said.

"You worry too much, you also know that I am true to my word."

"I seem to recall a few words you said to me the last time we were together." I said as I kissed him.

It was easy for him to submit to me this time, this time there was nothing to stop us and this time was different. Something different was in the air, we both felt it. As we held each other and kissed I felt his desires and needed to feel more.

With a carefree attitude we had a very remantic, uninhibited night of making love under a blanket of stars. A marvelous change came about this night, in the process of exchanging our love and feelings, I discovered the purpose of this power.

It wasn't new, it was a portion of our powers enhanced so that in the process of cneception, the child will acquire upon her birth the power and knowledge that the both of us share.

"I would give anything to spend eternity right here, in your arms."

"When everything that is going to happen comes to pass, we will." he said.

We stayed where we were for hours, he laid on top of me as we kissed, occasionally teasing and restirring our desires which were still burning strong. I couldn't stand it anymore, I needed to feel him once again moving around with excitement inside me. He knew it and kept teasing me before giving in.

"Marlin wants to establish his bond with you." he whispered in my ear.

"I know."

"Do you accept him as a worthy mate?" he asked curiously.

"Yes"

"Then before we leave he shall have his bond with you."

"Leave?"

"Before we start a family I want us to take one more trip. A trip that will hone your hunting skills, trust me you will enjoy it. After we will have our child."

I didn't know what was in store for me, thinking of that day was the furthest thing from my mind. After we satisfied the endless hunger of our desires we slowly made our way back to the house. I tried to get him to tell me where we were going but he just smiled and said I will find out.

There was still an hour before sunrise so after we cleaned up I made us some coffee and we sat outside watching the sunrise. I waited for the suns rays to become stronger, then I laid on the grass and felt the warm rays on the cool grass.

"That feels so good." I whispered to myself.

I put my hands behind my head and closed my eyes and let the rays of the sun blanket by body. I could feel tingling sensations all over, it felt good, some of them felt arousing. A gentle warm summer breeze was blowing and the birds started sing in full force.

As the breeze was blowing I laid there and listened for the whislpers, and I heard then, I hear one.

"Now the time has come for you to know your past, to know of the one you should fear. A man by the name of Raven should not be trusted, Liera made that mistake."

"What?" I said when I sat up.

"He is your grandfather. By the next centuries end his power shall be no more." and then I heard no more.

"What are you thinking?" Orrin asked as he sat behind me and then held me to him. "Your thoughts are confusing."

"I heard a voice, I got a warning." I said.

"What kind of warning?" Marlin asked when he came out.

"She said to beware of a man named Raven, he is my grandfather."

"Raven. No one questions his orders."

"Aparently Liera did, but by the end of the next century he will be powerless."

"We should wait until his demise before we try to have our child." Orrin said, and I agreed. There is no reason to try to bring up a child if there is a mad man running around that hates me for reasons unknown.

"That's almost twenty years away." I said.

"Yeah. We can take our trip." he said.

When nighttime came a light warm summer rain came with it, I stood outside and enjoyed felling the warm rain drops on my skin.

"Why are you standing in the rain?" Marlin asked when he and Orrin came out.

"It feels good."

"I know something else that will feel good." he said when he came up behind me and put his arms around me.

"And what would that be?" I whispered to him.

"Taking off that wet robe." he said as he open my robe and started rubbing his hands all over my body, slow and hard.

"What do you say we get naked and go sit on the grass." I said when I turned to him.

"I'm way ahead of you on that one." Orirn said when he walked passed me with no clothes on.

"Now its your turn." I told Marlin.

I went over and sat on Orrin, a few minutes after Marlin was standing naked in front of me. We didn't need any light, we used our hands to feel our way around. I felt Marlin fully aroused as I massaged my hands on him and gently pulling him down on top of me.

""That's much better. One in front and one in back, can't ask for anything better." I said.

We spent all night outside having sex in the rain, it was great. As I would have sex with one the other would watch or get turned on, I already knew Marlin had a perverted mind he took an overwhelming joy in watching me and Orrin and used that to his advantage when he had sex with me. Orrin liked it when the both of them could have sex with me at the same time.

My bond with Marlin was more spirit and soul, we could literally see the energy flowing from us and intertwining within each other. My body was so hot that when the raindrops fell I me they let off little amounts of steam.

I don't remember what happened after that, I woke up alone in my bed. The sun was shining, bird are singing, it's a beautiful day. I heard voices so I knew that the guys were downstairs, I couldn't make out what they were saying but I knew they were coming closer.

When I sat up I was dizzy, my head hurt and my vision was a little blurry. My throat was dry and so wasn't my skin, I put my head in my hands and fought the urge to get sick. This was not amusing.

"How do you feel?" Orrin asked when he sat down beside me. When he put his hand on my back it felt like a sunburn.

"There is no way I want to travel." I said without moving.

"Here, drink this." Marlin handed me a cold glass of water. "You've been asleep for three days.

I had all I could do to lift my head up. I was so hot and dehydrated, my body was weak, I couldn't even hold a glass. Marlin very carefully helped me. It was like they absorbed my energy.

"What happened?" I asked.

"I am so sorry, I never expected this to happen to you." Marlin said. When he touched my hand it burned, I had to move away. "I am so sorry. Apparently the timing for our bond was not now, but you will be fine."

"Why wasn't this forthcoming?" I asked.

"Somethings are meant for us to find out for ourselves, after all, what would our lives be like if we knew everything. We learn by our mistakes." he said.

"But you will feel better, in time. Your body has an interesting defense system." Orrin said.

"Meaning?" I asked.

"Meaning we are never going to attempt this again." Marlin said. "I don't want to chase you in the dark again."

"I don't remember anything." I said, then I looked up and got a better look at them two, it looked like someone beat the crap out of them. "What happened?"

"You happened." Orrin said, when I looked at him I seen that he had a fat lip. I was horrified. "Don't worry about it, we're fine. Besides it was fun wrestling you to the ground."

"I punched you?"

"You kicked me." he said, he also had a slight smile.

"You enjoyed it." Marlin said to him. "At least I didn't let her hit me in the face." then we heard someone at the door. "You've got company." he said to me before he left my room.

"You are going to love it when we take our trip." Orrin said as he tried to touch me.

Where I was feeling hot he didn't know if he should touch me or not. I made up his mind for him when I decided to try to get up.

"I need a shower."

"How about a bath in some cool water." he suggested. "This time if you want to fall back to sleep I'll be with you."

"It will help cool you off." Cileen said when she came in. "After what Marlin told me I just had to come over and see you."

"Do you know what happened?" I asked her.

"Your powers harness the energy around you, but their powers also protect them. You were trying to draw their powers." she said while she helped me up. "How do you feel?"

"A little better, I can stand with no problem." but taking a step wasn't very easy, I was still a little dizzy.

Cileen and Orrin helped me into a cool tub of water, it felt so good that I could have stayed there all day. Evediently Cileen had brought something with her for me and Marlin was supposed to be getting it so she sent Orrin down to find out where he is.

"You're not strong enough yet." she said to me when she gently poured water on me. "You need to be stronger."

"I don't think I have to worry about that." I told her. Marlin came back with a glass in his hand and the stem of a plant in the other. "What is that?"

"This will take the burn out of your skin. The pleasures of knowing your plants." she said when she took the stem and squeezed the juice out of it into the water and then used the stem to stir it with. "Drink this. It also makes a good tea."

It wasn't that bad, a little tangy once the initial bitterness was gone.

"You know, I'm feeling a lot better." I said to Orrin once Cileen and Marlin left the room.

"Yeah I know." he said kissing me. "When you feel better we are going home then we are going to get ready to leave."

"You can't wait for this can you?"

"Well, no. I made a slight change in plans, we're still going we're just going someplace else." he said with a grin.

"And you won't tell me."

"No, and we leave in a few days."

After I got out and dried off I put on a very soft loose robe, I wanted nothing touching my skin. Well almost nothing, I will tollerate a human touch.

Cileen stayed with us for the night when morning came she and I were the only two awake. After we made us some breakfast we sat down to a long morning chat as we ate. This conversation was a little different. She was talking about the changes within her and she was also mentioning doing things that she had missed in her life. She was looking for one thing and she was leary about asking me for a favor. I knew she wanted to ask me something but she kept going around it. It was driving me nuts.

"Cileen, ask me what it is that you want to ask me." I said when I cleared the morning dishes.

"I want to borrow something from you, only for a short time." she said hesitating.

"Well, what is it?" I asked her when I poured us more coffee.

"You know I want a child, the only thing is that I don't want the help of doctors and I don't want to search for a mate of my own. That's the last thing I want in my life, I just want a child."

"And?" I asked her.

"Can I borrow Orrin for a little while?"

I didn't know what to say to her, I know what she wants and I know how much it means to her.

"Why Orrin?" I asked curiously.

"Believe me I have been thinking long and hard about this. If you think about it differently like I am he's a perfect canidate, he's healthy and strong and smart, traits that would be passed down to offspring."

I just smiled when I looked at her. "And he's good looking and very hot in bed." I told her, which embarrassed her. "I can ask him, or you could ask him yourself."

"Oh no, I could never do that."

"How bad do you want a child?" I said picking on her. "And would it work?" I said when I got up to pour another cup.

"Would what work?" Orrin asked when he came in the kitchen. "Morning" he said when I gave him a cup. I looked at Cileen, she was getting a little more unnerved and even he noticed. "Are you alright?" he asked her.

"She has something she wants to ask you." I told him.

"Ariel!" she said.

"What? If I don't say something you won't and then you may miss your chance." I told her. "She want's to have a child." I told him.

"Oh I see." he said.

"With you." I told him when I sat down, I tried not to laugh, I tried not to smile. I knew how important this was for her, and how uneasy she was about asking. "And I'm okay with that."

"Ariel I could have done that myself." she said.

"Tell you what," I said when I got up. "I'm going to go and shower and change and I'll leave you two alone." I knew she would talk to him more if I wasn't around, at least I got her started. "I'll be back in a bit." I told him when I kissed him.

I was still trying not to laugh when I went upstairs, I passed Marlin in the hall and dragged him into my room to keep him from going downstairs. Then I started laughing when I shut the door.

"What is so funny?" he asked.

"It's not that it's funny, it's that I think it's sweet." I said. "You know how Cileen wants a child?" he nodded. "Well she was wondering if Orrin would give her a child."

In one way he was surprised and in another he wasn't. "What did he say?"

"I don't know, yet. She was afraid to ask so I kind of got her started and then I came up here to take a shower and change."

"And you're okay with that?" he asked when he sat down on my bed.

"Yeah, sure. I understand her reasons, they make sense. Why not? Besides I've seen what's around here, I don't blame her for that." I said when I got in the shower.

"That wouldn't bother you if he did do this and she has a child by him before you do?" he asked curiously.

"No. I have plenty of time." then I noticed how much my skin had started flaking since last night. "This is going to be fun." I said to myself while I tried to peel some of it off in the water.

"What's that?" Marlin asked when he came in.

"I'm peeling."

"So I see." he laughed when he looked at me, then he got into the shower with me. "I'll get your back." he gently rubbed my shoulders and back, it felt relaxing. "Your skin is a little darker, you got a nice tan." he noticed.

"That was a hell of a way to get one." I said when I turned to him.

"Yes, but that will never happen again." he said kissing me and caressing my body.

My quick shower became a little longer, not that I'm complaining, I would never pass up the opportunity to have sex in the shower. We may have been in there longer if it wasn't for a knock at the door.

"Ariel, I want to talk to you." I heard Cileen say.

Marlin got dressed and left the two of us alone, she was still a little nervious and I couldn't figure out why.

"Well?" I asked her when I got dressed.

"Well, he said yes." she replied.

"So what's wrong?" I asked her when I sat next to her.

"You two are leaving soon, time is short."

"Well yeah, but a lot can happen in a few days."

And a lot did happen in a few days, for her comfort in this we felt that it would be best if she was in her own home, so what we decided to do was Marlin and I were going to visit with his parents considering I won't be seeing them again for a long time and Orrin was going to stay with Cileen.

It was nice out so I spent most of my time outside, every now and then I would go over to where Squeaker and his mother are buried and place my hand on the dirt. My sad thoughts of losing him quickly passed when I thought of all the fun we had.

"Ariel, that was a nice thing you did for her." Mynera said when she sat next to me. "And what I would like to know is why you girls didn't tell me that I'm going to have a child."

"You know?"

"I do now." she said smiling.

"You're already pregnant?"

"Yes, we're going to have a girl."

"So the next time I come back you will have a little one running around."

The thought of children in these peoples lives is what they are living for right now. The need to know that their bloodline will continue gives them hope, and doing that without interference from doctors or scientest opened up new hope for them.

When Orrin got back the next day I couldn't resist picking on him about being with Cileen, I know he enjoyed being with her, I felt it. When I felt it I took my feeling out on Marlin and he loved it.

We returned to our home on kerrell and prepared for our departure from this solar system. It wasn't too bad, we took a starship that was going to take us close to our destination and then from there a small shuttle to the planet.

When we arrived we found ourselves a small secluded place on the edge of the city, it was a great spot because that was where most of the action was. The first few days we spent checking this place out. What law enforcement they had was considered owned, which meant that anyone with enough to offer could buy their silence. So whatever crime was committed would go unnoticed. Everything that you would think of as a crime was legal, and I mean everything.

"Welcome to Utopia." Orrin said to me.

"I am going to like this." I said as we walked the streets.

We found a place the people here call the Arena, for obvious reasons, it was considered an action bar. You could go and order a drink and watch two people fight until one of them was either dead or begging for their life.

This place fascinated me, we went there almost every night. I kept a good eye on the people who would fight, what interested me was the way that they would handle weapons or fight with hands only, depending on how drunk they were.

One thing that didn't feel right about this place was the girls, they seemed so young. One night I kept my eye on one girl that was with a man at the bar.

"What are you doing?" Orrin asked.

"That girl over there, she can't be no more than fourteen if not younger. That's not right."

"Then do something about it, just be careful." then he kissed me.

I did do something, I kept my eye on them until they left. I followed the two of them, making sure that neither one of them saw me. I also discovered very quickly that this is one place that you do not walk around without some kind of protection, I always carried a sharp blade that can be concealed very easily yet have my hands on it at all times.

I watched as he took the girl into a motel a few blocks away. Once inside he took her into a room, not too long I heard her scream as he beat on her. Another thing I learned quickly was how to pick locks, once I was inside the room the guy didn't even notice me.

The girl was on the floor in the corner, she seen me but didn't say anything. The man was standing over her taking his clothes off. I took out my knife and motioned the girl to move and when she did I tapped the guy on the shoulder.

When he turned around he smiled when he saw me, but he wasn't smiling for very long. I took my knife and embedded it in his throat.

"Interesting" I said as I watched him fall to the floor blood pouring out of his neck. I was so involved in watching his blood drip from my knife that I almost forgot about the girl. "Oh yeah, then there's you." I said when I ran my finger along my blade then tasting his blood. "Don't be afraid of me. I'm not going to hurt you." I said when I turned around to face her.

"What are you going to do?" she asked. In her mind she thought I was going to kill her.

"I said I'm not going to hurt you. Where is your family?"

"I ran away."

"Can you get back home?" she nodded. "Good I don't want to see you here again." I told her.

"I don't have anyway to get there."

I took whatever credits this guy had and gave it to her so she could return home. She was facing me when orrin came in, her fear returned when she seen him.

"He won't hurt you. Go home." I told her.

I stood there as she thanked me and ran out the door at the same time. I just hope she keeps her promise and returns to her people.

"You terrified that girl." Orrin said when he shut the door.

"She thought that I was going to kill her as well."

"I see you had no problem."

"He didn't even know what hit him, but then again he was drunk. There was no challenge." I said as I continued to clean my knife. "He's not going to be any use to us. His blood is full of alcohol."

"There will be others. How do you feel?"

"Great" I said when I put my knife away. "Just great."

As we made our way through the crowded street we talked about the opportunities that this place has for us. There was pleanty and we were ready for them.

I couldn't stand by and watch any more of these young girls being used by these horrible men. These girls were perfect, after I followed them and killed the men, I wouldn't see most of the girls after that. I didn't know if they went home or to another part of the city, all I knew was that nine times out of ten, I never seen the same face twice.

A year had almost passed, at first Orrin would follow me to make sure that I could handle myself, when he felt confident enough he would leave me to be on my own. I had a few men that would try to fight me but it always ended in the same way. Their blood fueling my desires.

Orrin and I would make love by day, satisfying our desires for each other, at night we would stalk our prey. Most of the time we would stick together, on certain occasions we would find separate victims, but that was rare.

By watching the fights and having a few of my own I ended up with one bitch that was constantly annoying me at the bar one night. Orrin and I were sitting at the bar minding our own business, we decided that it would be nice just to spend the time together, this drunk woman come over and was hitting on him. Eventhough he told her to get lost a number of times, she wouldn't listen, so I decided to make her listen.

I was sitting on the other side of Orrin and I reached over and grabbed her neck, then the bartender came over and got involved.

"Why does this look so familiar." Orrin said when he moved to the other side of me.

"No fighting at the bar. I ain't cleanin up no blood here. Take it in the ring." the bartender said.

"Hey that would be a great idea." one of the bar partons yelled, which sparked off half of the people there.

"A drunk is no challenge." I still had my hand around her neck, she was trying to loosen my hand as I pulled her closer to me. "How would you like to die?" I whispered in her ear.

She was starting to sober up a little. I pushed her away from me when I let go of her, someone had grabbed her and threw her onto the floor of the ring. Next thing I knew someone else had put their arm around my shoulder and forcibly led me toward her.

I waited until she shook herself up on to her feet, and she surprised me even more when she came after me. The best part was that she didn't know I had a knife. She found out when she when to slap me and ended up with my blade going through her hand.

"I don't think so. There is nothing that will let me get hit by you." I said when I looked at her, then twisting my knife before I removed it from her hand.

She backed off and held her wrist tight, she was in pain, but I was pissed.

"Want to make it a more fair fight?" I asked when I put my knife away. "Or to make it even more fair I could put one hand behind my back." which made a lot of people who were in earshot laugh.

"You bitch." she said getting closer to me.

"Mistake number one. You called me a bitch." then I punched her so hard that she fell to the floor. "Mistake number two. You got in my face you dumb bitch." when I back off she got up and came after me. I didn't want any more to do with her, I took out my knife and went for her throat.

This was a different feeling and I enjoyed it, and I knew Orrin enjoyed watching me. He also enjoyed the fact that I killed her because she was annoying him, he got the idea that I was protecting my territory. Which I was and he knew that I would do it again.

Over the next five years my skills in fighting became much more than what I had ever expected. I learned very quickly how to move and handle myself if I didn't have a weapon of any kind. I became sharp, quick and unpredictable. I never turned my back on an opponent or let my guard down. That was a rule that I lived by, that and never letting anyone live. I thrived on their fear, it was that fear that gave me my strenght, even in the ones who thought that they were brave. Everyone has fear, I just had to find out what it would take for them to show it.

As far as my bond with Orrin it became stronger with every passing day. Our bond was indeed unbreakable, our love strong, and we became more obsessed with each other. We never went anywhere by ourselves, we did everything together.

My worse day was when a woman decided to fight with me. She was strong and quick and knew how to handle herself. She fought well, but not well enough. I nailed her to the floor and stabbed her heart with her own blade. I made sure she was dead before I moved, when I stood up I had the look of disbelief towards her. She wasn't who she claimed to be.

Orrin came over and stood behind me. "What's wrong?"

"I think she may be Aquarian."

"Are you sure?" he couldn't believe what I said.

"I can feel her powers in her blood. I am very sure."

I didn't get any sleep that night. I sat in bed thinking about her and tried to think of a reason as to why she was here. I couldn't think of anything that made any sense.

One thing I did wonder about was if someone was going to question this.

"Forget about her." Orrin said when he pulled me down next to him.

"I can't, they will be looking for her."

"Then she shouldn't have been here." he held me in his arms and tried to get me to forget about her. To him it wasn't that hard to get my mind on something else. All he had to do was touch me a certain way. "Put it out of your mind for the rest of the night." he said as he stroked his hand along my leg, I felt myself giving in as he sucked my breast.

The good started to outweigh the bad in this part of the world. Our victims were people that had committed numerous crimes against the innocent. The people were starting to feel at ease for the first time in their lives. As the numbers of murders started to rise, people began to wonder for the first time as to who it was that was committing them, but they really didn't care. They called the dead undesirables that deserved to die.

Rumors on the streets were good ones, people were no longer afraid for the lives of their children and for once they are taking back what they lost so long ago, a peace of mind.

This kind of control wasn't quite what we had expected, but we didn't complain, we just had to be extra careful. After thinking about it for a while I realized the type of control I had was in the arena, I always came out on top. I had a few scratches but it was nothing to be concerned about.

I always won and I liked watching as the loser died. It got to a point where no one who knew of me would bother to challenge me. Even the bravest ones knew better.

"You know something?" the bartender said to me one night as Orrin and I were spending a quiet evening together and watching everyone else fight. "You keep this up and I will lose most of my best customers."

"Most of your best customers thought they could never lose." I told him. "They were wrong."

"You are a tough bitch, who taught you."

I leaned closer to him to whisper in his ear. "You gotta pick the right person to have sex with." I told him.

He moved back and looked at Orrin and started laughing. "There is someone over there who is looking for you." he said as he pointed to one of the tables."

We made our way over to a dark corner where a man and woman were sitting, he didn't look familiar but she was very familiar. She was the girl that I had met when we first got here.

"Long time no see." I said to the girl.

"We had to come." she said.

"To warn you two." the man added. "And to thank you for sending Lidia back home. She told me what you did and I am thankful, she's all I have left."

"What is it you wanted to warn us about?" Orrin asked.

"Rumor has it that there is going to be a massive restructuring of control on this planet. The government is finally going to do their job." the man said.

"That's good for you." I said.

"Yes and bad for us, we'll have to leave." Orrin said. "But, it is time that we leave here and return home."

"I wish you a safe journey." he said.

He shook Orrins hand and then he shook mine, but the feeling I got was not a good one, the vision I got was even worse. This planet is in for a very long hardship in this transition.

"You say your daughter is all you have, if you don't leave here soon then she will have no one." I told him when I moved my hand away.

The next day we planned our departure. We never acuminated anything so there was nothing to take with us or really destroy. In one way I was sad to leave but in another way I couldn't wait to get home, I also couldn't wait to see Cileen and her child.

When we returned home we wanted to spend a few days by ourselves and then tell people that we were home. When we did finally call them it was a one sided conversation with Mynera, she talked so much that I couldn't get in a word if I wanted to. One thing she kept stressing is that we have to come and see the children.

"Yes we will. I promise." I told her. "We have a few things to take care of and we will come. Besides I haven't even talked to Jennifer yet, she's next on my list."

"Well as soon as you can you two get down here." she smiled.

After I got done talking Orrin started laughing.

"What's so funny?" I asked.

"Did you add Christena to that list?" he asked.

"Yeah, she's in there somewhere." I smiled.

Not only was she on my list but a few days later she was at my door. I was even more surprised to see that Aries was with her.

"I thought that a captain never leaves his ship." I said to him.

"Well some exceptions are made." he said.

While he and Orrin talked Chris had another idea of conversation that she wanted to have with me. Why she took an interest in me I never really knew, I knew why Aries was interested in me but not her. It took a lot of prying to get it out of her and I was surprised when I did.

"Did you ever wonder why you could never read my mind, or know what I was up to?" she asked.

"No and I never felt it was my business to ask, but now I want to know."

"I actually want to show you, and to check on something else." she said.

"Are you going to tell me?"

"Well I thought of just working on your curiosity."

"Are you at least going to give her a hint?" Aries asked her when he and Orrin sat with us.

"No, I don't think so. But I will tell you this, I have a new scanner that I love using and I would so like to use it on you." she said.

"Scanner for what?" I asked.

"Here we go." Aries said. "We have a new medical scanner that she has used on everyone at least twice."

"Practice makes perfect." she said with a smile.

"So you tested it out on the crew first, isn't that a little twisted?" I asked.

"You really like your job." Orrin told her.

She was right, I am curious to see her new toy. After a few days she called me and told me to come and see her on the Orion, arrangements have already been made.

After sitting with us and explaining how the scanning system operates she showed us. It was increadable, it was like actually looking inside a person without having to open them up. As always there is always a surprise.

"Wow" she said. "This is fantastic."

"I'm laying here naked on a table and she's getting excited." I said to Orrin.

"And you will be too when I show you what I see." she said. She moved a smaller monitor closer to me and zoomed in on one area. "Do you see it? Very small."

The harder I looked the more I saw and the more amazed I was. I saw a tiny heart.

"I'm pregnant" I said.

We were astonished at how this baby looks inside me. She is so tiny and formless, the only thing we could identify was the heart and tiny little nubs.

"She has a heart." Orrin said with excitement.

"She?" Chris asked.

"Yes, we know the gender of the baby." I said as she drew blood from my arm.

"Now all you need to know is when." she said.

As she processed the blood sample she described everything that pertains to the good and bad things about being pregnant. She also asked if I wouldn't mind being monitored constantly, she loves her new toy, but she also informed me that there is something a little smaller that I can use.

Doc had a hand held scanner that just recorded information, you couldn't see it unless it was downloaded into a computer. She said is wasn't hard to use and it wasn't, if it wasn't for that she wouldn't have loved to have me there so she can do a day to day check to see this child grow.

"There was a reason why I wanted to do this." she said.

"When I was doing my exams I came across another person that had a similar chemical makeup that you do."

"Which means what?" I asked.

"Which means you two came from the same place." Orrin said.

"So this person is a crew member?" I asked.

"Yes he is. He's a pilot. His name is Derick." I was shocked, and she knew it. "You do know him?"

"Yes. Is he here." I asked.

"Not at the moment, he's on leave. Do you want me to let him know?"

"Sure, I know I will be back here again. I will see him someday. I'm glad he's alive." I said.

I figured that I had enough to think about and do right now that when I have more time I will see him and find out what happened.

No one was more excited about my pregnancy than Jennifer. I told her last, I waited until I got back to work and saw her. I thought that it would be more fun this way.

We knew that we had to go to Aquarius, we just wanted to get everything over with so we could go on with our lives. And of course another surprise.

Not only did we see Cileen's son for the first time but the look on Orrins face when he say him was priceless. A son was something that I knew I couldn't give him and I'm glad she could.

We were sitting outside at Mynera's when Cileen brought him over. He was almost ten, I thought to myself. He's a happy child, his hair is white like his mother's and he has Orrin's dark eyes.

As for as Mynera's child, she was a beauty. Her hair was long and blond and her eyes were a sparking blue, I could tell that Marlin spent a lot of time here. She got along with her big brother very well. They named her Star.

"My name is Jerrit." he said politely.

"Well, you get one of each." I said to Orrin as he stared at him, and then Jerrit looked over at me and smiled. "What?"

"You'll see it's a surprise." he said.

"And he's just like his mother." Jacob said.

"And what about this pretty little blond here?" I said while I played with her hair.

"She is like her father, loves anything that can fly." Jacob said proudly.

"Now about this baby business." Mynera said when she sat down and placed her hand on my stomach. She had a big smile, and it wasn't for me.

"Wow. Does Jacob know?" I asked her.

"No. I'm going to let him sweat it out." then her thoughts of being a mother again put a very happy expression of her face. "I can feel her move. She will be full of energy."

"It's fascinating watching the development of the baby." Orrin told her.

"There is nothing like feeling a child growing inside." Cileen said.

"Right, having a child may be painful to some, but it is one of the most pleasurable feelings to know that you have brought a life into this world." once again her excitement was overtaking her.

"With the way you're talking Mother, you would think that you were having a baby." Jacob said.

"Wouldn't it be nice," she said when she sat next to him, "to have another child?"

"Yeah it sure would." he said holding her, his thoughts were sad. As far as he knew there would be no more.

"Well," she said looking at him. "We will."

His expression dropped, his color became pale. For a few minutes he was speechless. I sat there and observed Jacob, children mean so much to these people.

"I was going to make you wait, but I can't." she said.

"You know, I'm beginning to wonder if this is all your fault." Jacob said pointing to me.

"Now what did I do?" I asked.

"Her getting pregnant. It rubs off you know."

"Don't blame me. Cileen started it. But with Mynera being pregnant, I'm not the last one to have a child."

We had a wonderful time talking about expectations of a baby, none of us could wait for either one to be born. When we returned home we continued our usual routine of work and preparing for our child.

As the child within me grew so did my anxiousness of wanting to hold her and my thoughts were more on the child than anything else. I'd be in my thoughts of amusment at being a mother, sometimes Orrin would say something and I wouldn't hear him. He also took a great interest in setting up one of the rooms for when the baby is born. With Chris helping him, I was all set for her arrival.

He enjoyed feeling the baby move around, but there was something different about this child. After numerous tests and looking at the monitor without any hint of what was wron, plus a visit from Chris, nothing showed up. I had an idea and kept it to myself.

As time got closer for her arrival Orrin was worried about me being alone. I had stopped working and started resting, when I was home alone I would read aloud and rub my stomach which was hugh, I was so uncomfortable. My back hurt, my feet swelled. I was in misery.

With my discomfort Marlin decided to come and stay with us, that eased Orrin's mind. I wouldn't be home alone if she decided to come. I still felt fine but I was getting tired.

I thought about my real parents as I laid across my bed. A short while later I sat up and as I held my head down rubbing my neck I felt a hand move through my hair. When I looked up I saw the form of a man standing in front of me in the darkness.

"Who are you?" I asked.

"I wanted to come and see you for myself." he said as he touched the side of my face. "You look so much like your mother. He taught you well. I am proud."

He left as fast as he came, he didn't have anything to say. I didn't question my father as to why he came, I was glad he did. Someday I will be able to talk with him. Talk with him about his world and tell him about mine.

"Are you alright?" Orrin asked when he and Marlin came in the room.

"I'm fine." I said.

"Who did you see?" Orrin asked.

"My father. He came just to see me for himself."

"He was curious." Orrin said when he sat next to me and held me.

"Yes, and I am glad." I said.

Every day I looked at my child inside me, Marlin was also fascinated by watching her grow. Her heart is strong and she is forming beautifully. Chris was watching every step, she wanted to do a live feed of what I was sending her but that is not in the best interest of security, so every chance she got she came over and spent hours looking at my stomach.

"This doesn't bother you?" she asked me one day as she scanned over me.

"Are you kidding? Look at me, I'm huge, I'm not moving. I am so miserable."

"I think if you and Orrin don't mind I would like to stay here." she said.

"Why, is anything wrong?"

"No, but I think you may have this child any day now. The baby's getting into position."

"So she can have the baby any time?" Orrin asked.

"Yes. And if you are going to have her at home then I should stay, unless you want to go to the hospital?"

"No hospitals."

I was glad she stayed, it made it easier for me knowing that she was around.

"Do you want anything?" Orrin asked when he came to check on me.

"No I just want to rest." I told him.

"You look a little pale." he said when he sat on the bed.

"Baby's taking a lot of my energy, she is going to be here tonight." I warned him.

The look on his face was priceless, the thought of the baby coming in a few hours was making him more nervious. I could feel the changes as she was getting ready. I could feel the contractions coming closer, they didn't hurt, but they were very uncomfortable.

I relaxed and let the baby take her course, Orrin tried to have a conversation with me but it was one sided, unless Marlin answered him, other than that I didn't listen to him.

"Do me a favor." I asked Orrin.

"What is it?"

"Don't take this the wrong way or anything but shut up, you're driving me crazy."

"I'm sorry." he smiled and gently wiped the sweat off of my face. "I was trying to keep your mind occupied."

"If you really want to think of something, I'd start thinking about delivering this child."

"Well will you look at that." Chris said. "I'm starting to see a baby."

It was better than I thought, now that her head was our and the rest of her came out with ease. Orrin cut the cord between me and the baby and wrapped her up quickly so she wouldn't get cold.

Chris took her scanner to check me and gave me a very surprised look.

"Oh yeah, by the way, there is two girls." I told them.

"Twins, we're going to have twins." Orrin said.

"There is another baby. She is a good little hider." Chris said as she got ready to deliver her.

"I thought I was, I just didn't want to say anything. I have a feeling that this is why Jerrit smiled at me." I said.

"He knew." Orrin said. "I am definitely going to ask him."

"You two are going to have your hands full." Marlin said as he held the first girl.

The second girl was easier but she took the rest of my energy. I laid back trying to catch my breath, I did not want to move any more.

"How do you feel?" Chris asked when it was over.

"Fine, tired."

"I think it's great." Orrin said when he sat beside me.

"This one will have my eyes and your hair." I said when I touched her little finger. "And the one Marlin is holding will have your eyes and my hair."

"How do you know?" Marlin said when he sat on the other side of me.

"I just do."

"What do you say that we name this one Katrina?" Orrin asked.

"Where did you hear that name?" I asked. "That was my mother's name."

"It came out of nowhere." he smiled.

"And I was thinking of Jessica." I said.

That was settled, one is Katrina and the other is Jessica. I could tell he was happy by the smile on his face as he watched both babies sleep. They also decided to let me sleep as well. Chris told me that she is going to stay a few more days, or until she has to return to work.

He was very excited about the girls, that I knew, and so was I. I closed my eyes and thought of the girls, and thinking of the look on his face when he heard there was two. I was resting peacefully only to be disturbed by a familiar touch.

"So what do you think?" I said without opening my eyes.

"Your girls are beautiful." Cileen said.

I sat up and smiled. "I do feel better, so I'm going to take a shower, and go see my girls."

"Take your time, right now they are getting plenty of attention from their big brother.

"The look I got when I said we were having twins is unforgettable." I said when I got in the shower.

"Your girs are going to be just like you. Are you ready for two?"

"So what you are saying is be prepared?"

She came in and handed me a towel. "Orrin is still a little bit out of it from the reality of two."

I put my robe on and looked in the mirror. "What a difference from this morning."

"You'll be back in shape in no time."

"We'll see."

When we got out to the living room Orrin was holding one child and Jerrit was holding the other, he was so preoccupied by her that he didn't know I was standing behind him.

"Now isn't that precious." I said looking over his shoulder.

"How do you feel?" he asked.

"Great" I said when I sat next to him, then Jerrit handed me Jessica. "So you knew?" I asked him.

"Yes. Surpise." he smiled. "They are going to grow fast."

"I don't know if I'm crazy about our girls growing so fast." Orrin said.

"Their groth is something that will have to be dealt with. Raven's powers are quickly fading. Our power stays within our own kind, his power is being dispersed within his bloodline." Cileen said.

"Are you saying my children will inherit some of his powers?" I asked.

"Yes"

"To be honest with you I haven't given my grandfather any thought. What will happen to him once he is powerless?"

"He will be tried for his crimes against the innocent, he will be condemned for letting things get so out of hand." Marlin said. "This is why I told you not to look too deep into things, you never know what you would have unknowingly stirred up."

"As long as one stays focused timeing is always everything. If you want a job done right the first time." Cileen said.

"You look tired. We're going to be here for a few days, why don't you get some rest." Marlin said.

"I will later. I want to play with my babies." my babies, what a thought. I can't wait to see what they are going to try.

They stayed for about a week, Jerrit had fun spending time with his father, they both like the relationship they have, it gives both of them more of an appreciation for each other. Cileen enjoyed helping with the girls, it didn't matter when it was, she had one. What I didn't realize and never given a thought to was that Marlin had never held a child until Cileen had Jerrit, so the look on his face when he held one of the girls is unforgettable.

I can't imagine being as old and never holding a child until now, I sometimes wonder if it was worth the price that science has caused on these people.

Chris stayed a day after them, she wanted to check me out one more time before she left. My power of healing amazed her.

Our first night just us was quiet both girl's are sleep at the same time for the first time. Orrin was sitting on the couch reading, now this was my time.

"How are you feeling?" he asked.

"Great, better than ever." I said when I sat on his lap.

"And full of energy I see." he carefully put his arms around me.

"You can hold me a little tighter. I'm not going to break." I whispered.

"I just don't want to do anything that will hurt you."

"Don't underestimate me, I'm a lot stronger than you think."

"Still, I can wait." he knows how impatient I am when it comes to certain things, he was doing this on purpose. His avoidance was a tease, so I teased back. "But I see you can't."

With a passion I kissed him and moved to entice his desires, they were there and needed to be satisfied and I had a desperate need to satisfy them.

I wasn't the only one with a burning desire, his touch and stare were a search. Deep within me the way that he had touched me for the very first time, those feeling were still there. Then for some reason he was laughing.

"What's so funny?"

"I should make you wait." he smiled.

"You wouldn't dare." I said tightening my hold. "You know what happens if I wait too long."

"I know." he said smiling,

He decided to tease me a little before giong to bed knowing how much it drives me crazy. I like it to a certain point, the point at which I lose control. That's one of the many things that he does very well to me, and he kept doing it.

"Keep it up and I'm going to tear you apart." I warned him.

"Promise?" he smiled.

"You can count on it."

"It seems your energy is very high." he said kissing my neck.

"Yes it is."

Full of energy, defiantly. Out of control, not yet, but I know that is what he is trying to attempt, he does it so well. I wrapped my legs around his and nibbled playfully on his neck in a spot that I knew drove him crazy. He surprised me when he moved a little so that I would nibble in a different spot.

"Why did you do that?"

"You'll see."

The more I nibbled the more he enjoyed it and the more carried away I got, instead of wrestling with me like he usually does he let me be. He put more pressure on me and as I continued his desires flared, I felt them burn.

Then I felt something else, it was a tender spot on his neck and when I broke throught the skin I tasted his blood then after the blood subsided something else came along and took its place. It was appealing, smooth and very addictive, it also made him very sexually aroused.

"What is that?"

"It feeds our need, it gives us what we desire. Remember that night in the hut? I was up before you, I never slept. The old man fortold me of this bond we will have." he said.

"And you love it."

He just smiled and kissed me and when he did to me what I did to him, I understood why his emotions were stronger than he could stand. It was a stimulating feeling and very arousing. The sex we had suring this process was wild and out of control, after a few hours I was out of breath.

It wasn't long before the girls slept through the night and stayed up all day. There were no naps in between, once these girls were up they were up. It was nonstop, Jennifer would come over once a week and help me, of just pop in after work for an hour or so.

Debbie on the other hand was suffering from empty nest syndrome, her youngest one left for an on campus school. She came over often, by the time these girls learned how to crawl, climbing was next. I'll admit keeping an eye on both at the same time was hard. When they are quiet is when I worry.

One time they freaked me out, I was putting their cloths away while they sat on the floor playing and when I turned to look at them they were staring at each other. They didn't move, they just stared.

I didn't want to disturb them, I went out and told Orrin what they were doing, he even thought it was strange.

"Do you think we should move them?" I asked.

"I don't think we should leave them alone." he said.

We sat next to them, after a few minutes I couldn't stand not knowing. I couldn't think of anything unless this is a way for them to talk to each other.

"Could this be their power, where they are twins?" I asked.

"If it is they could be little trouble makers."

"Well either way," I said when I put Katrina on my lap. "They can wait until they can talk to us before freaking me out."

It didn't bother her when I picked her up. She started smiling, she's laughed when I tickled her. Jessica enjoy climbing on her father and pullling his hair, that was her favorite toy.

When the girls started walking it became more of a competition. Katrina wanted to be the first one to cross the room and get to her father. One day Jessica had the advantage and Katrina pushed her sister.

"They are starting early." I warned him, then I sat on the floor facing him.

"She's jealous." he handed me Katrina and took Jessica. "I hate to think what they will do when they are older."

"They are sisters, they will fight. Now aren't you glad you work at home."

"There is nothing that would make me miss what these two are doing everyday."

"Especially when they do take that once in a great while nap." I said, which was only the few hours they sleep together at night.

I am grateful for Debbies help, she has no idea how much it means to me. Sleep was a rarity, it got to the point where Orrin made sure that I had at least one day a week to myself. It didn't matter what it was, sleeping or spending time at the museum.

Which I did for my one day, Jennifer loved it. She loved hearing my stories. Orrin took that time to spend with both the girls, he loved having his hands full, they wore him out.

In time the girls started to show they are independent and they started to show signs of rivalry, their petty squabbles were solved easy enough and they managed to say sorry to each other. Katrina still tried to put the point across to her sister that she was going to get all of her fathers free time and attention to herself, but it never worked and she felt a little resentment at the fact that she had to share her father.

Jessica tried her best to get along with her sister, one morning they really surprised me. I started to go into their room to get them up for breakfast and I saw them sitting on the floor playing as nice as they could. They didn't see me so I went back out and left them alone.

"Be nice if they would do that all the time." I commented to myself when I poured some coffee. In my amazement with them I didn't know Orrin was standing behind me until he put his arms around me.

"Morning. What has you in a daze?" he asked.

"The girls."

"And how are they?"

"Getting along great."

"And that surprises you?" he asked tightening his hold on me.

"Yeah, it's the first time they are not fighting." that's when he started picking on me.

"Now that is cause for celebrating." he grabbed onto my ear and nibbled. "The girls are playing quietly in their room so we could go play in ours."

"There's only two things wrong with that." I said when I saw the girls.

"What's that?"

"The girls are in here," then I whispered in his ear, "and you don't play quietly. But keep that thought in mind." then I turned my attention toward the girls. "Ready for breakfast?"

"We're not hungry." they both said at the same time. "We're going to play." Jessica added, then they went back to their room.

"Neither one of them said morning." he said.

"They are up to something." I said suspiciously.

"Why would you say that?"

"They are almost three, they act like they're ten. By the time I was their age I could read people like a book, and when I was five I knew what people were really like providing they couldn't block me out."

"You had that all set until I came along." he said mischievously.

"You were a mystery. Sometimes you still are."

"I know." he replied without changing his tone. "Sometimes you have no idea what I am going to do next."

The girls were so good playing together that I couldn't believe the morning we had. I waited for that one moment when one of them would yell for mom or dad. I waited so long that when I went to check on them, they both were sound asleep on the floor.

"Guess what daddy?" I said when I nibbled on the back of his neck while he worked at the computer.

"The girls are sleeping and I'm almost done. Good timing."

"They picked a perfect time for a nap." I said when I put my arms around his neck, then I noticed what he was working on. "Are you going to install this?"

"If I did, that would mean that I would be away from you and the girls for a few weeks." he said picking on me.

"Why would you want to do that?" I said when I tightened my hold.

"Nothing is going to take me away from you three. Roz will be over tomorrow to pick it up."

"This is for his new project. Marlin told me that he was around, that was a while ago. He should have been gone by now. I wonder what happened?" I said more or less to myself.

The afternoon was fun for us while the girls slept, when they woke up they continued to play in their room. Once again I thought that it was odd and both of us went in to check on them, they were sitting on the floor coloring.

"Are you two hungry?" I asked them.

"We're not hungry." Jessica said.

"How do you know your sisters not?" he asked her.

"Because I know. I feel what she feels."

"Is that okay?" Katrina asked.

"Yes it is." I told her.

"Is this why you two were not fighting today?" he asked.

"Sort of." Katrina said. "I don't like feeling it."

"I guess that means you won't be picking on your sister anymore." I hinted.

That idea was one I can live with. They had a light snack and cleaned up for bed only to wake up before the sunrise. They were very helpful, they went as far as helping with making their beds.

“"If you can do things, like clean up, with your powers, how come you don't?" Jessica asked.

"That's no fun. I like doing things myself, and you two help me. Besides, how else are you going to learn."

"You have company." Orrin said when he walked into the girls room with Roz.

"Twins. They didn't tell me you had twins." Roz said.

"Yeah and you didn't come see me sooner when you had more time. How come?" I asked.

"Well. Clair and I got married."

"Without inviting anyone." I said.

"You did the same thing. I hate to drop by and run but I really got to go." he said when he gave me a hug goodbye.

With the girls in their room and Roz gone we had some time to ourselves again so I decided to get playful. We had fun wrestling on the floor, the girls came out and decided to join us. My enjoyment was watching him with the girls, I found my opportunity and leaned against the couch to watch them.

"What do you think you're doing?" he asked me.

"Watching you three."

"Why should we have all this fun without you?"

He grabbed my hand and pulled me on top of him and at the same time Jessica jumped on my back and put her little arms around my neck and held me tight.

"Love you." she said.

"I love you too." I told her. "You're right, why should I let you have all this fun." I said as I looked for the only spot where he is ticklish.

"Don't you dare." he warned me.

"What are you going to do about it." when I had said that I didn't count on Jessica moving off me to sit on the couch with her sister.

"Now you're in trouble." he said with enthusiasm.

No matter how much I tried not to be pinned in under him and be tickled endlessly, it didn't work. He loved anticipating my next move to see if he was right and he usually was. The fun part was when I had started to get a little more aggressive with him. The girls enjoyed watching that, the only time they became concerned was when I had become overaggressive with him.

The intention was still playful and he knew that but they didn't. although we never leave anything this good unfinished we didn't have much of a choice when we heard a knock at the door.

Katrina and Jessica were sitting on the couch staring at me. They seemed offended somehow by the way Orrin and I had reacted toward each other, Jessica more than Katrina.

"Don't worry. Your father and I are always like that." I said to ease their minds.

"Actually your mother's worse." he said catching his breath after he opened the door.

They didn't know what to make of it or us, I think the girls are starting to realize that there is more to us than they knew.

"They will be surprised when they get older." Marlin said.

"This is a surprise. What brings you here?" I asked

"I tried to see Roz before he left. I figured where it was early I'd stop by and see how all of you are doing."

"That's nice, and I thought that you came here just to see me." I went over to hug him. "It's good to see you, I hope your visit is longer than Roz's. Sit and I'll get something for us to drink."

"I can't believe how much they have grown." he said when he sat with the girls.

"There is something new happening everyday with them." Orrin told him. He is still as proud as ever with his beloved daughters.

"So what really brings you here?" I asked when I handed him a glass.

"They found Liera. She's dying of old age. Her powers are gone, her memory is failing. She doesn't remember me or Roz." he explained.

"What does Roz think of that?" I asked.

"He doesn't. He will be surprised in years to come."

The girls didn't know what to make of our conversation and excused themselves to go and play in their room.

"The girls have a gift of art." Marlin said looking over at their pictures.

"They are excellent at it." Orrin said. "Jessica has a talent for animals and Katrina love abstract painting."

"We brought out our pictures." Katrina said when the ran back out to us.

The girls had about forty or so pictures to show him. We were amazed at the color coordination in the drawings. They do have a unique gift, I thought.

"Why don't you join us for dinner?" Orrin asked about an hour later.

"I'd love to but I have so much to do." he replied.

"Please" the girls said begging.

"Well how can I refuse these two pretty faces." he said.

"It's not easy." Orrin said.

"Of course not, they have you right where they want you." I said. "Besides, you always said that your work will always be there."

"I have slowed down."

"Well you should. You have a little sister and brother to play with." I said.

Our dinner conversation was enlightening, not only for the girls who heard stories of when I was a child, but for me as well. It brought back many memories of when Marlin and I would go and visit with his parents.

After we had gotten the girls into the bed for the night we stayed up and talked for so long that we lost track of time.

"You know you are welcome to spend the night." I whispered in his ear.

"That was not my intention when I stopped by." he said looking at me.

"And it's been a long time since we've been together." I reminded him.

"I know. I would rather hold you." he said putting his arm around me.

The only light in the room was coming from the fireplace, it was dark and quiet. Until we heard the girls screaming at each other.

"Fighting this late at night." I said.

We didn't have the chance to get up, Jessica came running out and sat with me telling us how her sister hit her with the pillow.

"She deserved it." Katrina said. "She's talking in her sleep."

"Well that's new." I said stroking Jessica's hair.

"You used to when you were young." Marlin said.

"I didn't know that. Why didn't you ever tell me?"

"I didn't want you to worry about it, you had enough on your mind."

"Do you think you two can go back to bed without fighting?" Orrin asked them.

"We'll talk about this tomorrow." I told them.

"Why were you at my door listening to me talk in my sleep?" I asked him when the girls went back into their room.

"Standing at her door listening?" Orrin asked.

"Wishing she was older." Marlin added.

They picked on me for the rest of the night, we didn't bother going to sleep, we had fun talking. Every now and then I would tease Marlin, in return he would hold on to me tighter.

When morning came the girls came running out to say goodbye to Marlin and to give him a picture they both did together. Sometimes they do know how to get along.

A year and a half had passed with remarkable results from the girls, they acted like they were much older. Mynera once told me to enjoy them as babies because it won't last long, now I knew what she meant. We miss our babies but we love our young girls even more.

They learned to read and write very quickly, their art also improved a great deal. Sometimes after the girls have gotten into bed we would hear them planning the next day. They also took an interest with computers, it was also time for them to start their schooling.

After I had finished cleaning up from breakfast one morning the girls cleaned up their room and sat quietly on the floor playing. I sat on the couch and wondered what they will be like in the next few years without realizing that they were standing behind me.

"Are we going somewhere?" they both asked.

"Not that I know of, why?"

"Because we heard daddy say that we'll be leaving soon." Jessica said.

"So are we?" Katrina added.

"What are you two doing listening to my conversations with others?" he asked them sternly as he stood behind them. "Go pack some cloths." he told them.

"Are you going to tell me?" I asked when they were out of the room.

"I could but I'm not. It's a surprise. I even packed for you."

"You've planned this very well, haven't you? Are you going to tell me where we are going?"

He kissed me and smiled. "No. have any of my surprises ever let you down?"

The girls came back with their bags in their hands and big smiles on their faces, those smiles stayed on their faces the whole trip. They liked it as they started to see less of the buildings and more of the trees. The further west we went the better they felt, the excitement of going on a surprise trip into an unknown place and seeing new things was driving the girls imaginations wild.

Their ideas of what they might see were crazier than what they will see, and after hours of listening to their thoughts, it became outrageously funny.

"You know, I'm going to enjoy this." I said as I moved closer to him, hoping that he would say something about this trip.

"I know you will and no I am not going to say anything." then he put his arm around me. "And we are almost there."

We pulled off onto a dirt road and looked for a spot to park, then from their we had a two hour hike in the woods. The girls loved this area, there were wildflowers everywhere and the path we were walking on was clearly open so I didn't worry about the girls running ahead of us. As we got closer I heard voices of other people and children laughing, then I started to wonder what kind of getaway this was. I felt something different, I felt someone's pain.

"Am I right?" I asked.

Before he could answer the girls came running back to us and there was a woman a little older than I was with dark short hair and a pleasant smile coming toward us.

"Did you girls do something you shouldn't have?" I whispered.

"No, but wait until you see." Jessica said.

"It's a beautiful sight, isn't it little ones." the woman said to the girls as she stood in front of us. "It's good to see you again, considering this time it's a good occasion." she said to Orrin.

"You should be thankful, father's passing has brought him closer to mother."

"Your father, not mine."

He was surprised with her comment. "You knew?"

"My real father told me everything before he died." then she turned her attention toward me. "I'm Sandra." I reluctantly shook her hand. "You're cautious around people."

"Ariel has always been careful around people." he told her.

"Suspicious is more like it." she said as she tightened her hold on my hand, and I returned her gesture.

"You have a strange way of approaching people." I told her.

"You have spirit." she said.

"And you, I feel it within you." I also felt a bit of intimidation from her. "My reason for not touching too many people, I feel a lot of their emotions and it can intensify with a touch." then I let go of her hand.

"Then someone has been expecting you. He will be pleased to see you." she said.

The path between the trees led to a courtyard with a wonderful view of the mountains. This place sat upon a hill and the incline was of moss and wildflowers, at the bottom of the hill was a beach running the shore of a small lake. Sandra is right about this place, anyone can see its beauty, but I wonder about what is hidden within.

"Can we go down to the lake." Jessica asked, which started both of them begging.

"In a minute." he told them.

"Take the girls down, we're fine." she told him.

Sandra and I stayed at the top of the hill and watched as the girls ran as fast as they could without falling. They were fascinated with the water and soon joined the other children that were playing on the sand.

"Your children are beautiful. You and Orrin are lucky." she said as we started walking.

"Do you have any?"

"No, I have yet to find anyone worthy enough to bare a child with."

Sorry I asked, I thought to myself. "You wish for a mate that is equal to you."

"It's not easy to find a male of our kind. Orrin went out of his way to find you. Considering what you are."

Her remark really didn't surprise me but I figured that she would have been happier for her brother.

"Sandra" an old man said as he approached us from behind.

"I'm sorry. My comment didn't sound the way it should of." she said with little sincerity in her voice and her heart.

"Think nothing of it. I have grown accustomed to the different opinions people have toward me. I have felt that their prejudice comments mean nothing when they do not understand." I said in a straight serious tone.

"Sandra, leave us alone." he said to her. She apologized to me again, this time I felt a little quilt from her. "I have been expecting you child. Do you not remember me?"

I was puzzled by his question. "We have talked many years ago." then he put his arm around my shoulder and together we walked a short way to sit on a stone bench under the shaded darkness of a tree. "You were so curious to know who I was."

"Now I remember." that's when I recognized his voice. "Are you the one I saw in my dream with Orrin?"

"Yes" then someone came over and handed us something to drink and left. "I know he was positive as to who you were, but I had to be sure."

"Sure of what?" I asked, then I took a sip of what I had without realizing it was blood.

"Are you surprised?"

"No. Nothing surprises me anymore."

"I know you can ease people of physical pain. Can you ease their emotional pain as well?"

"Yes, why?"

"My mother is one of the survivors from our true world, she is very old and tired. I feel that it is my duty to ease her pain so that she may have a peaceful passing."

"Does she know I'm coming?"

"Yes. She is down by the lake. She enjoys watching the children. She saw what happened."

"So did you."

"I was with her."

He told me of the day when his father was killed trying to protect his teenage daughter who was trying to find her mother. She was small and couldn't defend herself, when he tried to fend off an attacker he was killed from behind.

"He didn't even know what hit him." he said trying to constrain his tears, it was so long ago, but it was still a very emotional vision of terror that relived itself in his mind year after year. "You are a very sensitive person." he noticed when I tried not to cry.

"I have the same dream of my mother's death, I wasn't even born yet."

"Yes, you are lucky. Being from our world yet possessing the power of theirs through your mother."

"Lucky? How is it you know so much about me?"

"I knew your mother. I was on the ship that brought you here."

"How is it that with what my mother knew about survival that she was killed?"

"When she had seen your father and brother dead a good part of her died along with them. She had lost hope. I tried to stay as close to you mother as possible for as long as I could. When they took you from her I, with the help of others, tried to keep track of you. It was real easy after that woman you were implanted in went crazy." he explained.

"What? I never knew that."

"If word got out that Raven crossbred with another species successfully, they may look for you." then he paused for a moment. "Excuse me, I'll be right back."

As I watched him going toward the lake my mind was going throught what he had told me. Then I thought long and hard about myself, if I do belong to these people then where do I stand now. It's obvious Orrin's sister doesn't like me. By right I should have died with my mother, but thanks to science I'm still here.

As I looked up to the trees I closed my eyes and wondered only about my girls, I can't wait to see what they are going to do with their lives, then I felt Orrin as he kissed me on the neck.

"Your mind must really be working."

"Trying to understand everything that I have heard so far, trying to piece them together with things that I've heard in the past. Where are the girls?" I asked when I noticed they were not with him.

"They are down at the lake with Sandra. That gives us a few minutes alone." he said as he took my hand and pulled me off the bench. "Let's take a walk."

"A few minutes alone with you will pick up my spirits."

"How was your talk with Marcus?"

"He bares so much pain, but he only cares for the well being of his family."

"He consideres everyone his family. He and his mother are the elders of our tribe." then he turned to me and held me tight. "I love you."

I didn't answer, I kissed him instead. His hold on me reminded me of the very first time he ever kissed me, that lust filled emotion was still burning strong.

"I wish we were alone right now, I'd tear you apart." I said.

"There is plenty of time for desires later." a woman said behind me. I turned to see Marcus helping his mother as she walked toward us. "My name is Carla." she smiled as she extended her hand.

"I am pleased to meet you." not only could I see the pain in her face, I could feel it and it was very deep.

"I'm glad you came. We have much to talk about."

"In other words mother has much to say." Marcus added.

"It is beautiful here." I said when she sat down.

"Yes it is. This is why we moved here years ago." then she looked at Orrin. "Although some don't come around as often as they should have." she said to him.

"I had my reasons." he told her.

I got a better look at her, her eyes were dark like my fathers. Her skin was dark and wrinkled, but yet she retained a beauty of her own, her hair was gray with hints of black, either way, she is still a beautiful woman.

"Reguardless of your reasons, we are going to take a trip. On certain times the powers of the universe are open to those of us who can cross within the barrier of two worlds." she explained.

"How?" I asked.

"The same way that your parents have come to see you, except I'm not coming back."

"How long does this doorway last?" Orrin asked.

"On this side for one quarter." she said.

"We will be gone for that whole time?" I asked.

"Yes, and don't worry about the girls. Marlin will come for them."

"So that's who you were talking to." I said to Orrin.

"Yes, and he's excited about having the girls."

"Do the girls know that we will be gone for so long?"

"Not yet."

"Have the children ever been away for you?" Marcus asked.

"No, not for such a long time." Orrin said.

He gave me a kiss before he went to check on the girls, as he was walking toward the lake a frail looking woman was walking toward us.

"This is my daughter, Carla." she said introducing us.

"She looks so frail." I said.

"The ship I was on was not very strong. Some of us were contaminated, my future offspring were affected. But don't let her size fool you."

"She can fight." Marcus said. "Believe me I know. Some mistaken her looks for weakness."

"He's just mad because I have the upper hand." her daughter said when she shook my hand.

Her hand was bony but I could feel their strenght. "Your strenght must be in your bones."

"Mom look." I heard Jessica yell. We looked over and seen Orrin laughing at Kartina. "She fell off the end of the pier."

The older Carla touched my shoulder. "That's alright, the water's warm."

"Can we go swimming?" Katrina asked when we walked toward them.

"You two are going to be leaving." I heard Marlin say when he came over to us. "And the water's very warm at Mother's."

"We're not staying?" Jessica asked.

"Not this time." Orrin told them. "Go get cleaned up."

Carla showed Katrina where she can get changed. Jacob was with Marlin, Jessica didn't really remember him. I guess I should get home more often. They were excited about going.

"We can tell you all sorts of stories, especially about your mother." Jacob said to Jessica.

They didn't stay long after the girls were ready, the thought of staying at the lake for the summer was thrilling for them. Sad for us but it's a chance to be alone for once.

We took a walk along the lake shore until it started getting dark, we found a small clearing of moss that was soft and cool to the touch. We laid there for hours and watched the stars.

"Look at that." I said looking up at the new sun as it shined slightly in the sky. "There are no more pitch black nights."

"They say it has an orbit. No one can make sense out of it."

"A lot of unexplained things are going on around here. I think that sun is part of it."

It felt good to be outside, nothing was going to stop us. We stayed where we were all night long, we were still naked when when the sun came up so I had the idea of going swimming.

"You're serious." he said when I stood up and headed for the water.

"Sure, it's not that bad." the water was cool but it felt refreshing first thing in the morning.

He did eventually join me, it wasn't for very long because Carla had come looking for us. We did have enough time to have fun swimming.

"Mother is looking for you two." she hollered to us.

"It was a good morning for a swim." I told her when I got out of the water.

"Or having fun in the grass." she said picking on me. "You are going to love this journey. Have you ever been on a boat?"

"No"

"You are in for some fun." she said as we started walking back.

When we were closer to where the pier was I noticed a small boat docked that was taking us to a much larger ship waiting out in the middle of the lake.

"After you two get cleaned up and have breakfast we are going to leave." Mother said happily.

She's not mad, I don't feel so bad. I thought to myself. I didn't realize that she wanted to leave first thing in the morning. Where breakfast isn't my thing we got cleaned up and ready to leave.

The boat we were taking had an unusual appeal to it. It was old and rustic looking but it had modern technology for the drive system. We were informed that it is only used when necessary. Our cabin was small but we didn't stay in there.

I stayed with Carla, she spent most of her day's looking out at the open sea, inhaling the sea air. On the fourth day at sea Marcus atarted acting strange. He became quiet and didn't respond to anyone. When I asked Carla about this she said not to worry, he was just meditating.

That night I watched Marcus as he stood silently and stared off into the stars, a short while later a fog started rolling in, it was thick. It was then that I realized what he was doing.

"You're not meditating, you're casting a spell." I said to him.

He looked at me and smiled. "Our people possess a power of our own. I just happen to be able to open doorways."

"To where?" I asked.

"By morning we will have arrived at our destination."

I didn't go to sleep, I stayed with Marcus. When Orrin had come to look for me I told him what Marcus was doing. At least what I thought was the truth.

"I should have told you about him. He dabbles in black magic." he said.

"To say that I dabble is an insult Orrin." he said to him.

He has the knowledge to use the power, I thought to myself. That would make sense.

"Mother wanted to go home and you wanted to see your parents." Marcus said to us.

Just as it happened that one unusual morning so many years ago, this mysterious wonder in my hand began to glow with life. As I watched the fog clear I started seeing a shore line of a small island. The pier was good enough for the ship to dock.

"This place is quiet." I said looking over the rail as the ship was docking.

"This place is home." Carla said. Her skin was transformed into a radiant young woman. He frail body is strong again. "And I can't wait to go ashore." she smiled.

She was like a kid again, running down the pier, stopping when she saw a man coming toward her.

"That is my father." Marcus said.

As we stood on land I watched Carla with her mate, the reunion was so touching that I lost track of my surroundings, after a while Orrin put his hand on my shoulder, so I thought. When I turned around my father was standing there.

He put his hands on the side of my face and smiled. "We have been waiting for you, both of you." he said. "Are you going to give me a hug or what?"

I gave him a very tight hug. I didn't want to let go. It was the same for my mother when she seen me, she didn't want to let go.

As we walked I noticed my surroundings and paid close attention to everything. The colors were bright but not blinding. I could stare at the sun and it didn't burn my eyes. The air was fresh and sweet, the ground was more of a gold color with hints of white and silver, the only thing green was the leaves on the trees. Then I noticed a stream, but instead of the water being clear it was red.

"Your girls are precious." Mother said as we sat by a tree.

"They are our treasures." I said.

"They have changed our lives." Orrin said when he sat beside me.

"What is that river?" I asked.

"It contains the blood of every form of life in the universe. The ones that can live in harmony with each other. Since we are dead we have no need for blood to run in our veins." my father explained.

While Orrin was looking around he noticed two people coming toward us and recognized them immediately. His joy wasn't as much seeing his father, it was his mother that thrilled him.

"Don't get up." she told him. Then she sat down next to him and caressed his face. "It has been so long."

"Every creature is here at one point or another in their lives." my mother told me. "Even small ones." she said pointing to something in the grass.

I looked over and seen a little white ball of fluff jumping out of the grass.

"Squeaker"

I couldn't believe it when my beloved pet came running to jump on my lap. It was so wonderful to see him again, this time he had a little friend of his own to show me. In the distance another one of his kind came toward us, she kept her distance from us. I didn't know why, but I figured that she has never been around too many people.

"I have missed you." I said when I picked him up and hugged and squeezed him.

"So that was your little pet." Orrin said when he put his hand over to pat him on the head. "He loves affection."

"The only one he kept his distance from was Liera and I don't blame him there, I did the same thing, and for some reason, Clair." I said.

"Animals know people better than people do." my father said.

"He brought you many years of happiness." he said.

"That he did." stroking his fur brought back many pleasant memories.

"Let's you and I take a walk." Mother suggested.

When I got up Squeaker look at me then at his mate. "If you want to go for a walk with us then come." he ran towards her then he came back and walked with us.

Mother took my hand as we walked aimlessly around the area, not saying much of anything unitl we were away from everyone.

"I have always wondered what you life would have been like if you were born on our world." she said.

"So have I. I used to wonder if I would have been with Orrin if nothing had ever happened."

"I know for a fact that you two would have. He treats you well." she said looking at me.

"He is a wonderful man Mother, I couldn't ask for anything more from a mate."

"Yes he brings you much happiness. Your father and I were wondering if you and Orrin would consider being married while you're here?"

"I would be honored, and I know Orrin will also." I gladly replied.

She smiled and gave me a hug, I knew how much it meant to them and In a way it meant a lot to me as well. We continued to walk around for a little while, she told me how much their lives have changed since they were told about this new world.

I noticed another thing about this area, I didn't see any other people or animals, I could hear them and I could hear the laughter, but I couldn't see them.

"Where are all the people?" I asked.

"There everywhere, but they are not here for you to see. I am glad to have this time with you. Let's go tell you father."

"So Mynera was wrong about the origin of my father. Was she right about anything?"

"Yes, that ring you wear. That was given to me by your father." she said holding my hand and running her finger around the ring.

"You can have it back." I told her.

"Give it to me the next time we see each other."

"What does the inscription say?"

"My soul."

When we got back to the others Marcus and his mother joined us. Carla was so excited to be reunited with her mate, her face was glowing with excitement.

"I'm sorry to have left you so quickly." Carla said.

"No need to apologize." I told her. When her mate turned to face us I recognized him, then when he said hello to me I defiantly recognized his voice. "You're the one." I said in amazement.

"Yes" he smiled. "I knew that you are the one who would reunite us and other like us. You have the power to do so."

"As long as someone like Marcus can harness my powers." I said.

"Yes, he has the knowledge and you have the power."

So this is our leader, this is the man that has spoken to me ever since I was a child, another mystery solved. He was quite impressive, very strong or rugged even.

"Why didn't you tell me before as to who you were and why it was me that was chosen for whatever you wanted me for?" I asked.

"You were a child, even givin your situation, you were still considered a child. Would you have believed me?"

"I guess no more than believing that I spent almost a hundred and ninty years sleeping. Now will you tell me who you are?"

"I am Amedeus." he replied taking my hand. "I was right in choosing you. Let's go someplace more comfortable. I promise I will explain."

They had taken us to a shaded camp like area, I recognized the moutain range, it was the exact same as the world they once lived on. There were stone cabins centered around a bonfire pit. Not far from the pit was a common area for gathering. I know I'm going to like this.

"That name that you have called me, what does it mean?" I asked when I sat on the ground next to my mother.

"That was the name I was going to give you, have you been born in our world." she said.

"Dre also means giver." he added when he sat across from us.

"Of what?" I asked.

"You have the ability to fulfill ones greatest unselfish wish. Like Carla, she wanted to be young again, full of energy. The way she looked when she last saw her mate. Because of you, you granted her that."

"I possess the power but not the knowledge. How do I know when this happens?"

"You just will. Does everything have to have an answer? Sometimes we don't choose our destiny, sometimes it chooses us." Amadeus said.

What we have always wanted to do with our parents, was done. We sat and talked for hours, they told us of their world and we told them of ours. Something I'v always wanted to do was done.

We shared some very strong common interest, our children were one. After my father and I were sitting alone away from the others so that we could talk without being interrupted. We talked about how he loved to hunt, just as I do. He admitted to having killed a few chosen people.

"I'm curious. What did you feel when you killed?" I asked.

"That instant burst of adrenaline, the energy it creates was very satisfying. Or to put it better, a deep feeling of gratification."

Thinking about what I had felt brought back a lot of feelings. Some of them were very powerful feeling that tingled throughout my body.

"Maybe someday we can share the desire of hunting together." he said with a deep passion as he held my hand tight.

"I would love nothing more than to go hunting with you."

His eyes sparkled with that idea, I could feel his emotions growing with the anticipation of one day hunting with each other. It would be a glorious day for us.

"We should let them get some rest." I heard Orrin's mother say. "After all, they still need sleep."

"We are far from tired." Orrin told her as we walked back toward them.

Then I thought I saw something moving out of the corner of my eye, but when I turned to look there was nothing there.

As much as we hated to see our parents leave, we knew that we couldn't get them to stay with us longer. Marcus stayed with his mother, orrin and I had a cabin that was set up with anything we needed, even a hot shower.

We stayed up and talked about what we've seen and heard. My father wants so much to be a part of my life, maybe someday their will be a way.

As I laid on my side to gaze at him with a smile, studing his expressions, he became curious as to what I was up to.

"What?" he said with a slight laugh. I moved closer to tickle his lips with my tongue then I moved on him. "That's what." he said holding me tight.

As we were having made passionate sex I had many thoughts on my mind. Then what mother had said about the girls made me wonder.

"Do you think that our parents watch us?" I asked.

"I wouldn't doubt it."

"Do you suppose that they also watch us when we are having sex?"

He stopped moving and kept a tight hold on me and thought about that.

"I don't know. Could you imagine watching your parents having sex?"

"I did remember? It was in a place similar to this, I thought that it was very romantic." I said as I wrapped my legs around him.

He gave me a very inquisitive look. "What were you thinking when she showed you her and your father?"

"I'll never tell."

We were so full of energy that we didn't get any sleep at all, or I should say I didn't. I laid next to him and watched him sleep as I always do. He looked peaceful and relaxed. I moved my hand carefully along his chest then down his leg, even in his sleep I can arouse him with a touch.

"Don't stop." he said when I moved my hand away.

"I thought you were sleeping."

"And miss this? Never." he said replacing my hand on him.

"I never said that you would miss anything." I said playfully as I moved on top of him. "Besides, this is too good to ignore." I said slowly moving. "Can't let something this good go to waste."

"I couldn't agree more." he said caressing my body.

"Don't you two ever quit?" Marcus said when he walked in on us.

"No" Orrin said.

"What are you doing up early?" I asked.

"It's not that early." he laughed.

Our parents had something planned for us, but mostly for me. My mother never showed me a few things for some reason.

"Once this starts you can't change your mind. You will feel pain." she said.

"What are you going to do?" I asked.

"We are going to give you back what was wrongfully taken from you." she replied as she took my hand. The look on her face was enough to me that this means a lot to bothe of them. "You will share a bond with two worlds, you will see a much bigger difference. Not only with your powers but with Orrin."

"Orrin and I already share a strong bond."

"But this is much different." my father said when he stood beside me, then he put his arm around me. "It's time to start."

With his arm around me we walked over to the common area, as we sat and talked once again I saw something. This time I saw more of it.

"What is it that I am seeing?" I asked when Orrin handed me something to drink. It was blood with something else in it.

"You're seeing between two worlds." Amadeus said.

Whatever it was that I drank made me feel strange, numb in a way. I felt dizzy and my vision was blurry. My father held on to me as Orrin removed my shirt, with ease he laid me down on the ground. I barly saw my mother as she laid something strange on me. Whatever it was it was warm and slimey.

I don't think anything could have prepared me for the pain that she spoke of, the next thing I remember is feeling a sharp piercing pain in my chest. It was starting to burn, then that burning feeling went throughout my body.

"Are you alright?" my father asked when he sat by my head.

"Yes"

He held my head and caressed the side of my face. I could feel something sharp moving around inside me, I moved my head slightly and seen Orrin's mother say something to him, he responded by smiling and slightly nodding. Then I felt the pain my mother warned me about and screamed. I didn't know what it was that was causing it, all I knew was that it burned inside me. Both my parents held on to me tight.

"Soon this part woll be over." he said whispering in my ear. "And soon you will have what is rightfully yours." I sensed a strong desire in his voice as he said that.

With his hand he took my free hand and held it tight, I could feel something warm as it ran down on to my arm. It has to be my blood, I thought to myself. But it wasn't when he moved my hand toward his face I could see the color of the liquid that was burning inside me. It was white and thick, I could see it as it slowly trickled down my arm.

"What is that?" I asked.

"Their blood will no long flow through your viens."

"One more time and we're done. For now." my mother said.

Whatever he had done before he did again. This time it burned but not as bad. I had a strange feeling inside me, my emotions were confusing. I looked over toward Orrin and saw that he was smiling. I thought again as to what his mother could have said to him, he is very pleased about something.

He came over and sat with me, gently he moved my head onto his lap. Mother started to wipe my face with a soft cloth and cold water, it felt refreshing and I was drained. Orrin held me tight against him as he carried me, and very carefully he put me down and continued to hold me to him. I felt a little cold but not much.

"You should get some rest." he told me.

I look at him and saw that unmistakable look in his eyes,I moved to hold him better and the look was still there when I kissed him.

"Stay with me." I told him.

He leaned back enough to get comfortable and I laid on top of him and wrapped my arms around him tight. Once in a while we would be playful, but he didn't want me to overdo it. A few hours later I had some of my strenght back. When I tried to stand it was hard, Orrin held on to me tight as he helped me to keep my balance, that was the only thing that was hard for me to regain.

I rested my head on Orrin's shoulder while we sat and talked. I got a good look at my parents, they are happy together, I can tell they love each other very much.

"Are you ok?" Orrin asked me a while later.

"I'm fine. Why?"

"You're quiet."

"I have better things on my mind." I whispered in his ear.

He was smiling when he turned to face me better, I put my hand on the side of his face thinking if there was only a way to freeze this moment.

"Here they go again." Marcus said when Orrin kissed me.

"What are you, jealous?" I asked.

"No, he's just wishing Sandra was here." Orrin's father said to him.

"So there is something going on between you two." Orrin said. "That explaines her attitude."

When mother had awoken me early the next morning she carried something folded neatly in her arms. She took me where we wouldn't disturb Orrin.

"Take off your clothes, I want you to try this on." she said. When I obliged her she put on me a loose fitting robe that draped comfortable over my body. It was soft and a shinny light blue color. "it looks wonderful on you." she smiled.

"This is what you wore on your wedding day." I said when I recognized the robe.

"Yes, and I was always hoping to see it on you."

"You looked so beautiful the day you wore this." I heard my father tell her when he came in.

"It it makes him that happy, you should wear it more often I told her.

He kissed me on the forehead and smiled at me once more before he left. His thoughts were very passionate ones for her.

"Your hair is just like his, thick and long." she said as she watched him in the distance. I looked at him then I looked at her. My mind was going wild with questions. "What's wrong child." she said brushing my hair.

"When I was growing up I had so many questions that I wanted to ask both of you, now I forgot most of them." I said regrettably.

"But now you are here and that's all that counts." she said when we walked outside.

That's when I saw them, that's when I saw the people. This was my first time that I have been able to see my people. The children were running around enjoying themselves.

"You look lovely." father said to me when he hugged me. "And I know someone else who thinks the same thing." he said looking over my shoulder.

I turned to see Orrin staring intensely looking at me. "Wow" he said when I walked toward him. "You look beautiful."

"So do you." I said while I rubbed the muscles. "I always said you look good in leather." I told him when I moved my hands down his legs.

Which he did, what he was wearing hugged his body just right. Every curve of his muscles from the waist down was exaggerated just right, and the vest he wore with it was sleeveless and open in the front exposing his hairy chest.

"You look good." I said walking around him, feeling every curve. "You know what?" I said playfully when I got in his face.

"What?"

"I'm not wearing anything under this."

"Wait till later."

"We are ready whenever you are." his father said when he came for us.

It was beautiful outside, the birds were everywhere, different species that I knew I would never see again all converging to sing their morning songs.

There was a slim alter with a single flame coming from it, hovering over the flame was a small shiny object. We put our hands next to it and Amadeus pressed both our hands together. Not only was this small this hot it was very sharp.

Orrin smiled at me as it burned in our hands, it was painful but I maintained my posture. I watched as out blood dripped from our hands and slowly put out the flame. I had no idea what Amadeus was say or what he had asked me, but at one point my father leaned closer and whispered to me.

"What do you hold close to you?" he asked.

"My family." I replied without hesitation.

As I looked at Orrin I saw the distinctions that identifies us. It was there and it was strong within him, the markings of our people were there, the smoothness of his features were a bit more rough.

My only compulsion was to hold and kiss him, as I did he had a strong hold on me. We could hear Marcus's thoughts, it was very amusing to hear him picking on us, and he didn't understand why we were laughing at him.

"We can hear your thoughts." Orrin told him.

His expression dropped when he heard that, he stared at us and tried to think of nothing. In his mind he was a little embarrassed, he also wondered what else we have heard.

"Don't worry, we don't intrude on ones most intimate thoughts." I told him, which gave him a sense of relief.

It was wonderful, for a long time my father and I sat by the river and talked. He talked about mother and how much he loved her, and he told me about my brother and how he has been exploring the wonders of the universe.

"Where is he now?" I asked.

"Somewhere out there." he said looking at the sky. "He was one who was always full of questions about the unknown. Just like you. You always wanted to know."

"True, but I can wait to find out. I know that one day I will have the answers."

Something else happened in the course of the day, my father stayed closer to my side and had become very sad. I didn't understand why and asked him about it when I hugged him.

"What's wrong?"

"It's almost time for you to go. The doorway will be closing soon." he explained with a great deal of difficulty.

"We just got here?"

"I know, but here time travels faster."

When he held me tighter I started to cry. "I should of realized."

I felt mother put her hand on my back. "But it's not forever." she said. When Orrin came over he knew that I was very upset. "You have to be leaving soon." she told him.

"I know. My parents told me the same thing."

Mother gave me a kiss on the cheek and said goodbye, she was upset as well but not as much as my father was. He didn't want to let go, and I wasn't ready to.

"So will I, but we will be watching." he reminded me. "We should have told you that the time is different here, but I'm glad for the time we had. Even if it was for a short while."

"I have so many things that I wanted to say, I was hoping that I could have remembered them." I said as he wiped the tears from my face.

"One good thing about this," father said cheerfully, "there will be another time. That I promise."

"And I know you will hold true to your promise."

He looked at me one more time, I seen the pain in his eyes. He gave me a tender kiss on the lips before he let go. "Hold tight to her." he said when Orrin put his arms around me. "She is a precious creature."

It hurt too much for me to say goodbye, I didn't want to leave. I was so emotional that I could barely stand. I buried my head in his arms as I cried. I felt something nipping on my pants, when I looked down the face of one of the swans was looking up.

"They put us on Aquarius." Orrin said looking around.

Then we heard the girls holler when they seen us, when I turned Kartina was running so fast that she fell.

"Are you alright?" I asked her when I helped her off the ground. Then I noticed how tall she had gotten. "Wow, we missed a strong growth spurt. You're almost as tall as I am. Stop growing." I told them.

We were all sitting outside enjoying ourselves, getting caught back up, when we heard a comotion coming toward the lake. The swans took off flying as did all the birds.

We told the girls to get in the house and stay there while we checked it out. The did with no argument. I peered out at the water and didn't see anything, I heard something but I couldn't pin point it. The next thing I knew I heard a horrible scream and then I got knocked down by a girl.

She looked up at me, I could see that she was tired from whatever ordeal it was that brought her here.

"Commander?" she said to me.

Then I heard someone yell her name and tell her to stay down. The next thing I saw was a small flying creature going over us followed by a ball of flames. When she looked up she watched as the creature burned to death before getting off me.

"Who are you and where did you come from?" I asked her. Then I saw someone coming toward us.

"Good screw up." she said to him. Then I recognized him. It was Roz with the exception that he looks worse than the last time I seen him.

"Hey you'd be dead by now if it wasn't for me." he told her.

"And Jerrit would still be alive. You didn't mind your own business."

"Let's back up here." Orrin said trying to get control of their argument before their arguing got worse. "Who are you?" he asked her.

"My name is Cadie." she told him.

"Why did you call me commander?" I asked.

She was confused, but whatever her reason for taking a long time to answer.

"Because you are."

"Wait a minute." Roz said. "Something went terribly wrong. Cadie I'd be careful what you answer." he warned her.

"Well one things for sure, what we need answered is who are you, where did you come from and what is that thing that is burning itself out." Marlin said. "And so help me Roz, this had better be good." he said when he grabbed him and led him away from us.

"How did you get here. You came out of nowhere." I asked.

"We were chasing this creature when we got caught in some kind of distortion. Next thing I know, I'm on you." she told me.

"And you called me commander. Why?"

"You are in command of the Orion. I have been on that ship for the last twenty years. And I am thankful for it. My people usually live until their thirty, anyone older than that is lucky. By rights I should have died ten years ago." then some thought made her happy and she smiled.

"We have a problem." Jacob said. "It seems you are from the future."

"Now I know why Roz told you to be quiet." I said.

"It must be pretty far, it takes a lot to get command status and last I knew you had no interest." Orrin said to me.

"Great, so what does that mean for me?" Cadie asked.

"You mention that Jerrit is dead. How?" I asked. I felt her sadness when she thought about that.

"He thought he was saving me." she said sadly.

"She needs rest." Mynera said. "We'll talk to her after." then she took her inside.

"Well isn't this a surprise." I said. "Now what?"

"We need to find out when Aries is getting back. Whatever happened to them started on that ship." Orrin said.

"Last I knew the Orion wasn't capable of time travel." I said.

"No but it can slipstream through space. If they were doing that at the time we came back then we could have also been involved in their coming here." he explained.

"And I think Roz is a good place to start." I told him. "I don't want the girls involved in this."

"I'll take them to Cileen's until we get this straightened out." Jacob said.

I headed toward Marlin and Roz. He kept saying that he wasn't going to say anything.

"Jacob's going to take the girls to Cileen's and Orrin is sending a message to Aries. Eventually you are going to have to tell us what is going on." I told him.

"Go get cleaned up. We'll talk about this later." Marlin told him.

"I think we'll get more information out of the girl than him." I told Marlin when he went inside with Mynera. "It may be a good idea to keep them apart."

"No problem, I'll take Roz home." then he turned his attention toward me. "How was your trip?" he asked hugging me tight.

"It was great." I said with a big smile.

Roz kept giving Marlin an argument on why he should stay with Cadie. He didn't have much of a choice when Jacob got back by himself, he helped Marlin persuade Roz. I waited before they left before I said anything more.

"How is she?" I asked Mynera.

"I told her to get cleaned up and then we'll talk. She's very agitated, she is very angry at Roz. She has a very powerful block on her mind." Mynera said.

"So reading her mind is out of the question?" I asked.

"We're going to have to rely on her telling us the truth." she said.

"I wonder how much of it would be too much. It's obvious that she knows Jerrit, and Roz, and me. How many of us does she know?" I wondered.

"I know all of you." Cadie said when she came into the room.

"I figured that you would rest." Mynera said to her.

"I can't rest, I'm too tired to rest. I don't know where I am or how I can get back home." she said.

"Come and sit." Mynera said to her when she led her to the couch. "Let's start with Jerrit. How did you meet him."

"I ment him on my world. I had ran away from the people that my father sold me to. I didn't care where I was going I just had to go."

"Your father sold you into slavery?" I asked.

"It's what my people do. Anyway I took shelter from a storm one night and he just so happened to be there. After awhile he told me how he got here and I just thought that he was crazy, maybe got hit on the head. Until he proved it.

"What did he do?" I asked.

"He showed me the ship that brought him and Roz to my world. Apparently they crashed. It took a long time with what we had for resources for them to repair that ship."

"And you've been with them ever since." Mynera said.

"Yes. In the process of finding what they needed meant going back into the very town I swore that I would never set foot in. Jerrit's all don't worry, I'll be with you, nothing will happen. I got captured, dragged back and beaten for escaping."

"How old were you at the time?" Mynera asked.

"I don't know thirteen maybe."

Orrin came in and showed me a picture of her and Jerrit with two small children then sat next to her.

"Are these your children?" he asked when he gave her the picture.

"Yes they were around ten, we had twins. I carry this with me all the time." she said proudly. "It must have fallen out of my pocket."

"So twins run in your blood." I said to Orrin. "That means one of our girls could have twins." and then I saw her smile. "What?"

"Your girls, you say that all the time. Jerrit used to pick on me because I did that also, I didn't believe him until Aries told me that I did."

"You know my daughters then?" Orrin asked.

"How much about them do you really want to know?" she asked cautiously.

"Oh no, who's our troublemaker?" I asked.

"Well to be brutally truthfull, Jessica is a sadist morbid little bitch that likes to cause so much trouble. I knew what she was doing and I knew I should have told her mother sooner, but she always promised that she would straightening herself out."

"What's wrong with her?" Orrin asked.

"She has a few addictions, guys are one of them, and beating the crap out of them is another. She likes to fight. Katrina gets tired of helping her heal. Her last fight straightened her out." she explained.

"What happened." I asked.

"She pissed someone off, I don't know who or how, but whatever she did it pissed off her father because I stupidly walked into the middle of him yelling at her and I was a little too close because she ducked and he ended up hitting me. I hit the wall so hard that I woke up three days later down in medical and Jerrit thought that I was dead." she explained with a good tone of anger in her voice.

"Why did he feel there was a need to save you?" Orrin asked.

"Where I come from some of my people believe and practice blackmagic. Our high priest is very powerful, that creature that Roz killed was sent to kill me."

"Why?" I asked.

"Because I escaped again. We underestimated the amount of his power. He opened the gates of hell and let the demons through. But we could still send them back, and we did, but there were still a few stragglers. One of them got Jerrit. I saw it and he didn't, Roz didn't know what was going on and got in the way, he thought that it was coming after me and he pulled me out of the way. Jerrit thought that I was in trouble." she said with great pain. "That was five days ago. Commander Cayne is sure that this was the last one."

"When was the last time you were on the Orion?" I asked her.

"Two day's ago." she said looking at her picture.

"You need rest." Mynera told her, it didn't take much convincing to get her to go sleep this time.

"So what do you think?" I said when I sat next to Orrin.

"We have to be careful. Aries won't be back for a few days."

"She hasn't had time to greave. This time may help. But I can't help to think if this is a warning."

"We do what it takes to save Jerrit's life, and at the same time getting these two together. Sound's like a challenge." he said to himself, then he got into some deep thinking and he was not saying anything.

"Everything happens for a reason." I said.

"You know, it is summer time, and it is hot." he whispered in my ear.

"Yeah that it is."

We told Mynera what we were up to. It was actually the first time we really took a long walk along the lake. We found a nice place to sit and relax, and as hard as it was, not to think of what's going on.

"What do you do when you don't want to think about tomorrow?" I asked.

He looked out at the lake and smiled. "Easy, you go swimming." he said when he stood up and started to take his clothes off.

It was hot out and the water felt so cool, it did feel good but I still can't wonder. Then I remembered something.

"What is it your mother told you that put a smile on your face?" I asked when I swam next to him.

"Considering what is going on right now, I'm not going to tell you." he said then he dove under the water.

I dove in after him, it didn't take me long to ignore looking for him and start looking around the lake bottom. It was crystal clear, for a big lake it seemed kind of shallow. I followed a school of fish over to a sandbar that was waist high. While I was standing there looking around I noticed a small island close enough to swim to.

"What are you doing?" Orrin asked when he swam up from behind me.

"Want to go check out that island over there? I see a patch of sand." I said when I rubbed my body next to his.

The water was nice and he had other ideas. He held me tight against him and wouldn't let go, he was kissing and feeling me all over. When I looked at him he had the same excited look on his face that he did when he was talking to his mother.

"What," I asked when I faced him. "has got you so excited?"

"Mother told me one thing but my father told me another." he said holding me tighter to him.

He teasted me for the longest time, it's one thing that I love to hate, it get's to the point where enough is enough now I want more and he loves to fight with me for it. He had a pretty good advantage in the water.

I wrapped my legs around his waist and laid back in the water and floated. The sun was burning bright in the sky and the water was warm. It was so peaceful, birds were flying overhead and occasionaly I felt a fish swim by. He held me tighter, when I looked at him he had a more passionate look on his face. He was really enjoying what he was doing to me, so was I. His touch at times felt arousingly aggressive, I could feel his fingers digging into my flesh.

"I was also told something else." he said pulling me to him. He held me tightly to him and started kissing and biting my neck. "I have the knowledge to heal you under certain circumstances. And you naturally have the power to heal me." he said with a morbid look on his face. "I want you to dig your claws into my skin." he said when he held me hand tight against his chest.

He wanted to feel pain the the worst way, but I have also heard of a ritual that is performed which consisted of bleeding. The more we bleed the more we need to be satisfied, but he wasn't about to. I had my legs tightly wraped around him and he was not about to let me move to be satisfied.

Mother didn't tell me something, but he knew. He held me tighter scratching and digging as he went, and as our blood was mixing together in the water I felt something shape moving inside my chest. Then I felt something stranger.

He held me close and tightly wraped his arms around me and held my ass tight. I could feel him inside me moving slowly, then I felt something else moving inside me coming from him. It was moving slowly inside me body as if it was searching for a way inside me. The pain in my chest was subsiding as this thing moved closer to it.

The ultimate outcome of these two things uniting with each other caused a very powerful surge of relief. I could feel it in his body as his muscles loosed their tight hold on me. Eventhough he had his little secrets I also had mine.

"You know I have a few surprises myself. You think you're the only one who can have a joyous surprise." I said licking his chest.

"Really! Tell me."

"Father told me I had a special power of satisfaction that would please us. How much faith do you have in me?"

"You know my soul belongs to you. And you can do whatever you want to my body." he said with a devilish grin.

"Good, then come under the water with me." I said when I moved down licking and kissing him all the way then grabbing ahold of him with my lips to arouse him once more.

It didn't take long for him to colapse into the water to join me in a sex filled frenzy. He nailed me to the bottom of the lake bed holding me tight as he could while he kissed and sucked on my skin and occastionaly biting me. Nothing stopped him from bitting me when he got between my legs, by the time he got done with me I needed some air.

"Wow!" I said to myself when I floated to the top of the water. "That was wild." I told him.

"Yes it was." he said hugging me. "Are you ready to go?"

"No but we should."

We took our time going back, my legs were sore from the way he held me so I was walking real slow. By the time we got back Marlin had come back with Roz, it was a quiet day without him and it will be a quiet night with him.

"Well Roz, so what trouble do you get into?" I asked him.

"I can't tell you. We've been ordered not to say anything." he said.

"By who?" Orrin asked.

"We were contacted by the government not to say anything, as long as we comply we can stay here. At least for a few days, we have to stay out of sight." he said.

"I guess I can understand that. Why do something that would change ones future. But do they think they can send you back?" I asked.

He had the look on his face that he wanted to tell me something, but he knew better.

"You know we run the possible chance of being isolated for the rest of our lives, do you know how much that will suck?" Roz said.

"If they do it right, you two can be intergrated into the system." Marlin said.

"As long as we play along." he said.

"Wow. They are going to have you on a short leash." I told him. "There has to be a way we can keep in touch."

"Not if they send us to the dead zone."

The dead zone was a tiny little solar system way at the end of our universe, it was a great place to send people that have pissed the governing body off in some way and I can see this being one of them.

No one goes there, it's full of nothing. There is one little planet that is capable of life but it's always been considered too far out of the way to waste the resources for anything. It's a perfect nowhere land.

I heard that some people like that place, I also heard that it is very primitive. I have also heard that if they're not done with a person they have some kind of arrangement that if they studied the planet, then maybe they will be allowed back home. This place has no space travel, or electricity. No one can get off.

Cadie also knew this, she had a hidden fear of being sent there, because she is not technically of our world, they consider her an outcast, disposable would be more the correct word. She had to be careful.

Roz was calm when the Kerellian government came to the door to collect them. They wanted to know everything and wanted to know everything that was said. They studied the area in which they came here and where the creature was fried.

They spend days here, looking through everything, poking and proding, asking the same questions over and over. We at least had the pleasure of saying goodbye to Roz and Cadie, we were sorry to see them go, but we were also glad.

Our girls knew that something was up. Being teens they were very nosy, we managed to keep them quiet until we got back home. The only problem that I had about being back here was that they can watch us closer. When I'm at work I know that there are people around who have no business here. I was not surprised one night when I returned home from work and Aries was at the house.

"So what do we owe this pleasure?" I asked when I took my coat off.

"I have done a lot of talking with Roz, some of the things that he mentioned are a very long time away. By the time that this incident happens between Jerrit and Cadie meeting for the first time, she would have been long dead in this world." Aries explained. "If that eases your mind about anything." he said to me.

"In other words you don't want me to have any contact with them." I said.

"It would be in their best interests if you wouldn't. Roz understands this and he is staying with Cadie. After all her life span is very short. If she's lucky she may have another good forty years left in her before her body starts to die."

"That is understandable. Let her enjoy her remaining years. But I do promise you this, if what she said is true then we have it within us to make sure this doesn't happen again. But we should get her off that planet when the time comes." Orrin said. The thought of knowing how his son dies is not something that he wanted to know, but knowing how to potentally stop it, is something that he will make sure he does.

"Ariel, Chris has been asking about you. She would like to talk to you. On board the Orion of course." Aries said.

"I bet she does. To poke at me with her little machines. Did she get a new toy she wants to test?" I asked.

"The Orion is being reassested for it's next mission. We're going to be here for a long time. I can arrange it for a visit." Aries said, and the girls heard.

They were listening in on our conversation, they came running out of their room hoping that they were included in this visit. They were looking at me and their father saying please.

"We're not the one's you need to be begging to." I told them when I pointed to Aries. They turned around with big smiles on their faces. "Now how can you say no to that?" I asked him.

"Considering what I am easy. No." he said looking at them, which made their smiles dissapear. "But I do have permission to make accomidations for you two. I do have a sense of humor." he said to us.

"Yeah, we're going to have to work on that." I told him.

"Someone will be by in a few days to pick you up." he told us.

That was fine for us. I had to take care of things at work. Jennifer has know idea how much I love having her for my boss, if it was anyone else I would have been fired by now. But she always wants me to keep my eyes and ears open for anything odd that may be of historical interest.

"It felt like we just got home." I said when I was cleaning up our room.

"We did. Come here." he said when he grabbed me and threw me on the bed then landing on top of me. "So this may be our last night of quiet for a while."

"True. We should take advantage of it."

Just as we got our clothes off and attemped to do something our lovly girls barge right in with questions.

"If this can wait until moring, it had better wait." their father told them.

"Well it's not like we don't hear you guys anyway." Jessica said, trying not to laugh.

"No one told us what to pack." Katrina said.

"That's true, we didn't." I told him. "I'll tell you what, I pack a bag and you girls pack one and we can share clothes." I told them.

They love wearing my clothes, so it was just as easy for the three of us to share a closet. Shopping with them is fun, it takes us all day and for very good reason. Clothes are always something that the three of us agree on before we get anything.

Orrin took them one day and when he got back he told me that he would never do it again. It wasn't the idea of shopping, it was the idea that the girls have to try on everything and do a little mixing and matching before deciding. That's one thing that I will take the blame for, I got them into that habit.

We managed to finished breakfast and get things cleaned up before we heard a knock at the door. When I opened the door a was very surprised.

"Derick!" I gasped.

"When Aries asked me to come and get you I just couldn't say no. I'm also your pilot, so we have plenty of time to talk." he said. "Ready?"

The girls were excited, I was in shock. I never would imagine Aries sending him to pick us up. Usually it's someone from the ground authorities that take care of pickups.

On our way to the Orion he told me how he remembers being taken in the middle of the night. They brought him to another building and after doing days of tests the took him to another lab. In other words they took him to experment on.

Whatever they were doing to him disfigured him slightly. His face looks as if he had been in a lot of fights, and he said his body is the same way. Chris has been helping to rejuvinate his natural skin chimicals slowly, but when anything is done right, it's done slow.

The lab he was transferred to work with cybernetics, he was a victim to their experiments. Chris has been working with him in removing as much as possible. Much of his scaring is where they implanted one thing or another in him.

Other then that he's content with his life, he loves to fly and wouldn't give that up for anything. What amazed me is that we were so into our conversation that I didn't realize it until Orrin tapped me on the shoulder.

"You have two girls outside that are driving me nuts." he said.

I smiled when I looked out and seen the girls staring at me with eager anticipation. I seen Chris coming up from behind them, another one that had a smile on her face.

Chris told us that she would show us where we will be staying and Derick happily told the girls that he would be showing them around and answering their questions. After we got settled in Orrin went to talk with Aries leaving me alone with Chris.

"We need to talk." she said seriously. "First of all I want to appologize for my actions, I am loyal to my commanders orders." and then she sprayed something in my face.

"What are you doing?" I asked her when I wiped my face, then I started feeling dizzy. "What did you do?" I asked when I backed away from her.

"All I can tell you is that I follow orders. I am to put you and your family in hibernation for a while. That's all I know. I am sorry."

She said my family. What have my girls done to deserve to have their lives disrupted. It has to be because of Roz and Cadie. They said something, they had to. The Kerillan government knows their future, now is the time to get rid of obsticals.

My body was feeling numb, I could feel hands on me, laying me down. My vision was blurry, my hearing was going. She drugged me, they drugged my children. I let my guard down, I let my children down. They made my family disappear.